HEAVEN SENT

HEAVEN'S REJECTS MC #1

AVELYN PAIGE

CONTENTS

TRIGGER WARNINGS

This book contains graphic scenes of violence, gore, non-described sexual assault, death, kidnapping, drug use, and sexual encounters.

BLURB

Her nightmare is still happening. His has left him broken.

Dani Espinoza has a stalker. First he murdered her parents and now he's searching for her. So Dani does the only thing she can do. She hops the next bus out of town, and she runs. Leave it to her to run right into the middle of a biker war.

Tyler "Hero" Tobias is the Vice President of the Heaven's Rejects MC, and he takes his position very seriously. The instant he meets Dani, he knows he can't trust her. There are secrets in her brown eyes and lies in her sweet smile. So why can't he stop thinking about her when he should be focusing on keeping his club alive?

When Dani's secrets come out and her lies are revealed, Hero will risk his heart and his club to keep her safe and make her his.

Dedication

To Glen,

Thank you for supporting me throughout this entire author journey.

XOXO, Avelyn

Chapter 1

DANI

WARM, *sticky blood covers my hands…*

I scream as I wake up, huddling against the cool glass of the bus window. My eyes fall instinctively down to my hands, finding them clean. A sigh of relief escapes my lips before I peer up and notice several sets of eyes staring at me.

"I'm fine," I tell the others sitting around me on the bus. "It was just a nightmare. I don't sleep well in moving vehicles."

The lie spills easily from my mouth because I've practiced in preparation for my nightmares happening in public. If any of the people surrounding me knew the truth, I'd be in handcuffs immediately. I know my simple statement eases everyone, but it does nothing to ease the pain and fear enveloping my body. Every time I close my eyes, I see them. I re-live the night that changed everything for me. The night where my semi-happy life exploded into bloody chaos around me.

I had a family and friends that loved me, but love isn't something I can afford to rely on any longer. It can't keep me safe from *him*. That gruesome night set me on this path. I left behind the girl I was and the life I had in Cleveland. That's the only way I can survive this. Survive *him*.

A hot, wet tear slips down my cheek. Their faces and voices linger in the back of my mind for hours after each nightmare ends. Her dark hair and brown, kind eyes. The memories of laughter that resonated in our home before he came into our lives.

I can't let the darkness win. I need to fight to survive.

Wiping away the tears, I stare out of the window on the bus. It's been three days since I watched Cleveland shrink in the distance. Ohio has been my home my entire life, and I just left it in the past like a dusty, unwanted photograph. I had no choice but to leave. He left me with no choice. It could no longer be my home. The place where I had so many happy memories, which are now tarnished in the inky blackness of my last night there.

If I had stayed, I would've ended up just like them, anyway. No, this was my only option in a desperate attempt at survival. With nowhere else to go, I had taken a taxi to the closest bus depot in the middle of the night and never looked back.

The time I've spent on this bus has given me time to plan out what my new life might be like. I decided quickly that staying under the radar and finding a job will be the hardest part. Even if I manage to procure a fake ID, I will never be able to find work that doesn't involve the usage of my social security number. That will only draw a flashing arrow to my location. Being paid under the table and off the books is my only choice. I know the work will be shitty, but beggars can't be choosers in my situation. Money is money. No matter how I come by it.

I slide my hand into my bag, counting the few bills I have left. Seven hundred dollars. Not exactly a fortune, but it's what I have to work with until I sort out the job issue. Life in California won't exactly be as economical as it was in Ohio. My need to get away from the situation outweighed my ideal destination. I had grabbed a map and just hopped on the first bus that was leaving.

I used the travel time to research my destination. *Upland, California.* I'll be honest when I say that it looks promising on paper. It's a small suburb on the outskirts of the city, and has everything. It is also far enough outside of the city that it will be the last place anyone would look for me, and that is exactly what I need.

Using the free Wi-Fi on the bus, I have browsed housing options on my recently reset iPad and new e-mail address, and I contacted some of the listings seeking a roommate. One woman had emailed me back and even offered to pick me up from the bus station to look at the house. The rent was affordable at four hundred dollars per month for a split, two-bedroom furnished apartment. The landlord even pays the utilities, making it more appealing. As long as it isn't a whorehouse or a drug den, I'll likely be calling it my home in a few short hours.

The bus cruises through the desert at a record pace, and soon, I find myself stepping out of the bus and into the sweltering heat. They may not have humidity here, but even without it, one hundred degrees is still hot. The bus depot has beautiful flowering trees everywhere, which surprises me. I assumed with the heat that nothing but cacti could even grow here. Only having the picture she sent me to go by, I search the crowded station for my potential roommate.

I finally spot her leaning against a post. Her bleach blonde hair is drawn upward into a ponytail, and her crop top outfit screams stereotypical California girl. I watch as she scans the crowd several times looking for me before I approach her. She spots me and waves frantically before stalking over to me

"Are you Dani?" she asks, flipping her long ponytail behind her.

"Erica?"

A huge smile spreads across her face. "That's me! But please, call me Ricca. I hate being called Erica."

Her excited tone instantly puts me at ease. A pang of jealousy wafts over me. I used to be that carefree. Would I ever be again?

"Are you ready to go see your new place?"

"Sure," I reply.

Her lips turn down slightly at my lack of enthusiasm for meeting her as my prospective roommate. She sidles up next to me as I hoist my bag over my shoulder, following along beside her.

"First time in California?"

"Yes," I say, the word coming out flat.

"Where are you from?" she inquires.

"Midwest," is all I offer to her.

She eyes me carefully, then laughs. "Be prepared for a culture shock then. A big one."

Her laughter is loud and contagious, and a smile forms on my face for the first time in days.

She directs me to her bright yellow jeep, where I slide across the warm seat and toss my bag between my feet. Ricca jumps in on the driver's side and starts the engine. Before I can even get another word out of my mouth, she peels out of the parking lot and turns to merge onto the freeway.

I try to count the cars passing us on the crowded freeway, but after a few minutes, I give up. The amount of people I see driving on the highway blows me away. Sure, Cleveland has its periods of rush hour traffic during the workweek, but I've never experienced anything like this at one o'clock on a Wednesday afternoon.

Ricca weaves through the traffic like a seasoned pro, and finally takes an exit ramp. She laughs when she sees me clutching the seatbelt strapped across my chest. This woman drives like she could be in the minor leagues for NASCAR. We make turn after turn, until finally, she pulls up alongside a small apartment complex. Just like the bus depot, the streets are lined with flowering trees and dotted with large palm trees. It doesn't seem to be too dangerous of a neighborhood. There are kids playing basketball in the small park next to the complex, and all of them seem happy and safe.

I note that one palm tree in particular looks odd. "What's wrong with that tree?" I ask. "It looks different than the others."

She laughs hard when she sees what I'm pointing at. "That's not a tree. That's a cell phone tower."

I peer at it again, more closely this time, and I see the wires hanging out of it. "Huh, you don't see that every day."

"It's all a part of the glamour of Hollywood," she replies. "Nothing is as it appears around here, Dani."

And with that, she jumps out of her jeep and motions for me to follow her. We snake through the garden linking the buildings, until we pass a doorway with the number three crookedly nailed onto it.

"Now, I want to warn you about something before we go in. The previous tenant really liked colorful paint. I'm like ninety-nine percent sure she was a hippie, because the place reeked of weed when I moved in. It took me weeks to get the apartment aired out and not smelling like Woodstock."

She makes quick work of the lock and ushers me inside. The apartment is just as small as I figured it would be for the price. A couch and a single easy chair sit in the living room, facing a small flat-screen TV. She leads me through to the kitchen. It has a small counter-top, stove, microwave, and an apartment-size refrigerator. It's much smaller than the kitchen I had in the house in Cleveland, but I doubt I'll be cooking anything bigger than a microwave meal until I can save up more money.

Next, she leads me to the bedroom and I realize what she meant about the bright colors. A vivid blue that could probably be seen from space covers the walls.

"Shit, that's bright. It's like the face of the sun is shining from the walls of the room. You need sunglasses to walk in here. How you do stand it?" I declare, squinting at the brilliant pigment.

"I warned you the old bat was an extreme hippie. My room was a neon-orange with yellow swirls before I repainted it hot pink."

How is that much of a difference? It's like trading one neon monstrosity for another.

We both laugh as I step into the room. It's simply furnished with a bed, small dresser, bedside table, and lamp. There's even bedding on the bed that seems to be clean. How has no one snatched this place up? Cheap rent. Fully furnished. What's the catch?

"How many people have come to see this place?"

"Too many," she laughs. "All of them have given me the creeps. I've had so many scumbags trying to move in with me. It's like my apartment is a half-way house for the lost and perverted, but you seem pretty normal. No skeletons in the closet I should know about?"

My heart stops momentarily at her question. Her innocent question. She has no idea about what skeletons I have in my closet. *She's merely making a joke. Get it together.*

"You okay?'

"I'm fine." The lie comes so easily the more I say it. "Just exhausted from my bus trip."

"Well, what do you think? Will this work for you?" Ricca asks, hope building in her eyes.

Is this what I want? It's the only affordable place I found online that came furnished, and she seems pretty nice. I weigh my options, before announcing my decision.

"I'll take it."

Ricca jumps in the air, screaming like a teenage girl at a boy band concert.

"I'm so excited! Once you get settled in, we'll go grab dinner at In N' Out. Everyone needs to christen their first day in California with a burger from there. Tomorrow, I'll take you to meet the landlord and get the paperwork signed. My last roommate was paid up until the end of the month, so you won't owe rent until the first of the month."

She leaves me to unpack the meager bag I brought with me. I put the few outfits into the small dresser and place the picture of my parents next to the bedside lamp. Just looking at my parent's photo brings a rush of painful memories and fresh tears. They'd want me to try and be happy, and that's what I'm going to do. I may have to work my ass off to do it, but I will. The past that lies hidden in Cleveland will always linger, threatening to take away my freedom, but I can't think about that. I had survived its horrors.

No one will take away my choices again. I'd rather be dead than go back to that life.

Chapter 2

HERO

TODAY STARTED off just like any normal damn day. Woke up hungover as shit, fucked the woman I had picked up from a local bar last night. When I was done with her, I went to Church. Pretty typical day. But as soon as I walked into our meeting room, I knew today was going to be fucked all to hell.

"Nice of you to join us, Hero," Raze, the president of our club, calls out. The smirk on his face tells me he knows what I was doing. Most of the guys in this room probably got their dick wet this morning, so the fact he's calling *me* out is odd. Shrugging my shoulders in return with a shit-eating grin on my face, I can't help myself from not dishing it back.

"Sorry, Prez. Just had to get my daily dose of vitamin T & A for breakfast. I'm a growing boy, you know," I fire back with a laugh, while taking my seat next to him.

Raze just shakes his head, while the other men surrounding our table all laugh. Tyson, our club treasurer, nods in agreement and leans close to me.

"Was the pussy worth being late?" he whispers.

"Isn't good pussy always worth it, Ty?"

The night's activities might have been hazy, but the pretty little pussy I pounded into for over an hour this morning was satisfying enough before I kicked her out of my bed. Although her pussy was pretty good, she had all the signs of a clinger, and that's not my kind of relationship. She had to go, and she had headed right on out of the door with the help of one of the club girls.

"Fuck yes, brother. You never pass up a chance for that grade-A choice pussy you picked up last night. Wish there was more of it around here," he laughs. "Think we can get her to stay on?"

I smirk, then Raze clears his throat, interrupting our side conversation.

"Now that Hero's gotten his rocks off and his ass in his seat, we can finally start," he orders.

The meeting moves on as normal. We discuss our upcoming charity runs to raise money for a local kid with cancer. He's on the road to recovery, but his medical bills have nearly bankrupted his parents. The Heaven's Rejects MC may be filled with tattooed, meat-head bikers that would make even a devout nun faint, but we take care of our friends and neighbors. The club was established in nineteen eighty-six by Raze's father and our former Vice President, Jagger. At that time, thugs hiding from the authorities called Upland home. But once Raze took over the club, everything changed, and the area was cleaned up. He made sure they were the first to go once he settled all the differences. They hurt our business, and we couldn't have that shit happening when we met with clients.

Our business was our lifeline, and nothing would threaten the cash flow coming into the club and into our pockets. And business was fucking good.

Our phone rings off the hook with business proposals from concerned rich daddies worried about their perfect little whore daughters going out for a night on the town, to the occasional politician needing some muscle for a back-alley campaign money deal. You can say we cater to all walks of life. Our lack of a one-percenter patch works in our favor. We are legal enough to appease the local police, even though we don't exactly follow all the rules of decent civilian society. That made us the perfect fit for protection, and we are paid well for it.

Our club meeting is about to adjourn when I hear a yelling coming from outside. Ratchet, our Sergeant at Arms, busts through the doors.

"Where the fuck have you been?" Raze questions.

Ratchet says nothing, but holds up his hand. In it, a

bloody leather cut, our club patch clear as day on its back.

Raze sees the cut and moves across the room in long strides before I even realize what's going on. Raze rips it from his hands, flipping it to the front to see the name patch. His eyes harden as the name comes into his view.

"Where did you find this?"

Ratchet hangs his head. "Prez, the cut isn't all that I found. You need to come out back to the storage shed."

The entire room empties out the back doorway of the clubhouse to avoid alarming the old ladies and club girls in the main room. If this is as bad as I think it is, they don't need to know about this until we get whatever's in that shed out of here. We all walk across the dirt parking lot of the clubhouse toward the small shed we use to store spare Harley parts from our repair shop in town.

Rounding the corner of the building, I can smell Jagger before I see him. A pungent smell of old blood, decay, and rotting flesh permeates the air around us. The heat of the day didn't waste any time cooking his body. My stomach wretches when I see his lifeless body hanging from the rafters of the shed like he'd been crucified. Seeing my friend hanging up there sends bile hurtling up my throat, but I manage not to throw up.

His face is nearly unrecognizable under the blood and bruises that mar his flesh. But it's his stomach that shows the calling card left by his murderers. Two thick T's are gouged into his flesh, just above his navel.

Fucking Twisted Tribe. Our long-time rival MC.

Our brotherhood stands in silence for what seems like an eternity.

"Prez, we have to do something about this," Ratchet snarls, his body vibrating with the rage we're all feeling. "They killed Jagger. We have to hit them back."

Things had been quiet with the Twisted Tribe after our last run-in a few years ago. Raze and their president had come to a paper-thin agreement to keep away from each other and to let the dust settle. Killing Jagger and leaving their mark on his skin just threw all of that out the fucking window.

Raze turns to Ratchet and charges towards him. He stops just inches from his face before he speaks.

"We all lost a brother today. Twisted Tribe will be dealt with in time. I know how you feel, Ratchet, because every man here feels the same fucking way. They will *pay* for this."

"Raze is right," I declare, showing my support of his decision. To go now would be reckless and exactly what they would expect. "Today, we mourn. Tomorrow, we will burn Twisted Tribe to the fucking ground."

Looking at the men around me, I see the rage and sorrow in their eyes. These men need their leaders to stay strong and command them. As much as I want to rage with them, I have to keep my cool.

"Ratchet, grab Slider, and get Jagger down from there. Clean him up the best you can, and call Morton's Mortuary. He owes us a favor."

"What about Darcy?" Ratchet asks in defiance. "What are you going to tell her and the boys?"

"I'll take care of it. It should come from me," Raze mutters.

He nods and stalks back to the clubhouse to retrieve our newest prospect. A short while later, Ratchet returns with Slider in tow, heading towards the shed as the rest of us move back into the meeting room.

The mood has sobered with our discovery. Raze makes a quick vote to offer to pay for Jagger's funeral expenses, as well as set up a fund for his boys. The vote passes unanimously, and we file out of Church into the main room. Maj, Raze's old lady, is behind the bar inventorying the damage we did at the party last night. Her eyes lock onto Raze, and I know she can tell something is up. She leaves from behind the bar, and the King and Queen of Heaven's Rejects head back to their suite in the clubhouse. He needs time to process this before he tells Jagger's wife. Darcy and those boys will be devastated. I don't envy Raze with that task.

I head to my room and pace, trying to make sense of everything. My body is a coiled mass of energy, just seething to break free every second I relive that scene outside. My mind spirals out of control, knowing the last minutes Jagger had on this earth was with someone from Twisted Tribe carving into his flesh. My stomach twists into knots.

They tortured the only good man amongst us to death. They'll pay for this. They'll pay for dumping his bloody body right on our doorstep like a fucking Christmas present.

Goddammit. He didn't deserve this. His wife and kids didn't deserve this.

I continue pacing, but the feeling of the impending rage inches closer. The last time I felt like this was in Iraq, listening to my brothers writhing in pain after the roadside bomb, unable to do anything about it because of my own injuries. My heart rate ticks higher and my skin feels too tight. I'm a ticking time bomb. The therapist I had met with off and on for years didn't do any damn good, so I learned to cope the only way I knew how. Alcohol and sex. Was it a good way to cope? No, but it did the trick in a pinch. And that was not in short supply around here.

Is it a good idea? Fuck no, but I have to do something. I have to vent off some of this rage before I do something stupid. Before more people get hurt because of me.

I open my door and head out to the main room. I see

Ruby, one of the club whores, lounging on the couch with a couple of the other girls.

She'll do.

Grabbing her by the wrist, I drag her back to my room. She doesn't say a word as I shove her to her knees the instant the door closes. I unzip my jeans and force my cock into her pretty painted mouth. My mind needs a distraction and Ruby is just what the doctor ordered. Grabbing onto the back of her head to increase the force of my thrusts, she moans at my touch, the top of her big tits brushing against my thighs.. Her tongue swirls around the tip of my cock as I pound into her willing mouth.

I continue to thrust, and her eyes lock onto mine. I don't know why that shit turns me on, but it works. Her green eyes watch me as I increase my speed. She moves one of her hands from my hip and grasps my balls, rolling them between her fingers like the expert that she is. She lightly grazes her teeth against the head of my dick as cum shoots down her throat. A smile grows across her face as it sticks to her swollen lips.

I'd planned on coming on those tits of hers, but I was gone as soon as she used her teeth. Ruby knows what I like. She's the only club whore who has warmed my bed more than once, and it will likely stay that way. I don't need to drag anyone else into this shit show that is my life. It helps that Ruby isn't looking to settle down either, so she's the only one I've allowed to stick around after the first fuck. Well, and that heavenly mouth of hers. Good blowjobs are hard to come by anymore thanks to the augmented realities of the porn industry in the valley.

I shove my dick back into my pants as Ruby gets off of her knees and stands. It doesn't take a rocket scientist to decipher the look she's currently shooting my way. She knows something's bothering me. Ruby may be a club whore to everyone else, but to me, she's more like a friend with benefits. I can fuck her anytime I want, and she knows me better than anyone else.

"Who was it out in the shed?" she asks, keeping her eyes on the ground.

"How in the fuck did you know someone was out in the shed?"

"I watched out the back window."

Her admission rattles me. She can't even look at me when she's telling me about sticking her damn nose where it doesn't belong.

"Had you said that to any other patched member, your ass would have been out on the street or dead. I won't fucking break club rules to protect you just because we're good in bed together."

She still refuses to look at me. I know she has to realize she fucked up by admitting that kind of shit to me, but she needs to understand how serious I am. I pull her chin back up until her eyes meet mine.

"Ruby, you can't keep digging into the club's business. One of these days, the wrong brother is going to catch you and I won't be able to save you."

She nods and, without another word, heads toward the door. I know I need to tell her about Jagger. I just don't know how to tell her. She was close with him, and not in the usual way. Her entry into this club was atypical. She wasn't a bike bunny or a good girl trying to piss off her rich daddy by slumming it around with one of us. This club saved her life, and she stayed to repay us for that despite being told that her debt was paid in full. But she stayed, because we are the only family she has. Especially Jagger, who was like a father to her, and his death will hurt.

Just before she reaches the door, I stand up, stalk over to her, and push my hand against the wood to stop her from opening the door.

"It's Jagger, isn't it? If it were anyone else, you'd have just told me. You're hesitating."

"Do not say a word until Raze announces it to the club. Darcy doesn't know yet."

"Who did this?" she turns to me with tears welling up in her green eyes. My answer is silence. She sighs before shoving my hand out of the way and walking out of my bedroom door.

I lock the door behind her and return to my bed. My mind spirals out of control, trying to make sense out of the chaos swirling inside it. Ruby managed to take the edge off, but it did nothing to calm the storm inside of me right now.

Jagger was the best of us. He was my sponsor when I was a prospect. He turned me into the man behind the VP patch on my cut today. He managed to tame the wild beast I was when I walked into this clubhouse like I owned the place at just twenty-two years old. I had no idea what the life of a member of a motorcycle club was, but I was lost after leaving the Army. An MC seemed like the right place for me, and after Jagger educated me, I knew I was right. I needed a strong brotherhood and a bit of chaos from time to time to keep my inner demons in check. This club was an outlet and my home. He made sure of that.

Seven years later, I'd moved through the ranks and became VP, succeeding Jagger after his health started to decline, and he'd needed to step away from his leadership duties. Raze wasn't happy he was stepping down, but he understood his need to live the rest of the years he had with less stress. He had a young family, and he deserved more time with them.

If I'm honest, I always thought it would be his heart to take him, but never did I fucking think it would be a knife from a Twisted Tribe member that snuffed out his life. The thought of Jagger's last fucking memory being a Tribe member's face sends rage rocketing back through me again.

Slow your roll, fucker. Don't go ape shit now. That's not what they need.

I've got to keep my anger in check over the next few days. Jagger wouldn't want me or any of the guys to ruin his funeral for Darcy and the boys. Once we've laid him to rest, I can't guarantee I won't set the Twisted Tribe's world on fire in plain sight. Consequences and incarceration be damned.

These fuckers need to pay, and I'll be the one to send them all back to hell.

Chapter 3

DANI

TWO WEEKS after moving in with Ricca, we're finally getting used to living together. I knew that living with a complete stranger would be difficult, but her bubbly personality has helped me settle into our new domestic life more easily than I originally anticipated. Before everything happened, I was outgoing. Living with her brought that part of me back, in a way.

She was like me more than I could have ever imagined. Though she never spoke in specifics, the hurt on her face was clear enough when she talked about her past. She had dark secrets, just like I did. It was a quiet bond of painful solitude that was an invisible tether between us. Maybe one day, we would share our experiences with each other when we finally felt safe again in this world.

We spent much of the first week I lived here, running

around to local thrift shops to find clothes for me. The few things I had stuffed into my bag in a panicked hurry wasn't going to be enough to get me by. Goodwill became my best friend, and fifty dollars later, I had a few more outfits, shoes, and a coat. Shopping might have brought us together, but it was the conversations while we browsed that really bonded us.

The biggest surprise for me was how old she is. I'd assumed she was a lot younger than me, but I was shocked to find out she's actually thirty years old. Five years my senior. She doesn't look a day over twenty-two, but who knows if it's because of good genes or a good doctor.

The only bad part about being her roommate is that she comes home drunk as shit after working her shift at a local bar nearly every night. She just passes out wherever she lands in the house. I have no clue how she can live like that night after night, but every single morning, she wakes up perky and ready to take on the day. I've had my brushes with Jack Daniels over the course of my life, and let me tell you, my frumpy hot mess of a hangover is day and night compared to hers.

The one plus side of her working nights is having the place to myself to relax and watch something other than one of her many reality TV shows. There's only so many times I can take watching the same group of rich women get into a catfight about what came out of their mouths.

Unfortunately for me, tonight's her night off and, as usual, she's back on my case about applying for a waitress position at the bar.

"Come on, Dani," Ricca pleas. "I promise it will be fun. Red's been dying to meet you. I bet once he sees your sexy ass, he'll drop to his knees and beg you to come work at the bar."

I roll my eyes, and she crosses her arms, giving me the sad puppy eyes.

Like that will work.

It's not that I don't want to work with her, but it's the exposure I'll get working in a bar. I really don't want to work in a public place, but after fourteen days of California living and pre-paying for next month's rent, I'm down to two hundred dollars and some change. It's not like I haven't been looking for a job since I got here, but no luck so far, other than the listings I saw for a topless house cleaner on Craigslist, and that's a no in my book. I knew there were some screwed up people in this world, but the lifestyles of the rich and famous are far weirder than I imagined them to be.

Fucking Hollywood.

"I said no, Ricca. It sounds like a strip club."

I've noticed she isn't one for giving up her arguments, and frankly, running this low on cash is clouding my decision-making process. For a split second, I consider her offer of asking about a job before I come to my senses. A bar full of drunk assholes with grabby hands isn't where I want to be.

"Dani, you need a job, and Red's offering to give you a shot and pay you under the table. What's the harm in coming in with me on my day off and just checking the place out?"

Ricca stands her ground as I try to bypass her in the kitchen doorway.

"No."

She doesn't budge. Goddammit!

"Move, Ricca, or I'll move you."

Her eyes narrow, and she plants her feet against each side of the door frame. "Admit it, you're curious. It's just one night out. Just come with me. We'll go out and have fun. You do know what fun is, right?"

I forcibly shove against her again, but she doesn't budge. She's keeping me from the couch and re-watching *The Hunger Games* for the millionth time. I really don't want to give up trying to get out of this, but she's bound and determined to cancel my macaroni and cheese date with Peeta and Gale.

"Oh, for fuck's sake, Ricca. If it lets me out of this kitchen, fine! I'll go," I relent.

She jumps up and down, screaming like one of those rich housewives she likes to watch on television, before bolting down the hall to her room. "I bet some of my party clothes will fit you," she yells.

"I have my own clothes," I call. Just as I sit down to take a bite of my dinner, she walks in the room and jerks the spoon out of my hand.

"No time to eat! It's time to get you looking bootyli-cious," she shrieks.

Fuck my life.

Three hours later, I emerge from Ricca's room painted and stuffed into a flimsy silver and black mini dress that barely covers my ass. My level of discomfort in this get up is off the charts, but Ricca wouldn't budge. The moment I voiced my displeasure, I was met with a pissy glare and another layer of lipstick before she weaved a fishtail plait braid with my unruly hair.

Why the hell did I say yes to this?

She shoves me in front of the full-length mirror in our shared bathroom, and I barely recognize myself. The dark circles under my eyes, left from the endless onslaught of nightmares, have been expertly covered with a layer of concealer and accented with a dark eye shadow that would rival that of a vampire in a Holly-wood movie. The dress hugs my curves like a second skin. My boobs are pushed up so high, I feel like Wilson peering over the fence on the *Home Improvement* reruns I used to watch with my grandpa growing up. One false move and my boobs will spill over the top of this dress. Ricca returns with a pair of black stiletto heels, twirling them in her hands.

"No way are those going on my feet," I protest, but my words fall on deaf ears as she kneels down and shoves them onto my feet in a few quick movements. "I'm going to kill myself trying to walk in these things. Can't I just wear my flip-flops?"

"You'll be fine," she assures me with a smile.

"I'm not so sure about that."

My eyes shift to focus on my reflection in the mirror. The entire look is one layer of overkill after another. I lean forward and stare into the hollowed-darkness of my own eyes, feeling a familiar tremor ripple just below the surface of my skin. Before I can contain the thought, a vision of my mother staring at me with displeasure rockets into my mind.

No. This isn't happening right now.

The visual of her angered face probes at my brain, and my heart beats wildly inside of my chest as I try to force down the darkness trying to take over.

You're fine. It's just one night, like Ricca said. What's the worst that could happen?

I take deep breaths in and out, and just as I find my calm center again, Ricca drags me from the bathroom, out of the front door, and shoves me into her jeep. She hops in the driver's seat and then we're flying down the street.

Red Rocket's is only a few miles from the house, so it doesn't take long to get there. The bar looks like a dump from the outside. The grass is dead and brown, but that seems to be a trend in Southern California with the water shortage. The parking lot is filled with potholes, but nevertheless, it is full. Ricca pulls her jeep into the employee parking lot around back, parking it next to a row of shiny black Harleys.

"You ready to have some fun, Dani?" she asks with excitement sparkling in her eyes.

I can't help it. My mouth to brain filter fails, before I can reign in my sarcasm. "Oh, Ricca, I'm so overjoyed to be here. What's next? A trip to the emergency room to get the roofies pumped from my stomach and a tetanus shot?" Her smile fades into a scowl. "Fine, yes. I'm so excited," I lie sarcastically.

"That's better. Now, push those tits up and let's go eat, drink, and be merry. I bet Red gives you that job before you even tell him your name."

She walks around the car and pulls me out of the seat. Ricca drags me up to the door, and the bouncer waves us in without ever checking my ID. Walking into the bar, I can instantly tell this place is a dive. The wooden floors are scuffed and dirty, and it reeks of sadness and broken dreams. As we walk further into the door, the smell of greasy fried bar food hits my nose. The food might have smelled good if I had been drunk, but since I'm sober, it stinks like week-old roadkill.

The patrons of this fine establishment are randomly

perched at the bar top and in various booths. I see a group of bikers looming in a secluded corner, surrounded by scantily clad women. That's one section of the bar I will be avoiding. That kind of attention is exactly why I don't need to work in a place like this.

Ricca parks me in a seat at a high-top table near the bar and orders us two tequila sunrises before I can protest.

"Isn't this place great?" she asks, leaning in by my ear. "Red has really updated the place from when he first bought it."

I plaster a fake smile on my face while she goes back to her drink.

This is updated? The place looks like it's one strong wind gust away from disintegrating. What did it look like before this?

Rolling my eyes at the thought, I pull my drink to my lips and let the tequila work its magic. Ricca waves at someone, and a short, pudgy, bald man walks towards our table. I can smell his overpowering cheap cologne before he ever gets close to us. Its pungent scent is nearly enough to make me throw up.

"Red, this is Dani, the girl I was telling you about for the waitress job," she says, pointing to me. Pulling me from my stool, she practically shoves me at him in her semi-drunken state.

God. Was she drinking at the house before we left? How did I not catch on that she was already two sheets to the wind?

"Meet your new waitress, Red. Isn't she perfect?"

Red's eyes scan up and down my body, and I struggle to keep the tequila in my stomach.

"She sure is, doll face. She'll make all the boys howl. What do you say, Dani? Want to join the Red Rocket team?"

He's joking, right? He makes it sound like a five-star restaurant. This isn't a team atmosphere. It's a train wreck waiting to happen.

"I told you he'd like you," Ricca drunkenly whisper-yells into my ear.

Shoving her away, I stare at them both.

"Come on, Dani. You'll make a metric shit ton of tips, judging by the guys watching you tonight. You know you need the money," she continues, swaying to the music blasting from the speakers.

Red moves closer to me and runs his fingers down my face. I shudder at the connection.

"Come on, baby. I'll make sure you're taken care of here. I'll pay you under the table, just like Ricca mentioned. You can be my dirty little secret," he says, as the smell of the liquor on his breath fills my nose. I try to move away, but he grabs me by the arm and yanks me closer to his putrid smell. "I don't know what you're running from, but I can take care of you, sugar. The options are… well… less than desirable unless you're into that kind of thing."

He's right. I know he is, but it doesn't make this decision any easier. I need the money desperately. If I worked here, at least I would have Ricca with me most nights. How bad could that be?

"Fine," I say, pulling my arm away from his grasp. "But there's going to be some ground rules."

"You're not exactly in the position to be issuing ultimatums, Dani."

"I won't be a fucking plaything for you or any of your patrons. I'm here to do my job and get paid. That's it."

"Anything you want, darlin'. As long as your ass will be here at eight tomorrow night. Ricca will show you the ropes." His eyes roam my body again. Jesus, I'm regretting this decision already. He starts to walk away but pauses, turning to us both. "Wear something revealing and shove your tits in their faces. You'll do *just* fine." He grins before turning his attention back to Ricca.

"You make sure she's looking this good tomorrow. The only ugly woman we have working in this bar is my wife, and I plan on keeping it that way. Drinks are on me tonight. Consider it a welcome aboard present." He disappears, and the brave face I had put on for him fades away quickly. Ricca seems oblivious as she raises two fingers to the bartender.

"He's not so bad, right?" Ricca asks, as two more drinks show up on our table.

"Not so bad? The man is a pig. How do you stand to work for him?"

"He's not that bad once you get past the smell and the grabby hands. Just keep his customers happy and you'll be fine."

Downing the drink in two gulps, Ricca waves at the bartender for another round and shoves my drink into my hands.

"Drink up. We have some celebrating to do."

Three buttery nipple shots and two more tequila sunrises later, she drags me out onto the dance floor. The alcohol blurs my vision, and my inhibitions fall away. Dancing by myself, I see Ricca is grinding against one of the bikers from the corner. His hands roam her curves and dig into her hips as her ass circles his crotch. I can tell she's into the man groping her when she leans back and kisses him. I wonder what her boyfriend would think about that guy's tongue shoved into her mouth. Dipping to the floor, she rubs her ass on him harder as his fingers slide under her short dress.

Is he…? Is she…? Oh, god.

Determined not to watch, I quickly turn and run smack dab into a hard, broad chest.

"Dance with me," a gruff voice demands.

Chapter 4

HERO

IT ISN'T until today that Jagger's death really hits home.

The news spread like wildfire through the chapters, and within days, eight more clubs came rumbling up to the clubhouse to pay their respects to one of the Heaven's Rejects founding fathers.

I look around the clubhouse and take in the sight around me. These were the men that served beside him as our club was birthed into existence, followed by the creation of each additional chapter throughout the years. Jagger was a legend amongst our club, and he was one of the most respected men in its history. He held the club together, along with Raze, as they forged a new path for us, after the shit show Raze's old man left behind when he died. The years that came after it were messy, but with Jagger and Raze at the helm, we had survived it.

The mood in the clubhouse has been dampened from the usual boisterous atmosphere, ever since Raze announced Jagger's passing. Calling his murder a passing was just sugarcoating the truth for the women and children, but using that word was like a knife to the heart. It wasn't a passing. It was a fucking murder that would be avenged as soon as we had the chance. Jagger had to have gone through hell during his last moments, and just the thought of that makes me sick. He didn't deserve any of that shit. The man had basically retired to enjoy the family life, and the mother fucking Twisted Tribe denied him that.

After the dust settles, Twisted Tribe will understand why you don't fuck with my club. Jagger's death will result in far greater losses for them in the end. I just have to bide my time and wait to strike. The beast raging inside of me demands revenge, not only for Jagger, but for his family and our brotherhood. You don't take from us and get to walk away scot free.

Despite my arguments against it, Raze lied to Darcy and the kids, writing it off as a hit and run on his bike. But I suspect she knows the truth. I couldn't help but notice her eyeing his Harley sitting in front of the clubhouse with his cut draped over the seat. It doesn't have a scratch on it. As a longtime old lady, she knows not to ask questions. It's the nature of club life. She, along with every other old lady, knows the rules, but I can see it in her eyes that she won't let this go. She's too strong of a woman to leave it be. It's one of the very reasons she and Maj are so well-respected amongst the men.

When we enter the Heaven's Rejects brotherhood, one of the oaths we swear is to protect and help our own. Jagger's family will never want for anything as long as I live. *I'll make for damn sure of that.*

While the club has surrounded his family with love, Ratchet and I have stayed to ourselves by choice. My brand of rage wasn't what anyone needed right now, and Ratchet, as our enforcer, was in the same boat. We have both taken his death hard. Jagger was Ratchet's fucking hero. He had pulled both of us from a tailspin and helped us back to our feet. Now, he's just gone. Truth be told, it was better for us to be in the shadows than in the spotlight right now. Not until Raze gives us the go ahead to finish this. We need the time to process and work through the rage before stepping in front of his family.

The memory of his marred body will likely stick with Ratchet for the rest of his life, just as the mangled bodies of my brothers in arms in Iraq, who were sent home in wooden boxes with a flag, has with mine. The sight, the smell, and the look on the faces of their widows and children are fresh in my mind, even now, years later. It's not something you can easily shove into the back of your mind and move on with life. It affects you every single fucking day until you draw your last breath. I'm proud that I served our country, but I couldn't take losing my brothers anymore. When the time came to re-up, I left without ever looking back. I wanted that part of my life over with, and I wanted to find peace again, without having the world blow up around me. But sometimes life has a funny way of shoving irony down your throat when you least expect it.

Finding myself in a motorcycle club after returning stateside is something I never imagined happening, but these men are my family, and this clubhouse is my home. My therapist would probably tell me I had exchanged one war for another, and that's why I never told her about the club. She wouldn't understand, and then she would likely put the police on our tail for some of the more questionable actions we've done.

The men around me today are clothed in black from head to toe, with just our cuts on our backs to identify us. Darcy had brought us a couple of Jagger's old Harley shirts, and the other old ladies cut them into strips, and fixed them around our arms when we had gathered in the parking lot this morning. Now, it feels as though Jagger is riding with every single one of us.

Walking back to my black beauty of a bike, I notice the prospects must have been busy the last few days, while the rest of us mourned for our fallen friend, because every Harley belonging to our club is cleaned and polished. Jagger would be proud of how we look, while representing our club and honoring his memory. He was a neat freak when it came to his two-wheeled baby, but I swear, there were days when that damn bike was cleaner than him. Thinking of the good times with Jagger brings a smile to my face, but it soon fades as Raze's bike rumbles into view with the club's Harley hearse attached to it.

The ride to Oak Park Cemetery is somber. Raze leads the procession with Jagger's casket in the hearse. Darcy and the boys follow him in a family car the mortuary had lent to us. I fall behind them, with Ratchet riding beside me. The trail of motorcycles following us spans for miles. People line the streets, watching us ride by. An older man even stands and salutes our procession as we pass by the town square. Jagger may not have served in the military, but he protected his city like a goddamn trained soldier. It makes me happy to see him honored in such a way by perfect strangers.

Raze must have called in yet another favor, because when we pull into the cemetery, the Upland Police Department is blocking off the street surrounding the entrance. Twenty minutes after we enter the cemetery, the final set of motorcycles park in one of the parallel drives. As the crowd gathers around us, the club officers and I slowly remove his casket from the hearse.

Darcy's choice in casket is honestly perfect for the man we're about to bury. The black and gray brushed metal shines in the California sun, as Harley casket corners adorn it. As we walk him to his final resting place, a hushed silence falls upon the crowd. Raze leads Darcy to the center seat, with the boys following quietly behind. I drape Jagger's cut across the casket, and everyone settles around us. The rest of the crowd falls in behind the row of seats as Raze walks to the head of the casket. Jagger wasn't religious in the least bit, but next to Raze stands a Catholic priest in full regale. A stark contrast against our club president in his leather cut.

The priest steps forward, but Raze throws out an arm, stopping him. The priest slinks back to his former position and watches with wide eyes as Raze goes front and center.

"Brent Kyle was more than just a friend to many of us standing in this crowd today. He was our brother. He was with my father from the day this club was born, and he served as my VP during my early years as president. He was the kind of man you knew would always have your back, even if his ass should have stayed the hell out of the way."

A somber laugh escapes my lips as I think about all the times in our club's history that Raze is referencing. Looking to the other officers, they nod in agreement. Jagger had a way of landing his ass into unnecessary trouble with both his brothers and his wife. I don't know how many times we'd narrowly escaped some of our more reckless pursuits, back when I'd first joined the club, only to return home to a pissed off Darcy waiting for us. When Jagger and Darcy had an argument, you'd have thought they hated each other, but we all knew differently. He loved Darcy like she was his only reason for living. He was a better man because of her.

"Brent saved me from myself more times than I like to admit. He was the voice of reason in my head when I couldn't think clearly out of anger. His nickname may have been the reflection of his wilder and younger years, but he was still the front man of this MC. Without him, I doubt this club would have lasted to my generation."

A few sniffles from the women in the crowd fill the air.

"Losing Brent came far too soon. He told me once that it's old men like us that live forever, and I just wish he would have been right. He may be gone from this life, but his spirit will forever live with the men standing here today, and the stories we pass on to the next generation of Heaven's Rejects." Raze's eyes scan the crowd, a tear glistening as it rolls down his cheek.

"I know you're looking down on us today, shaking your head, yelling at me to stop fucking crying and go get a beer. Well Jagger, the beer I drink tonight and every night until my last will be for you. Put in a good word for me up there, brother, because when I get there, we've got some hell to raise. May the roads in heaven ride smooth, and the wind be at your back. I'll see you again at heaven's gates. Just make sure you tell the bastards to let me in."

Soft laughs murmur through the crowd as Raze lays his hand against the head of the casket. His head hangs as he mutters quietly to himself.

Picking up the cut, he walks to Darcy and kneels before her.

"On behalf of the brotherhood of the Heaven's Rejects Motorcycle Club, we present you with Brent's cut as a symbol of our brotherly love and commitment passing from him to you and the boys. This brotherhood will never forsake you and will care for you from this day forward." Pressing a soft kiss on Darcy's cheek, Raze slides Jagger's cut into her hands. "I promised Jagger that if anything ever happened to him, I would take care of you. From this moment on, you and the boys are my responsibility. If you ever need anything, you call me above everyone else."

The crowd murmurs, before Raze shoots us all a shut the fuck up glare. He knows damn well that's not how we handle a fallen brother's cut after his death. We burn it so no one else will wear it. I just hope Raze realizes he is going to piss off some of the other chapters. I've seen the bastard rip a cut from a grieving widow's hands and burn it like our club rules decree. There will be a backlash from this.

Just what we fucking need.

Darcy brings the cut to her face and sobs into the worn, black leather. Stepping back from Jagger's weeping widow, Raze instructs the crowd that the service has ended and dinner will follow at the clubhouse. The motorcycles rumble to life as they depart, leaving only the club officers and Jagger's family behind. We each take turns hugging Darcy as we say our last goodbyes. I silently walk towards Jagger's final resting place and lay my hands over the head of the casket.

"You may be lost to us, Jagger, but I promise you'll never be forgotten. I'll make those bastards pay for you, Darcy, and the kids," I whisper to the sky.

Raze helps Darcy from her seat, and we step away to give her and the boys time alone to say goodbye. She walks away a few minutes later and settles into the waiting car. Morton, our club's go to man for funerals, brings me over the corners from his casket as Jagger's family pulls away, then returns to finish his work. Stowing the corners carefully in my saddlebags, I start my bike and ride back to the clubhouse with the others.

Entering the club, I notice that the club girls look almost normal today as they carry platters of food out of the back door. They've stowed their tits and short skirts, exchanging them for simple black dresses. Maria, Hot Shot's old lady, stayed behind to supervise the girls for Maj, and made sure the food was ready by the time we got back from the graveside service. I need to thank her for that later.

The tent we'd rented has been set up in the backyard and is filled to the brim. The chatter of the other chapters and their families fill the tent, while my brothers and I eat in silence, surrounding Jagger's mourning family. As I shovel in a spoonful of food, Darcy's face catches my attention. Her eyes are circled with dark rings as she shifts her food around from one side of her plate to the other. She doesn't want to be here in this big crowd. A feeling I know all too well myself.

"Irons," I mutter to our newest prospect, who is seated next to me.

"What's up?"

"I think Darcy and the kids are over this. Why don't you and Slider give them a lift home and watch over the place?"

It's the least we can do until we know the coast is clear from anymore Tribe surprises.

"You got it, boss."

Irons takes one last bite of food before slipping away from the table and placing his hand on Darcy's back. I watch as he leans down and whispers to her. She glances up at me with the tiniest smile of relief on her face, then nods a quick thanks. She slides away from the table with the boys, Irons, and Slider in tow.

Over the next several hours, people begin to disperse

and head home to await orders on our plans. Every single chapter president had pledged all the manpower they could spare to help us with the upcoming attack on the TT's retaliation. They respect Raze's decision to wait until the time is right to strike. Everyone knows it's pointless to stick around waiting while Raze calculates our next move. Voodoo, our club technical expert, has spent the last few days tracking their moves, and like we suspected, they've gone underground.

Once everyone is gone but our own club, Ruby and the girls work to clean up the mess from lunch, while some of the guys and I head into the main room. Ratchet plops down next to me on the worn leather couch and flips the television to ESPN. Raze joins us, parking in his favorite recliner, and together we sit in silence, blankly staring off into space in the general direction of the TV.

"I can't fucking take the silence anymore," Voodoo declares. "I'm getting the fuck out of here and heading to Red's. I need a change of scenery. Who's with me?"

"Shit, man, I'm in. I think we owe it to Jagger to celebrate his life," I reply. He'd hate seeing us like this. He was always the one who picked us back up when shit went south. Raze is right. "Let me change into some normal fucking clothes, and I'll meet you outside."

Jumping up from the couch, I walk down the hallway to my room at the clubhouse and fling the door open. I retrieve a pair of my worn, ripped jeans from the dresser, along with one of my Harley t-shirts. I slip off my cut and toss my dress shirt into the hamper by the door. I pull the jeans up my muscular legs that are littered with scars. Seeing the jagged lines on my skin makes me think about my time overseas again, but I don't want to deal with that shit right now. After throwing my riding boots back on, I grab my cut and head out the door.

Most of the club is sitting on their bikes waiting for me. I spy a few of the club girls and old ladies happily perched behind a few of my brothers.

I guess this is going to be more of a family outing than a brother thing. Not exactly what I had in mind, but whatever.

Raze and Maj are the last to join us, and as I start the engine of my bike and feel it rumble to life between my legs. The hum of the engine soothes me like a mother's lullaby.

Following Raze, we pull out of the club's parking lot and cruise towards town. We drive around to the back of the bar and park our bikes in the employee parking lot. Kellen, the bouncer, waves us in, and we settle in our usual corner. Bobby brings over our normal round of beers and a whiskey neat for me without even needing to be prompted. Red's may be the shittiest bar in town, but they treat the club right. We've taken care of some problems for Red over the years, so he indulges us whenever we come rolling in.

The bar is pretty empty for a Friday night, but it'll

liven up the later it gets. Sucking down the whiskey, I lean back into the booth and watch the girls dancing to shitty pop music. I don't know how anyone over the age of twelve could listen to this bullshit, but the club girls seem to love it.

Raze orders a round of Johnny Walker for us, and Bobby brings over the whole bottle and several shot glasses. Picking up the bottle, Raze pours the whiskey into each glass, doling them out to the five of us.

"It's only right that as a brotherhood, we drink in Jagger's honor." He raises his glass in the air as he speaks. "Jagger, this shot is for you. Ride free forever, brother."

Clinking our glasses together, we drink to our fallen brother, letting the whiskey burn down our throats. The first of many drinks to come.

The alcohol flows freely as the night goes on, and it doesn't take long for my buzz to take hold. My brothers and I reminisce about the old days, telling stories about Jagger and our more perilous exploits.

"Do you remember that one time, when Jagger stumbled into Church naked, after a patch party?" Voodoo jokes. My brothers chime in, but my attention is immediately drawn elsewhere when a tall blonde walks into the room wearing just a scrap of a dress.

She sure as fuck isn't leaving much to the imagination in that getup.

But it's not her that draws my attention. It's the olive-skinned beauty standing next to her. While the blonde looks like a typical California bar slut, the raven beauty next to her is far from the normal view in a place like this. Her exotic look is fucking sexy, and my dick approves as it starts to strain against the fly of my jeans. My night just may be looking up after all.

Ratchet notices my eagle eye on the dark-haired one. A knowing smirk grows on his face, but I can't pull my eyes away from the raven-haired mystery for more than a few seconds. Annoyed by my lack of attention, he throws a wadded-up bar napkin at my face.

"Hey, fuckface. Did you hear what I just said?" he yells across the table.

"Yup."

He glares back, knowing I didn't hear a fucking word. "You want the blonde, or the other one?"

"You know blondes aren't my thing."

"Fine by me," he says with a shrug. "Blondes are more fun, anyway."

Rolling my eyes, we both sit back and watch our prey. Red corners them both almost immediately. Fucking asshole thinks he has a chance with a woman like that. In his wildest dreams. But if I have my way, she will go home with me tonight.

Ratchet slips from the booth and makes a beeline for

her friend. I take my chance and move in for the kill. Just my luck, she smacks right into me.

"Dance with me," I demand of her.

She hesitates, but I don't give her the chance to protest. My hands fall to her hips, and she sways against me to the music. We remain silent as our bodies sway together, but my dick is screaming to come out to play. This woman's curves are like none I have ever seen. She's a dangerous mix of exotic and soft perfection, unlike the harden plastic-filled women you usually see around this place. I spin her just as a waitress slides over to us with a shot glass in her hand.

"I didn't order this," she says, peering up at me under long lashes. Her hazel eyes scan my face, and I can't help but notice that she's checking out the rest of me.

She's into this. Good. It'll make taking her home easier.

"One of his buddies ordered it for you," the waitress informs her before turning away. I turn to see Voodoo smiling back at me. Motherfucker is going to pay for this.

I watch as she shoots back the blue concoction in one swallow

"What's your name?" I demand.

"Like that's what you really want to know?" She laughs over the sound of the pounding music. "What's it to you?"

"I want to know the name of the woman I'll be fucking tonight?"

"And who says that will be me?"

She's feisty and beautiful. Definitely a dangerous combination that I want to taste over and over again in my bed later tonight.

"I'm still waiting on that name."

"My name is—" Her friend pulls her away before I get my answer.

"I don't feel well," her friend gurgles and gags.

"I'll be right back," she tells me, before her friend drags her off the dance floor. I move to go after her, but her friend pukes all over herself and the floor, sending them in the direction of the bathroom.

Fuck it. I can wait until she gets back.

Ratchet shrugs his shoulders, and we head back to our seats. Red's leaning against our table, talking to Voodoo as we approach. Ratchet slaps Red on the back before sliding into the booth.

"Red, who are the two women you were talking to earlier?" I ask. I need to get as much information on my target before sealing the deal. "She belong to someone?"

Red turns to me with a confused look. "Are you talking about the blonde?"

"Fuck no, the one with the black hair that was with her. Need to know if I'm stepping on any toes by dragging her off later."

Red throws his head back and laughs. "She's my new waitress. I think her name's Dawn, or Debbie, or something like that. I was too busy checking out her rack to catch her name. She's a feisty one. That spirit is going to make me a ton of money."

The thought of him touching her flares rage in me, and I reach out and grip the front of his shirt, yanking him to me. "She's off limits," I warn through clenched teeth.

Red straightens his shirt once I let him go. "Sure, Hero. Whatever you say, man. But you should probably know that the blonde with her is Ricky's girl."

Ricky mother fucking Alvarez. President of the local TT chapter. Fuck. Ratchet straightens in his seat upon hearing the club's name. He starts out of the booth, and I know he's going after the girl. She has value to Ricky, and when he sees a way in to get TT back, he won't walk away from it. He's like a bloodhound when he sees a way to solve our club's problems. A bloodhound with zero conscience. Grabbing him by the arm, I stop him from going any farther.

"We can't do that shit in here, and we sure as shit won't use a woman as bait. Get your fucking head on straight, man. This isn't the way our club operates."

He jerks away from me and charges out of the door.

"I guess playtime's over, gentlemen," Red says, watching Ratchet leave.

"I think you're right. Doubt you want blood staining on your floor tonight. By the way, I'll look into what you mentioned earlier," Voodoo says, then he leads the rest of the group away from the booth.

Following along behind them, I search the crowd to see if she emerges. I can't believe she's likely tied up in the Twisted Tribe bullshit. I guess I dodged a bullet by not acting on my earlier ideas, but tell that to my aching dick. He wants the taste of the forbidden just as badly as I do, but even I know not to fuck with another club's woman. It's not worth starting a war over a bit of new pussy, even if it's beautifully packaged.

Chapter 5

DANI

"ORDER UP, DANI," Rick, the bar's head cook, yells.

Scuttling back to the dirty kitchen prep area, I grab the plate of loaded cheese fries and head out to my table to deliver them. It's been three weeks since I started working at Red's, and I'm finally getting in the groove of working at a dive bar. It's easy work. Take orders, serve beer, avoid Red, and ignore the inappropriate sexual remarks of the sleaze ball regular customers. At first, I thought telling the grabby patrons I batted for the other team would deter them, but I soon discovered that made them even more interested. I don't know how many times they asked if they could watch. Creeps.

Most days, Ricca and I get to work together. It only took me two days of working here to realize why she comes home drunk every night. Every single man in this bar tries to buy her a shot, hoping they can get into her pants after closing. Why refuse a good drink if they offer the expensive hooch as an incentive? She never says no, but I do. I don't need to chance getting slipped a roofie and date raped for a free drink. That's not worth the risk. I'll stick to my glass of ice water that Bobby keeps behind the bar for me. I don't feel like I need to worry about him drugging me, since his boyfriend would kick his ass for hitting on a woman.

The part of this job that *has* disappointed me is that the man I drunkenly danced with hasn't returned. Deep down, I was hoping he was a regular here, and I would get the chance to see him again. There was something about him. Something I haven't been able to shake since I danced with him.

The feel of his body against mine. His hardness pressed so tightly against me. His eyes.

The dark green orbs were framed by his tanned skin and light brown hair. The way they stared into me, like they were reaching inside my body and coiling around my soul, drew me in. I've never had a man affect me like that before, but I want to see him again.

Every time I heard a motorcycle pull up, my eyes dart toward the door, hoping it's him. But it never is. What it is about him that makes me feel this way? I had danced with him once. I don't even know his name, but here I sit and watch that door like a hawk every night, hoping he walks through it.

Pathetic. I am utterly and hopelessly pathetic.

After dropping off the fries to a group of drunken frat boys, I saunter up to the bar and deposit myself onto a seat. Tonight has been slow, and there's no use checking on my two tables, since they are already blitzed. I doubt they can find their own feet.

"Tough night?" Bobby asks, while wiping down the bar.

"Yeah, you could say that. Those frat boys have spent two hundred dollars on drinks tonight, but I can tell already they won't be leaving me a damn tip." I sigh and spin around on the bar stool to face Bobby. "Remind me why I do this again?" I say, planting my face on top of my arms.

"You need the money, D," I hear Ricca say from behind me. She sits on the stool next to me, laying her head on Bobby's nice clean bar. Swatting her off the freshly cleaned wood with a bar towel, Bobby slides two glasses in front of us.

"You okay?" I ask.

"Yeah," she says with a sigh. "Boyfriend problems, but it'll be fine."

"I think it's time to celebrate, ladies," Bobby says. He pours two shots of tequila for us, and then one for himself. "Dani has made it three whole weeks in this shit hole, and she hasn't stabbed anyone with a rusty fork. Cheers!"

All three of us laugh as we slurp down the shot. The heat from the tequila travels down into my stomach before I can even set my glass back onto the bar for Bobby to refill. He looks at me with an inquisitive look before pouring another.

"Definitely a bad night. Dani's having two shots of tequila." He fills my little glass and grins, then corks the bottle and sets it back under the bar. "No more for you tonight. We don't want you to lose focus on how to avoid Red when you go to get your pay from the office."

Tipping back the shot, I flip Bobby off, then stalk back to my table to check on my customers one last time before the last call. Thankfully, they don't stick around, and the bar is finally empty fifteen minutes later. After I finish sweeping up my area, I head back to the office. Creeping quietly around the corner, I peek into Red's office. He's nowhere to be found. *Thank god.* I slip into the room undetected.

The envelope containing my pay lingers on his desk, and I snatch it up, bolting for the door to make my exit before he gets back. Unfortunately, my plan fails, because I literally run right into the pervert as I try to escape.

"Well now, Dani baby. Looks like you were trying to give me the slip," he drawls. I quickly take a step back, trying to backpedal away from him. His hand slides across my ass as I move.

"Oh, uh. Hi, Red," I stammer. "Didn't see you

standing there." The way his eyes are watching me sends uncomfortable chills down my spine. Waving my pay envelope in the air, I stuff it into my back pocket. "Well, I got my last week's pay, so I better get out there before Ricca leaves without me."

I move to get around his figure looming in the door. His hot, smelly breath oozes down my chest as I attempt to squeeze past him. He rotates, just as I'm about to make it back into the hallway and away from him, pinning me to the door frame with his beer belly.

"You know, Dani. You could be making much better money if you would agree to be my secretary," he whispers, his lips now just inches from my face. I try to turn away, but he grabs my chin, pulling it back to face him.

"Your pretty face and nice ass are bringing in new customers for me left and right, but I don't like sharing you with the world. Maybe I'll just chain you to my desk. I think I'd like watching you helping me with the bar's paperwork. You'd like being my baby doll, wouldn't you, my beautiful Dani?"

"Your wife works here," I recoil. "Ask her."

"Don't worry about her. She won't mind."

"She might not, but I do. I'm not interested."

The idea repulses me just as much as the touch of him on my body does right now. He must notice the fear in my eyes because he lets out a hearty laugh. Shoving against him one last time, I break free of his grasp. I can hear his laughter as I scurry back down the hallway, toward where Ricca should be waiting for me.

"Remember my proposal, Dani. I'll make it worth your while," he calls out before closing his office door.

The bar area is empty now, except for Kellen, the bouncer. Damn it. She left me.

Kellen's face nearly confirms it as he saunters up to me, carrying my purse from behind the bar. His build is that of a professional linebacker. Big, wide, and terrifying. He may look scary, but he's the sweetest person I've ever met. Every night, he waits for me to leave before locking up.

"You ready to go, Miss Dani?" he says with his thick southern drawl. With no idea where Ricca is, I can only nod my head. He opens the bar door and walks outside with me. "Red didn't hurt you, did he?"

Kellen knows I don't like Red, or being anywhere near him. Especially after the first run-in I'd had with him a few days into my employment at the bar. Red got a little too handsy with me for Kellen's liking, and he got me out of that situation before it got worse. He's my savior in this place.

"No, I'm fine. He didn't hurt me, but thank you for checking on me. Did you see Ricca leave?" I ask.

"Someone came to pick her up. She wanted me to tell you that she left the keys under the floor mat of the jeep. She said to take it and just head on home. She'll get a ride back in the morning," he says, as we near Ricca's jeep. He opens the door for me, and I feel around the floorboard for Ricca's keys. I finally feel the cool metal and pull them out of their hiding spot under the mat.

"Do you want me to follow you home?" Kellen asks.

"You don't have to do that, K. I'll be fine. I can get myself home," I reply with a soft smile. I step up into the jeep and settle into the driver's seat. He shuts the door for me, and I slip the seatbelt around my waist. Starting up the engine, I put the car into reverse.

"Lock up when you get home, Dani," Kellen yells over the noise of the engine. Nodding in agreement, I back the jeep out of the spot and shove it into first gear, heading for the parking lot exit. I wave to the watchful Kellen, and then pull into the street and head for home.

Safely arriving at my apartment a few minutes later, I lock the door and toss Ricca's keys on the counter. I wonder what the hell is going on. Why couldn't she tell me where she was going? She was off the entire night, and her ghosting on me doesn't exactly put me in the bests of moods. If she had plans, she could have just told me.

Pulling the envelope out of the back of my jeans, I count the cash and put half in my secret hiding spot, behind a loose baseboard between my bed and the TV stand. The rest of the cash I deposit into my purse on the side table. I had discovered my hidey hole after an extreme cleaning session.

At first, I took to hiding my cash from Ricca, because sometimes you just never know a person's true intentions until it's too late. Now, I hide it from her elusive boyfriend. I still find it odd that I have yet to meet the man she claims is the love of her life, but it's not my prerogative to inquire about him. I'm not about to leave my cash lying around when he could stop by any second, though. I've learned my lesson about trusting too soon. Cleveland is proof of that.

Stripping off my work clothes and depositing them into the ever-growing pile of laundry by the door, I slip into a shirt and shorts, then climb into bed. An hour or so later, I hear the door of the apartment open and foot-steps coming from the living room. I settle back when I hear the door to Ricca's room open. I think for a split second about having it out with her for leaving me before she passes out, but it won't do any good. Not until she sobers up. My eyes close and exhaustion takes me under again almost immediately.

"Who the fuck are you?" a male voice screams. Suddenly, I'm ripped from my bed and thrown onto the floor. I scramble to get my wits about me, but my attacker doesn't wait for me to wake up fully.

"I'm not asking again, bitch," he roars. "Answer me!" Before I can even reply, he presses a gun to my temple. "I'm still waiting for that name. I'll give you until the count of three to give me your name, or I'm going to pump this pretty fucking head of yours full of lead." He clicks the trigger as he pulls back. "One… Two…"

"Dani!" I yell. "My name is Dani!"

Feeling the gun pull away from my head, I can finally breathe again. My vision is still blurry with sleep, but I just can make out that his muscular, tanned arms are covered in tattoos. His jean-clad legs are powerful and huge.

"Well, that wasn't so hard now, was it, Dani? Where's Ricca? I know you know where that bitch is."

"I don't know." My voice comes out uneven and full of fear.

"Bullshit," he seethes. "Tell me where the fuck she is."

"I don't know! She left me the jeep and told the bouncer she had somewhere she needed to be," I shriek, just before he kicks me in the stomach, knocking the air out of me.

"Tell me where she and my money are and this all stops," he growls, then lands another blow to my midsection.

"I don't know!" I scream. "I saw her just before I left the bar. That's all I know."

Kicking me a third time, I feel something inside me

snap. A pain-laced scream rips from my throat, and my hands fly to protect my blisteringly painful stomach.

"Maybe she's with her boyfriend," I sputter out. "Maybe he knows."

"I'm her fucking boyfriend, bitch." He curses at me in Spanish, striking me with the butt of his gun on the back of my head as I try to crawl away from him. I hear the crack as it connects, followed by a searing, radiating pain. My world dims under the weight of it. Black, inky edges throbbing in my vision. His rough hands grab me, dragging me back. Then he shoves me on my back, his legs straddling my waist, pinning me between him and the ground.

"I swear, I don't know where she is. Please, stop kicking me. Please!" I cry.

"Oh, puta," he says, leaning down closer to me. "Please doesn't work with a guy like me. If you think a few shots to your stomach are bad, just wait until we get you back to the clubhouse." He calls out through the door in Spanish, and four more men walk into my bedroom. The men surround me, while the man with the gun hauls me to my feet by my hair. As he rips me from the floor, the pain from my stomach shoots through my torso. It limits me from my ability to fight back, but it's not going to stop me.

I flail my feet outward, hoping to connect with his groin, but I miss completely. One of others grabs me, his fingertips digging into my shoulders, but I bite his hand as hard as I can. Before I can move, another hand grabs me by the throat and squeezes, cutting off my air supply and killing the fight left in me.

"You're a feisty little bitch. I like that. Maybe there's some use for you, after all. I guess you'll have to pay her debt," he says with a sinister laugh.

I fidget, trying to break free from his grasp before he chokes the life of me.

"I hope you like dick, puta, because you are about to become our newest whore. The guys will have fun breaking you in," he says, his voice laced with evil as he increases the pressure on my throat.

The room blurs, and his laughter continues. Darkness takes over my vision just before I pass out under his grip.

The hum of an engine fills my ears as I slip back into consciousness and the pain shocks me awake. Time moves slowly, and I try to keep my eyes open. Where am I? The thump of the prison surrounding me and the honk of a car horn outside gives me an answer. I'm in a car, and it's fucking moving.

With each jostle of the car, pain radiates across my stomach. I need to calm myself down before I pass out again. I won't be taken prisoner by these bastards. I try to move my hands, but duct tape binds them in a prayer position.

I wrack my brain for ideas on how to get out of this,

when suddenly, the car comes to a stop. The door's slams shut, and footsteps walk away from the car. The muted male voices radiate through the metal panels, growing quieter, and then I hear the ring of a door opening.

Are they all out of the car?

I remain silent and still. Minutes tick by and only silence comes from inside. This might be my only chance to escape before they bind me to a bed and make me their sex slave. I'd rather die than let one of these fucking bastards touch me.

While wiggling around in the car, I discover that my feet are unbound. I thank God for small miracles, or in this case, their stupidity. This oversight on their part is my only shot. I'd be a fool if I didn't take it.

Using my unbound feet as leverage, I shift gently to my side to avoid injuring my aching ribs any more than necessary. I feel around the dark compartment with my feet, hoping to find the string attached to the trunk release.

Yes! They didn't remove it.

Finally, I feel a piece of corded material in the corner by the trunk lid. Maneuvering the string between the toes on my left foot, I clench it tightly and pull. I can feel the cord trying to release the latch, but I need more pressure. I clamp down harder on the string, maneuvering my other foot to flank the side, and pull with all the energy I can muster. The string yanks back hard, and I hear the latch click. Pushing up on the lid with the side of my right knee, the trunk slowly pops open.

As fast as I can, I scoot to the edge of the trunk and peer out. It's pitch black outside, which is to my advantage. There will be fewer people on the streets to alert the kidnapping bastards inside of my escape. I push the trunk lid higher and slip my legs over the edge of the trunk. Gingerly, I lift my upper body off of the trunk's carpeted floor and sit upright, then with one last look around, I slide out of the trunk. My feet shake beneath me as I try to regain my footing.

Closing the lid with my bound hands, I cautiously jog away, trying to ignore the pain radiating from my stomach with every step. Broken glass and rocks dig into my bare feet. The car is parked in front of a diner, but there's nobody outside. I make my way around a corner a few blocks away. I lie in wait for my captors to drive off, crouched behind what has to be the smelliest dumpster I have ever encountered in my life.

Ten minutes later, my former prison roars to life and speeds past my hiding spot. Minutes tick by, and I sigh in relief that they haven't yet discovered my escape and doubled back. Using a rusty and jagged edge of the old dumpster, I cut the duct tape wrapped around my hands. I know from watching forensic shows with my step-dad that they can pull fingerprints from the sticky side of the tape, so I stow the evidence into the waistband of my pajama shorts for safekeeping. Maybe I could use it to identify the bastards later.

I push myself off the dirty ground and make my way back to the street. I check out my surroundings, keeping to the shadowed corners.

Where am I? How long was I out?

Just thinking about home sends a thick layer of fear settling over me. All my money, clothes, and meager possessions are all there, including the photograph of my parents. I can't go back, and I can't exactly go to the police for help, either. Not without shining a bright beacon on me screaming, "Here I am!" for my Cleveland demons. I don't even know Kellen or Bobby's number to help me get out of wherever I am, even if I did have a phone.

I am alone, with no one to call and no place to go for the second time in a matter of months. Truly helpless.

I wander the streets until I finally spot an abandoned house next to a salon. Looking through the boarded-up windows, I get the idea that no one has lived here in ages. Wooden slates cover the ground level windows and doors. I test each one, until finally, a board slips free from an old nail. Sliding between the gap I just made, I step into a dust-covered room. The place is unfurnished, but at least it's off the street, and secluded enough that nobody will see me hiding in here while I figure out my next move.

The rising sun illuminates the room just enough that I can maneuver in the space. Just as I determine I will have to sleep on a dirty floor, I spot a cot propped up in the corner. Looks like someone else used this old house as a sleeping place before me. Hopefully, they don't come back and find me poaching their territory.

Sliding the cot from the wall, I set it up and use my foot to test its strength. It seems surprisingly sturdy. I get as comfortable as I can on the rough canvas covering of the cot, but my mind will not stop replaying the day.

You have to rest, Dani. Just get some rest, then we'll see how big of a fucking mess Ricca has gotten us into.

The thought of my roommate has me seething with anger. She brought this on me. I was finally settling into life here as best as I could, and yet again, someone rips it away from me. I'm so tired of running from the evil in this world. My life of hiding in the shadows has finally caused me to hit rock bottom. I'm homeless and broke. It's at this moment I truly realize how far from grace I've fallen. My mother would be so ashamed of what a colossal screw up her daughter has become.

It's probably a good thing she's not alive to see it happen.

Chapter 6

HERO

THE THUNDEROUS SOUNDS *of explosions shake me awake. My body is frozen in place, and I watch my brother's bodies erupt into flames. Their hands are outstretched, reaching towards me as they cry for help. Their scorched bodies pop and crackle from the intense heat. I try to escape the invisible bonds that bind me in place. The bright flash of another bomb blinds me, and louder screams pour from the fire-bombed area surrounding me. More inflamed bodies crawl towards me, and their burning flesh assaults my nostrils the closer they get. The smoke finally clears, and the faces of my brothers have changed to a female face surrounded by a hazy smoke.*

Her beautiful, dark body is marred by slashes and holes, while blood pours from her wounds. "Help me," she cries. A man follows closely behind as she runs towards me. She stretches out her hand to me, and just before I can grip it, the man jerks her back. His maniacal smile beams as he runs a knife across her throat, sending blood spurting everywhere. She falls to her knees, her eyes never leaving mine as the blood pours from her body like a fountain.

"You didn't save me, Hero. You failed me," she whispers. And then he pumps a bullet into her head.

"No!" I wail, rushing from bed to fight for her. I make it halfway to the door before I realize I'm in my room at the clubhouse, and not in Iraq. The smell of their burning flesh still lingers in my nostrils, and my body trembles from fear, my chest heaving with adrenaline. *Fuck. The nightmares have never been this vivid before. Just fucking breathe, before someone comes up here to check on you.*

For the weeks since we had laid Jagger to rest, I've been dreaming about the IED explosion that had claimed my brother's lives and left me scarred. I've relived that day repeatedly, but tonight is the first time the woman was there. The woman from the bar the other night. The women who may have ties to my enemies. Forbidden fucking fruit. As much as I'd like to find out how good fucking her would feel, she's off limits. My club has enough to deal with right now.

I can't have her. Plain and simple. My club's needs will always come first over my own.

After a quick shower, I head downstairs for breakfast. Ruby walks over, handing a plate of food to me.

"Thanks, Ruby," I say. Kissing her cheek, I take the plate of bacon and eggs from her and plop down on the leather sofa next to Raze and the rest of our motley crew. I take a bite of the crispy bacon and realize every man in our circle is staring at me. Putting down my fork, I toss my full plate onto the side table.

"Did I grow a big pair of tits last night? The fuck is wrong with all of you?" I stare them all down, but no one seems to want to speak. "Out with it," I growl. Raze shifts uncomfortably next to me.

"We heard you," Raze answers. The dream. Fuck. Just what I need. "I know you went through some shit overseas, man. Do you need to talk to someone about it?"

"I'm fine. Jesus. Can't a man have a bad night?" I snap.

How dare these bastards sit around in a goddamn prayer circle judging me? I've seen more bad shit in a single day than they have experienced in their entire civilian lives. Yes, I have fucking demons in my past, but they're no one's business but my own.

"We're being serious," Ratchet says. "You good?"

"I'm fine. Jagger's death just dug shit up. I'm dealing with it."

"I'm sure the VA could set you back up with your counselor again," Tyson adds into the conversation.

"No, I'm good. Just need to work shit out on my own."

"My door is always open, Hero, if you ever need to talk," Raze offers. The cool seriousness of his face stays locked on mine, driving his point home.

"Same here," Voodoo offers, followed by each of my brothers.

"I appreciate it, guys. I really do, but this is something I need to work out on my own."

"All we need to know, Hero. We just needed to clear the air."

Grabbing my discarded plate, we settle in and catch up on sports news for the next hour, before heading into Church.

I'll admit, its weird being in this room without Jagger. He was the guy who made sure our meetings never got out of hand. With him gone, the room feels uneasy. Like a ticking time bomb ready to explode at the drop of a hat.

Something's up.

I peer over at Ratchet, whose face is tightly coiled with a frown. He feels it, too.

Raze moves to the front of the table and throws down a stack of papers, sending them sliding down the table.

"The fuck is all that?" Voodoo asks.

"It seems like some of our upstate brothers are pissed that we didn't burn Jagger's cut," he grumbles.

I knew from the moment he gave Darcy that damn cut we'd have problems. The original chapter sets and enforces the entire club's rules, and our president just broke a cardinal rule because he felt like it. Shit doesn't work like that in an MC.

"It's not surprising. We've never broken that rule for anyone before."

Raze crumbles the paper in his hand and slams his fists onto the wooden table. "Jagger was our brother, and a founding member of this club. He presented me with the cut I have on my back now. Forgive me for wanting to honor a piece of our history, but I'm not backing down. Darcy and the boys deserve that cut more than the earth needs its ashes," he declares.

"You know this could hurt our reputation with the other chapters," I say. "Fuck, Raze. They could call for your President's patch for this. Some of the other clubs were already questioning our chapter's decisions before Jagger, and this might just cut the thin tether we still have over them."

"Yes, I fucking know that, Hero. I'll take the hit for it because it was my damn decision."

Raze is pissed. More so than I have seen him since we found Jagger. *He should be here.* Jagger was the only guy who could settle him down. Just another reason to miss the fucker. It's my job now, and hell if I know how to handle him. He's a hair-trigger away from setting the world on fire to get what he wants.

How in the hell am I going to diffuse the situation? I'm not good at this shit.

"What if we amend the club charter to say that cuts of founding members may be given to their surviving family if their chapter votes in favor?" I suggest. Raze's eyes narrow at my suggestion, while the veins in his arms constrict. He's either going to clean my clock with a right hook, or he'll see my reason. Either way, we're still fucked. Even if he takes this back-door deal to amend the rules, some of the chapter presidents aren't going to like that we didn't include them in the vote. We're damned if we do, and damned if we don't.

"The clubs are going to be pissed any way we play this, but at least this will cover our ass for the time being. I'll forge the papers to pre-date his death, and I'll lie out my ass that we didn't get it sent out because we were dealing with Jagger's murder. It's not a perfect plan, but it's that or deal with the backlash. We need their support for taking out Twisted Tribe, and I'm not about to lose the manpower over a bunch of grown ass men whining like little bitches about a cut."

Raze pounds his fists down on the table before walking away from us. His hands go to his brow, and he rubs his temples as he thinks.

"Do it, Hero," he says a minute later. "I assume we don't need a formal vote to use this half-cocked plan to cover my ass, or would you like to vote to make it kosher?"

"Nah, we're behind you. But maybe next time you decide to break a founding charter rule, you'll let us know before shit hits the fan," Ratchet says. "We all miss the fucker, but we can't collapse as a club because you want to honor his memory for his wife and kids. He knew what he signed up for when he took his pledge."

"I know, Ratch," Raze sighs. "But his death wasn't exactly accidental. Darcy was finally getting his health under control before those murderous sons-of-bitches killed him. I wanted to reassure her we were handling it. We all know she didn't buy my cock and bull story about a riding accident. She's too fucking smart for her own good."

"I get that, Raze," Voodoo says. "But maybe we should just send flowers next time, instead of pissing off our back-up."

"Noted," Raze grumbles. "Any other business we need to discuss?" The room stays silent as we look at each other. "Dismissed."

As one, we all stand and file out of the room. Raze had actually taken my suggestion. I'm not sure whether to be flattered or dumbfounded.

He's a hard-headed bastard, but he has a good heart when he wants to unleash his nice side. It's just that sometimes his thoughts come out a little convoluted. I head towards the bar to talk to Ruby about going out on a ride with me, when Maj's shrill voice cuts through the noise in the room.

Could this day get any worse?

Chapter 7

DANI

FOOD, water, and shelter.

The three basic needs of survival. Shelter? Check. Water? Check. That is the one saving grace I have, because this old house still has running water. It isn't exactly warm, but I can clean myself and my clothes in the old sink. Not to mention that I don't have to resort to using a bucket as a toilet. I've never been so thankful for water in my entire life.

Food is proving to be a bit harder. Having no money eliminates sneaking out and buying supplies, if that were even an option. I don't know if those guys are still out there, canvasing the area to find me. No. I have to stay put for now. Scraping by the best I can.

My ribs aren't helping the matter. Any movement sets off the pain. I'd found some old curtains that I had washed and bound around me to stabilize them the best

I could. I'd broken a rib before, playing soccer as a kid. The pain was nothing like this now.

Between food and my battered ribs, I'm in trouble. Big freaking trouble. That trouble is the only reason I sneak out every night, searching the local business for supplies and food scraps. Luckily, there is a local mom and pop diner down the street that has decent garbage to dig through for food. It might be half-eaten, but it still fills my grumbling belly.

Methods of survival.

Tonight has been a particularly good night for dumpster diving. The diner had thrown out a few bags of apples and oranges that are only soft in a few spots. Snatching the bags, I immediately rush them back to the house, stowing them just inside the door for later. They will last me a couple of days at least.

I start down a different street and find a few more household items to add to my stockpile, including a nice blanket for my bed, which I stuff into a trash bag I collected to keep it clean. I continue to search the street, finding an old shirt that is clean enough to use for binding my ribs until I figure out what to do with them.

Giving up for the night, I slink back to the house. The sunrise is just starting to come up, and the sky is turning a pretty shade of pink and orange. As I round the corner, I spy a tall man lingering in the shadows by the neighboring salon's back door. I can't make out his features, as he stays in the shadows, but I can make out orange and green writing with a white skull on the back of his jacket. Just like the one my captors were wearing.

Shit. They've found me. Panic sets in immediately. My heart rate picks up like I'm running a sprint, beating wildly in my chest.

Sliding behind a set of trash cans to avoid detection, I watch as the man jiggles the lock on the door, then raises his foot and kicks it in. He retrieves a flashlight from his pocket and steps into the building, shutting the door behind him. I can hear glass breaking and hard objects hitting the walls. Suddenly, he exits the building, tossing a match behind him. Fire bursts from the ground, moving quickly towards the interior of the structure. He jogs past my hiding spot and hops into a battered gray pickup truck, then peels out into the street, leaving the scene of the crime.

A fire is not what I need right now. It'll attract the local authorities and fire department. So not what I need right now. I pause, considering my options. I could go back to the house and hide, hoping not to be found, or I can try to deal with it, covering up my existence. Neither is a good option, but it only takes a second for me to realize there's really only one thing I can do to lessen the risk of discovery.

Rushing towards the burning building, I spy a discarded towel near the trash can. Grabbing it, I try to smother the flames the best I can. The smoke fills my lungs with each toss of the towel, while the fire singes it. My ribs scream in pain with every labored swing.

"Fuck!" I cough out, sucking more smoky air into my already burning lungs. I have a few minutes at the most before the carbon dioxide in the air completely incapacitates me. Pulling my shirt up over my nose as a makeshift mask, I beat down the flames until I reach a hair-washing sink. I cough harder into the foul smoke as my fingers feel for the handle of the spigot. My fingers finally find it, and I use the sprayer to douse the last of the flames. The charred wood sizzles from the heat and water being sprayed over it. My heart thuds when I hear sirens in the distance, growing closer by the second.

I have to get out of here. They can't find me.

I bolt out of the salon and into my makeshift home just as the fire truck pulls into the alley. Sliding the wood slat over my secret entrance, I slide my body to the floor. My lungs heave for fresh air as I force myself to catch my breath and slow the adrenaline pumping through my body. The exertion of trying to put out the fire has taken its toll on my damaged ribs. The adrenaline was enough to mask the pain temporarily, but as it leaves my body, it is replaced with searing pain that nearly cripples me with each breath.

I really need to take care of these soon. Somehow. Some way.

I watch the firefighters buzz around the semi-burnt structure for hours, my eyes trained on them until they finally leave the scene. The police linger, however, securing the area with barricades, and inspecting the scene outside. I stow a silent curse when one of them spies my bag of discarded treasures and rummages through it. I don't breathe again until he tosses it aside and resumes his search.

A short time later, the police leave the scene, and I can finally rest easy, knowing I will not be discovered. I pad into the old kitchen and pull the smoke-filled shirt and shorts from my body, depositing them into the water-filled sink to soak.

God, I wish I had some good soap.

I'm pretty sure my only pair of shorts is now ruined. Pulling on one of the old worn-out t-shirts I had found in my nightly scavenger hunts over my head, I drink a couple glasses of water, then head to bed. I know it's not a smart idea to sleep without being monitored after inhaling so much smoke, but I don't have a choice. I need to rest my body, and more so my ribs. I slide onto the soft, but worn, couch cushion and pull the blanket around me. Falling asleep comes easily.

A voice startles me awake.

No. No. No! Hide. I have to hide.

Scrambling to hide, I slide off the bed and run to the closet under the stairwell as quietly as I can, shutting the door behind me. I huddle into the darkness, hoping it's enough to mask me. Heavy footsteps enter the room.

"Do you see anyone, Voodoo?" The feminine voice comes from the kitchen.

"No, Maj. There's a bed in here, though," a male voice responds. The heavy footsteps move closer to me. "It's still warm, so whoever this belongs to is not very far away." I hear the cot's metal legs scruff against the hardwood of the floor. Heels click into the room as the noise from the cot stops.

"They've got to be here. The soot footprints led into this house. Are you sure you've checked everywhere downstairs?" she asks.

"Yes. I'd go check upstairs, but I'm afraid those steps are rotted out, and I don't want my ass to fall all the way down to the basement. Think we should roll and try again later?"

"No," she snaps. "I know they're still around. You're not leaving until you find them."

"I'm not the hands-on guy," he protests. "Call someone else."

"Do it, V," she snarls, then the heels click closer to my hiding spot. "Have you checked in here?"

The door flings open, and I'm exposed. A middle-aged woman with dark hair stands before me, her dark eyes peering down into the darkness. I still, ceasing to breathe, but it's like she has night vision goggles on. She smiles down at me, as I cower away from her.

"Well, what do we have here? Found a girl, V. Help me get her out," she yells behind her.

The man walks over to her and shoves her aside. Thrusting his hands into the closet, he captures my arms.

I try to press as far back into the closet as I can to get away from him, but it's no use. "Please," I beg. "I didn't do anything."

"We'll see about that. Out you come," he orders, then pulls me from my hiding spot.

Extracting me from the closet comes with a price for the man, though. I kick and bite, trying to free myself from his large-handed grasp.

"Jesus, woman!" he screams, as my teeth rip at his flesh. In one swift movement, the man twirls me around, pulling my back against his torso and wrapping his arms tightly around my chest and broken ribs. The fight leaves me as the pain floods back in. The woman walks closer and inspects my face.

"Judging by the smell of smoke on you, I'm betting you're the one whose sooty tracks we followed from the salon. Did you start it?" she asks, watching my face for what I can only assume is guilt.

"I saved it," I whisper.

"Is that so?" She looks skeptical.

"It was a man wearing a leather jacket, with orange

and green writing and a white skull on the back," I reveal, nervous as I wait for their response.

The woman's eyes light up and instantly flick to the man holding me. "You sure about that, sweetheart? Was it a white skull, or a red one?"

"It looked white from where I was hiding," I reply. *God, I hope my honesty doesn't end with me back in the possession of those bastards. Death is a better option, if that's the case.*

"It was the same symbol the men who kidnapped me wore," I whisper.

The man holding me suddenly lets me go and jerks me around to face him. His face is mere inches from mine.

"Kidnapped? Men wearing those colors kidnapped you? When?" His face is red with anger. "Why would they kidnap you? Are you one of their whores? Do you run drugs for them?" He continues to bark questions at me in rapid succession. "Answer me, woman."

"Because of my roommate," I cry. "I don't know why they wanted her, but they took me instead."

The woman edges closer. I fight the urge to recoil, but the man releases me just as her hand touches my shoulder, sending me scrambling away.

"If you're here to kill me, just fucking get it over with."

"Kill you, doll?" the man says, nearly laughing with

each word. "What do you think, Maj? Do you buy her story, or should I call the boys to bring over the other cage to dump her body?"

The woman's eyes narrow as she evaluates me. She walks around me like I'm on an auction block, about to be sold. She suddenly stops and motions for me to come closer. I do what she says and move forward, just close enough so she can't grab me.

"What's your name?"

"Dani."

"Well, Dani. Since you say you saved my salon, I think we have more things to talk about. Voodoo here is going to take you back to our clubhouse under my protection. What do you say?"

"I'm not a fool," I argue. "Why should I agree to go from one prison to another? Why would I fucking agree to that?"

"Because you don't have a choice, I'm afraid," the woman almost coos. "The way I see it, you can either come back with me, under my protection, or be forced to come with us without it. You're far safer in our club-house than you would be on the streets. They'll never look for you there. You're coming with us one way or another."

"Forgive me if I think this is all bullshit," I say, my eyes narrowed on her. "What's from stopping you from selling me out the second we leave this place? How the fuck do I know you aren't one of them?"

"We aren't like those bastards," the man hisses. He inches closer to me. I'd set the trap, and he'd taken the bait like I suspected he would. The woman throws up a hand, stopping him from getting closer. "You helped me out, so I'll help you out. You earn our trust, and we'll make sure you stay safe and out of the Tribe's hands."

I really don't have a reasonable choice at this point. The man who'd manhandled me is strong. Far stronger than I am, even without the broken ribs. I had no chance against the likes of him if I tried to escape. The choice was made the second they found me.

"I'll go with you to your house."

"It's not just my house, baby doll. You see that guy?" She points to the Sasquatch next to her. "There are fifteen more just like him who live there. My husband is the president of a motorcycle club. They eat mouthy little bitches like you for breakfast, so I'd stow the attitude."

"Yes, ma'am," I utter.

"That's what I like to hear. Obedience will get you far in our lifestyle," she says. Turning to the man, she barks more orders at him. "Take Dani here back to the clubhouse and get Ruby to help her clean up and put her into one of the guest rooms. She's off-limits to the guys, unless she says otherwise. You got that, Voodoo? You make sure every one of the guys knows that. Someone fucking with her is like someone fucking with me. Heads will roll if one hair on her head is harmed."

Off-limits? Do I even want to ask what the other women do for these guys if she's branding me off-limits?

The man grunts and drags me out of my temporary home, pulling me behind him and straight to a truck parked on the street. He all but shoves me into the cab before sliding into the driver's seat. He starts up the engine and pulls away from the salon. The man stays silent during the entire drive. We twist and turn down the streets before he passes an Upland sign. Holy shit, he's taking me back towards the city I lived in with Ricca.

"Do you guys live in Upland?" I ask.

"Yes," is the only response I'm given, and then he turns to head up into the mountains. Since moving to this town, I have wanted to see Mt. Baldy. I never imagined I'd be seeing it for the first-time, riding in a truck with a tattoo-covered biker. Thinking about our surroundings gives me hope that once the smoke clears, I might be able to make it back home to retrieve my money and my possessions. The thought of the photo of my parents lying there in my room, waiting to be stolen or thrown out, sickens me. The last photo of my parents could already be gone. I can't think about that right now.

Voodoo pulls onto a dusty dirt road and drives deep into the mountains. A few minutes later, a metal structure comes into view, with several motorcycles dotting the paved lot out front. He slams on the brakes and veers into a parking spot to the left of the bikes. He jumps from the truck before he even turns off the engine. Throwing open the door and pulling me out, Voodoo walks me to the front door and shoves me into a room filled with leather-clad men and women wearing tiny little outfits.

The room falls into stunned silence upon seeing me. Looking around, I notice worn leather couches in the center, along with beer and Harley neon signs lining the walls. The worn hardwood floors under my feet have seen better days, just like some of the older men in the room. The smell of stale beer, cigarette smoke, and cheap perfume lingers in the air.

"Did you bring us a new plaything?" a large man says with a grin. "Pretty little thing, isn't she?"

"This is Dani. She's under Maj's protection," he announces. "Keep your hands to yourself."

Voodoo wastes no more time, and shoves me off towards a hallway. A doorway appears to our left, and he pushes me inside.

"Stay in here," he demands. "Once I leave, this door will be locked."

"You can't keep me caged in here like an animal," I protest.

"We can, and we will." He shifts to step out of the room. "Take a shower. You smell. One of the girls will bring you clothes." He grabs the door and slams it shut. The lock clicks into place, and then his heavy footfalls stomp away.

I bang on the door until my hands ache. A pointless reaction. I'm trapped in here. I made this bed by trying to protect myself, and now I have to lie in it. Slumping against the door, I cry. All the anger, fear, and sadness pour out of me in big, fat tears running down my face. I sob until I can't anymore. I have nothing left inside me.

I push off from the door and wander into an ensuite bathroom. Quickly stripping off my dirty clothes, I turn on the shower and step into the hot spray. The water feels like heaven as it washes away the stress of the last few days, and the filth coating my skin. I stay under the water until it runs cold. Pulling out a towel from under the sink, I wrap it around my body and walk back out into the bedroom. A perky little red-headed woman is sitting on my bed, a bundle of clothes in her hands.

"Who are you?"

"Ruby." She smiles. Jumping up from the bed, she prances over, shoving the clothes into my arms. "I brought you some club shirts, sweatpants, and under-wear. It's not much, but it's what we have on hand."

"It's great, thank you," I force out a smile. I start to lose my grip on the items in my hand, and my towel begins to slip. She gasps when she sees the bruising around my ribs.

"Did V do this?" she hisses, her hands shifting to the delicately bruised skin.

"No," I answer, shaking my head. "I was kidnapped."

"You need a doctor." She's not wrong, but that decision would be left up to them. My new captors.

"I think I just broke a rib." The answer comes out nonchalantly, like having broken ribs is no big deal.

"Holy shit. You've been dealing with a broken rib, and just now thought to say something? Hang on," she says, then she exits my room. Taking the chance to change while she's gone, I strip the towel away from my body, then throw on the sweatpants and one of the shirts. By the time she gets back, I've settled on the bed and started to doze off.

"Here, take these," she says. She shoves two large white oblong pills and a bottle of Coke into my hands. Depositing the pills into my mouth, I swallow them with the pop. Ruby sits down on the side of the bed, observing me. The pills quickly take effect. My vision clouds, and the room begins to whirl. She remains still as I lose all ability to form words. Darkness creeps along the edges of my vision, and I feel my body go limp before I completely black out.

I've been drugged.

Chapter 8

HERO

MY MIND IS RAGING a war inside my head, and there is nothing I can drink or fuck to make those painful memories go back into that box in my brain. In hindsight, I should have probably taken Voodoo's spot on salon fire duty. The work would have taken my mind off the nightmares, and I would have found a useful purpose to ignore them again. The need to compartmentalize is growing by the day, but seeing my therapist is out of the question. At least until this war with the Tribe was over. I can't abandon my brothers for my own needs. For now, I just have to suck it up and cope. Weakness isn't an option.

While Voodoo and a few others were heading out with Maj to see about her salon, the rest of us had stayed behind on high alert. Was this an effort to drive us out of lockdown? The odds of that being the case were high.

Especially after the little care package we received this morning. A piece of Jagger's bloody clothes had been mailed to us, along with a photo of his body hanging in the shed.

The rage brewing inside me had reached an all-time fucking high as I stared at the photograph in my hand. Every second I looked at that photo, I was another second closer to losing my shit. We need to move against them and soon, but not until we're prepared. There were too many unknowns in this fight. Those were our priority before we strike. Voodoo has been practically living in front of his computer the past few days, trying to track down more information, but he hasn't found anything concrete. Knowing what we were likely to face in the coming days and weeks, we could only operate on absolutes.

The only absolute that I need to operate with is the absolute certainty that I will put down the men responsible for killing my brother. Personally, I want their last vision of life to be me snuffing it out.

And I will have it. One way or another.

Hours went by before Raze sent a few of us off to get a few hours of shuteye. I had protested, but his orders were firm.

Sleep never came, though. The nightmares did. All fucking night.

Every time I closed my eyes, I saw the carnage of my

brothers, and then the woman from the bar dying in my arms. Her face filled my mind as I paced the floor, thinking back to that brief encounter with her. Her body pressed against mine. The way her hazel eyes, though slightly glassy from the liquor she had consumed, shining back at me. The way her breath had hitched when I whispered to her what I wanted to do to her that night. She was perfect until Red's revelation. She was in some way associated with Twisted Tribe. Whatever possibilities for a little playtime between us were null and void. We were on opposite sides, and it was a line I refused to cross. Brotherhood and loyalty to my club meant more to me than anything in the world. I lived, breathed, and would likely die for this club without hesitation. I made the oath, and no pretty little piece of ass would make me change my mind.

I give up after pacing the floor for a few hours and do a few reps on my hand weights before hitting the showers. The hot spray does nothing to relax my body. Not that I expected it to. This kind of rage and anger isn't something that can be cured with hot water. I step from the shower and wrap a towel around my waist, when suddenly, there's a pounding on my door.

"What the fuck do you want?" I bellow, throwing open the door to find Voodoo standing there. He scans me up and down, then shakes his head.

"This the way you greet everyone when they come to

your door, or is this just for me?" he asks, smirking.

"Nope, just for you, shithead. Trying to show you what a real man's body looks like when he takes care of himself," I quip.

"Hey, don't insult my baby beer gut. It might get offended. Not all of us have the time to work out like you, VP." He leans his head into the room.

"You going to tell me why you were working on beating down my door, or did you just want to see me in the towel?" I start to loosen the towel from my waist, and he jerks back.

"Hero, you're not my type," he says. I glare back, and he just smiles like an idiot. "Prez wants you downstairs. Got some intel that Twisted Tribe is the one that set fire to the salon. Church starts in five minutes."

"How'd you determine it was Twisted Tribe? Did you pull video from the neighboring businesses?" I ask. Voodoo was our tech guy, and he is damn good at it, too. He may not be the strongest of us, but he makes up for it with the other shit he can do.

"Oh, that's the best part. I brought you home a surprise." He laughs and turns on his heels, then makes his way back down the hall.

A surprise? Why do I get the feeling shit is about to hit the fan?

Not even closing the door, I walk to my dresser and pull out a pair of jeans and one of my club t-shirts. I quickly get dressed, adding my cut over the top. I have no idea what this surprise might be, so I grab my riding boots and lace them up before walking out of my room.

Hustling down the stairs, I see Ratchet and Voodoo waiting outside the door. Ratchet's mischievous smile raises my suspicions. I'm not going to like what's behind the Church doors. I can tell. That bastard isn't one for cheery smiles, so I know shit's about to go down. Sliding by them and through the door, I'm shocked to see Maj and Raze screaming in one another's faces at the head of the table.

Why the fuck is she in Church? Women are barred from our official business dealings. Has this club gone to hell in a hand basket in just one night?

"You crazy bitch!" Raze exclaims. "What were you thinking, bringing someone here? I run this fucking club, not you."

"That colossal fuck up you're talking about gave us the only solid evidence against the murdering bastards. I thought you'd be happy I just delivered you the information you need to take them out on a pretty little platter," Maj replies. "Excuse me for thinking about the club and not servicing your dick for once."

"You brought an enemy into our home. You could have at least called me, and we'd have taken her to one of the interrogation houses. Not deposited her in our goddamn home, where she can report back to them."

Oh shit.

Knowing this is about to hit the point of no return, I run into the fray and slide between them. Voodoo grabs a hold of Maj and jerks her back, while I try to hold off Raze. How have these two survived being married so long?

"You're a fucking bastard. I'm trying to help you, but you're too jaded to see it. You know, I'd love to see things from your point of view sometimes, but I can't seem to get my head that far up my ass," she yells, as Voodoo drags her to the door and shoves her out, slamming the door in her face. She punches the door and screams more insults at Raze before she walks away.

Turning my attention to Raze, I can see he's still seething in anger. "You care to enlighten the rest of us about what we just witnessed? What did your old lady pull this time?" Raze moves me aside and punches the wall behind us.

"That bitch brought someone associated with Twisted Tribe here and offered her fucking sanctuary under our roof in exchange for information."

Shock runs through my body. "You've got be shitting me, right? She brought a traitor into our fucking clubhouse? What the fuck was she thinking?"

"That's the problem, Hero. She wasn't thinking. She thought she was bringing us a gift, but instead she brought a bigger fucking headache. She didn't even have a clue who the bitch is to those assholes, but she brought her here, anyway. What if she's an old lady, or one of their whores? We'll be at war for this, and we're not ready to strike back. Maj may have single-handedly stamped out our time of death if this chick is important enough to them."

Shaking my head in disgust and frustration, I don't even know what to say about Maj's deception. She has a good heart most of the time, but even a dumb fuck doesn't bring in an enemy without telling Raze first.

"What do you want to do, Raze?" Ratchet asks. "Do you want me to handle the bitch?"

"My wife put her under her protection. We're fucking stuck with her for the time being. The only thing we can do is keep her under lock and key and watch her twenty-four seven. Have Hot Shot strip everything from her room she could use to communicate. Any requests she makes come through me and no one else. I want this bitch watched at all times. She doesn't take a shit without one of us there watching," Raze instructs.

"Hero, you might try getting some of the girls to be buddy-buddy with her to see if she'll talk," Voodoo suggests.

"I'll talk to Ruby. She'll be on board with it."

"One more thing. Watch what you say around her. Club business talk shuts down as soon as she steps foot in the room. You got it?"

"Yes, Prez," the group collectively murmurs. Slapping a hand to my back, Raze and I leave Church, heading down the hallway towards the living quarters and guest rooms. I follow behind him, but stop him before he opens the door.

"Raze, are you serious about keeping this woman here? She's a liability if Twisted Tribe finds out she's here," I say. I don't mean to open the can of worms Maj brought home again. Not now that he seems reasonably calm, but I need to ask. "Is this a smart move for our club, with the other chapters PMS-ing about the cut situation?"

"There's nothing we can do until she talks. Hell yes, she's a liability, but until she fucks up enough we can justify killing her, Maj's protection stands."

"If that's how you want to play this, I'm good with your decision, but like you said, we've got to be careful around her until we know for sure."

Raze reaches for the handle and opens the door. The woman lying on the bed is comatose as we walk into the room. She's buried beneath the blankets. We stalk closer, but she doesn't move.

Jesus, what did they dose her with? Elephant tranquilizer?

Grasping the blanket in my hand, I jerk it off of her and freeze into place.

It can't be her.

The fucking traitor is the raven-haired beauty from the bar.

Chapter 9

DANI

A FEELING of being watched wakes me, but there's no one else in the room. Suddenly, I recall the events that took place before I passed out.

That red-haired bitch drugged me.

I need to get out of here before she comes back with the next dose. Edging to the side of the bed, I feel my abs constrict.

What the fuck?

I slip down the blanket that is tightly wrapped around me and find that my torso has been wrapped in an ace bandage.

When the hell did that happen?

Sliding out of bed and onto my shaky feet, I toddle my way to the bathroom and flick on the light. I pad inside, closing the door behind me. My reflection peers back at me from the mirror, and the visual sucks the air right out of my lungs. I knew I felt like shit, but this truly reflects how I feel. Dirty and broken. My black hair is matted into a tangled mess, and there are stitches across my brow.

I peer into the mirror for a few minutes longer, and then I hear the door open, followed by heavy footsteps. The sound of each step moves closer to the bathroom, sending me scurrying into the corner, away from the noise. I don't know what's coming for me, but at least my back is covered. The heavy steps stop just outside the bathroom door before it's kicked in. I scream as the wood crashes against the tiled walls.

A large man with a buzz-cut stands before me. His arms bulge out of his black t-shirt, matching the muscular legs wrapped in tight, dark-wash jeans. Tribal half-sleeve tattoos peek out from under the sleeves of his shirt on both of his arms. A gray, short scruff covers his face, contrasting greatly with his deep blue eyes. He stands with stiffening authority, demanding respect with his stare. He's the kind of guy you see standing on the street, and you walk to the other side, just to avoid him.

"Well, I see Sleeping Beauty is finally awake," he says, as I huddle deeper into the corner. He laughs as I struggle to shrink away from him. "Cat got your tongue, doll? You look like I just beat your dog in front of you."

His deep voice shocks me just as much as the smile on his face. He outstretches his hand to me, but I refuse to take it. "Why don't you come out of there? The position has to be killing your ribs."

I stare at him with a calculated gaze, sizing up the threat. He's at least twice my weight and six inches taller than me. My chances to get around him are about a million to one, even if I was healthy. He reaches towards me, and I slap his hand away.

"I'm not going to hurt you. Maj would have my balls."

Hearing the woman's name, I relax slightly. The man who brought me here said I was under her protection. He announced it to everyone, so it had to mean something. Maybe she's the one who sent this guy.

"Maj?" I whisper. "Can I talk to her?"

"No can do. But seeing as how she's my wife, you can talk to me about whatever you need."

"No. I only want to talk to her," I say, not budging an inch.

"You will talk to her when I say you can. Now, are you going to come out of that corner, or do I have to come in there after you?" He shoves his hand into my personal space, but I swat it away as I slide from my hiding spot. He tries to grab me again, but I dodge at the last minute.

"I want to talk to Maj," I insist. "She brought me here, and I want to know why I was drugged."

"You were drugged because I ordered it. If you want

to blame someone for your three days of undisturbed sleep and medical care, you can blame me. How are the ribs feeling, by the way?" he asks, eyeing my mid-section.

Three days? I was out for three fucking days. What in the hell did they give me?

"They're fine," I answer with clipped words. "Do I get my next dose of elephant tranquilizers after we finish our little chat here, or does the Red Bitch come back with it later? I'd like to at least be lying in a comfortable spot if my choice to stay will be revoked again."

"I can't wait to tell Ruby your little nickname for her. That'll fire her up," he chuckles.

If he thinks for a second that I'll let that woman drug me again, he has another think coming. They'll have to pry my mouth open, shove them in, and force me to swallow before I will go so easily into oblivion.

He stares back at me and my inaction.

"I get it. You're in a strange place with strange people, you've been drugged, and you're looking for a fight. If it were any other circumstance, I would admire your spirit, but the bottom line is you're in my club-house, under my wife's protection. How about this? You get cleaned up, and then you and I will have a little talk. Maybe a little lunch."

"So you can drug me again? I'll pass."

"It wasn't a request. And before you get any ideas, there's a guard outside your door. There's no running."

I remain silent, considering his demand. Though his entrance was a little over the top, he seems more reasonable. Knowing Maj is his wife, there is another factor in my corner. "Fine," I relent.

"You have ten minutes before Slider here will come for you. I suggest you make sure you're on time. I'll replace the door later."

The brooding, gray-bearded man stalks out the door and barks the same orders to the man stationed outside.

"Nine minutes left, girly," he bellows. "I don't hear the shower running."

He laughs from out in the hallway as I rush back into the bathroom, stepping over the shredded remains of my door.

Stepping under the hot spray, I rinse off the multiple days of coma-filled sweat and grime. I can't believe I was out that long. There's no medicine on this earth that would knock me out like that with just two pills. Either they dosed me again, or they injected me with something stronger. I don't sleep well as it is, so to sleep for several days is far-fetched, even with drugging me. My hair will need extra work with a wide-tooth comb, but I know I don't have time for it. Stepping out of the shower, I dry off and pull my knotted hair into a wet, messy bun to deal with later. I find a small pile of clothes and a new strip of an ACE bandage on my bed. Someone must have brought them in while I was in the shower. I gently wrap the bandage around my tender ribs, tucking the end in the top row to secure it. Next, I slip the sweatpants over my wide hips. I reach for the t-shirt and wince when I lean a little too far forward.

"Fuck," I hiss.

Slipping the shirt over my head, my head gets stuck. I tug hard against the misbehaving fabric, when a rough pair of male hands grabs the hem and yanks it free of my hair. His touch startles me. Shock must register on my face, because the tall man backs away with his hands held up in surrender.

"Sorry. It looked like you needed help. The Prez will be pissed if I bring you down late. Let's get going," he says, grabbing my arm and aiming me towards the door. He lightly heaves me out into the hallway. Pointing to the left, we hustle at a quick pace.

"I'm Slider, by the way," he says, as we make our way down the stairs.

"Dani," I tell him. "Is that your real name?" He completely ignores me.

We walk in silence, weaving along the hallway and through the large, crowded main room I had been dragged into a few days earlier. Finally, we enter a side room, where he deposits me into a wooden chair, then exits, closing the door behind him. Being left alone is a scary notion, especially in this kind of biker-filled hell. I drum my finger against the wood of the chair, and after a few moments, the door abruptly swings open and in walks King Gray Beard. It's the man that shuffles in behind him that takes my breath away. His face is blocked from my vision, but my body instantly responds to his presence.

It can't be him. There's no way. He's not one of these assholes.

I continue to stare at his hidden face as the temperature of the room rises past boiling. I break out into a shock-induced, nervous sweat. My body launches into shakes that ripple through my bones. Whether it's in fear or anticipation, I don't know. A familiar cologne wafts over me as the man shuts the door behind him. His face continues to stay shielded, until finally, he turns around.

Fuck. It's the man from Red's.

He's taller than I remember, but I wasn't exactly sober that night. If I took a guess, I'd say he is probably close to six feet five inches. Every muscle on his body is toned, and the tattoos snaking up his arms are just an added bonus.

I plead internally for him to look up at me, and when his eyes finally lock onto mine, neither of us move. The tension in the room rises as my blurred, drunken memory comes back to me in waves. His body swaying against mine mentally seduces me all over again. The memory of his touch on my body sends arousal shooting through me. Someone out there in the universe has a fucking horrible sense of humor for putting him in my path. Even though he hasn't said a word, I want to fuck him and kick him in the balls, all at the same time.

King Gray Beard watches, trying to decipher what's going on between us.

"You're the man from the bar," I state, hoping to still be wrong.

He says silent.

"You are, aren't you?" I ask again, hoping to illicit a response from him.

"You tell me."

"All right," Gray Beard interjects. "Let's start with the easy stuff. Who are you, and where the hell did you come from?"

"You can start by telling me who the hell you are, and where I am," I reply, mentally smacking myself for being so rude right off the bat.

"I'm the president of the Heaven's Rejects Motorcycle Club, and you can call me Raze. The woman who deposited you into this predicament would be my wife, Maj. The man to my left is Hero. Now, it's your turn to tell me your name."

"My name is Dani."

"Well, Dani, I'm going to need more than that. How about the second question? Where are you from?"

"I'm from the Midwest," I state, giving minimal details. I don't need to give him, or Hero, any more information about me. I don't know if wanted posters have been issued for me, and I'm not about to paint a red arrow over my head, screaming, "Here I am," if one of these assholes searches my name.

"Midwest, huh? What brings you out here?"

Shit, what do I say to that? Think, Dani. Think.

"I'm waiting, Dani. Answer me," he demands.

"I needed a change of scenery. Figured sunny California would be a good place," I state.

Keep it to minimal details. You don't want to lie elaborately in case you forget it later. You can do this, Dani. Keep it simple, and maybe you'll survive.

"How old are you?"

"Why the hell does my age matter? I'm legal, or does your club like things a little less legal?"

Raze leans into the table and stares me down.

"Let me make myself perfectly clear. I don't know what kind of fucked up idea you have about an MC and how we treat women, but if you call me or another member of this club a sick fuck, or a kiddy fucker one more goddamn time, I will put a bullet between your eyes. Do you understand me, Dani? My club and my men will be respected."

"Yes, Raze," I whisper, his threat hanging in the air and making me regret my attitude. "I'm twenty-five."

"How'd you end up in that abandoned house next to the salon?" Raze asks.

Hero re-adjusts his position against the wall to a crouch before me. "I'd answer him very carefully, Dani. You don't want to lie to us. You won't like the consequences."

"Back off, Hero," the man demands, sending Hero back into an angry silence.

I look right at Hero when I answer. I won't back down or show I'm intimidated by him.

"A group of Spanish men kidnapped me from my bed as collateral for my roommate. They locked me in the trunk of a car, but only after they beat me into a blackout. I escaped from them and holed up in the abandoned house. I was trying to wait them out, so I could go back to my apartment and get my things. Then, I walked up on a man setting fire to the salon next to the house."

"You don't buy this crock of bullshit, do you, Raze?" Hero asks, looking up at him. "Sounds a little too convenient for me. Like a goddamn fairy tale."

"Tell me," he says, ignoring the guy next to him. "Did you see the guy who started the salon fire? Notice anything about him at all."

"Like I told the guy that was with your wife, he had on a leather jacket with a white skull and orange and green writing on the back. It was too smoky to make out the words, but it was the same jacket the guys who kidnapped me were wearing."

The mention of the colors stiffens him, just like it had with Voodoo.

"Are you one-hundred percent sure about that emblem on his jacket? If I showed it to you again, would you recognize it?"

I nod my head, and he pulls his phone from the back pocket of his jeans, flicking his finger across the screen. Once he stops, he shoves the phone in my face.

"That it?" He waits as my eyes adjust to the bright screen.

"Yes," I reply. My answer must please him, because he returns the phone to his pocket. "I've answered your questions. I'd like to leave now. You got what you wanted."

"You'll be staying here until we can verify your story."

"I don't want to stay here. You can't keep me."

"That's where you are wrong, Dani. I can, and I will, until I'm damn well ready to release you. You're an unwanted guest here until I say otherwise. And there are a few ground rules you're going to need to follow. You go nowhere alone in this clubhouse, or outside. Slider, who you met, will be your personal shadow from the time you leave your room until you return. If a man with a cut like mine tells you to do something…" He indicates the leather vest on his torso. "You do it. You can only be in the main room of the clubhouse, or the kitchen outside your room. Do you understand me?"

"Yes, I understand. I'm a prisoner here until you deem me fit enough to fuck or kill."

"I see you still aren't getting with the program," he snorts, turning his attention to his partner. "Hero, have Slider get her a plate of food, then lock her back in her room. Maybe some isolation will do her well."

Raze quickly exits the door, and I stand to leave myself. Just as I reach the threshold, Hero's hand wraps around my arm, jerking me back into the room. His face is mere inches from mine.

"Tell me what you know about Twisted Tribe?" he orders. I look out of the door, praying that Raze or Maj are still nearby. He jerks my arm harder.

"Twisted who?" I sputter. "I don't know who that is."

"Bullshit. Your roommate is a side-piece for them. They kidnapped you, or so you say. Seems to me you're very well versed with them."

"All I know is that I was kidnapped, assaulted, and then kidnapped again. I'm tired, hurt, and hungrier then hell. If you think for one second I would withhold information about those bastards, you're delusional. Now," I say, jerking away from him. "Let me pass."

He steps in front of me, blocking my escape once more.

"Don't let that night at the bar cloud your opinion of me. I'm not a good man. If my president says to end you, I will. Despite what you think you know about me. It was a dance. Not a wedding ceremony."

I have no words to answer his threats. I don't know who this other club is, or if Ricca really is involved with them. I'm just as pissed about being kidnapped as they are about whatever this club has done to them. I may be far from innocent, but I have nothing to do with these accusations, or this other club. I just have to bide my time and behave as they expect me to until I can be allowed to roam free.

Why do I feel so fucked already?

Chapter 10

HERO

THIS IS NOT how I pictured her interrogation going. Not her feigned innocence, my anger, or my dick screaming in my pants from just being around her. I shouldn't want her, yet I do. From the moment I saw her at Red's, something inside me changed. What changed exactly is still a goddamn mystery, but I can feel the difference. Is it attraction? Maybe. Lust? Fuck yes, but the feeling is foreign. After years of being closed off to the world, I had started to imagine not spending my life alone, with only a revolving door of women in and out of my room. And not just with any woman. No, it was her. A complete fucking stranger that has barreled into my life twice in a matter of weeks. A stranger who could have ties to a rival club. If this isn't being in deep shit, I don't know what else I could say to describe it.

And try as I might to hide the chaos swirling inside

my mind, I'm doing a shit job of hiding it on the outside. Raze knew, from the moment she pegged me as the guy from the bar, that something was amiss. His puzzled look, paired with a we-need-to-talk glare, was clue enough.

Each time he asked a question, I could feel him watching me, clearly noting my reaction to her. I know he's trying to downplay my rage and insistence on being an asshole towards her to get her to talk, but this little hellcat has a mouth on her. She questions Raze at every turn, challenging him. My dick throbs with each sarcasm-laced word that spills from her mouth.

Keep it together, jackass, and do your job.

As soon as she said her name, I was fucked. Dani. It fits her. My brain goes off the rails, and I imagine what I could do to her soft body. Her voice calling out my name, as I pound into her. It sends chills through me.

She could be in bed with the men who murdered Jagger in cold blood, and I still fucking want her. I need to break the spell she holds over me. Somehow.

Her origin surprises me. Well, I guess it would, if I believed that's really where she's from. Her exotic coloring, dark eyes, and dark hair don't exactly scream small-town Midwestern girl. No one is who they say they are out here. Not in the land of plastic tits and Hollywood dreams. This is place you come to start over. A new life, a new look, and a new name. The latter would be easy enough once Voodoo is looped in. Either she's innocent or guilty. Only time would tell for sure.

But until I can prove otherwise, I'll be watching her every step. She's a prisoner within the walls of this clubhouse, which makes it easier for us to keep an eye on her. After Slider dropped her off in our nicest interrogation room, I pulled him aside and assigned him to spy duty. He's quiet enough that she won't notice him hanging around if we let her go any farther than the salon.

I start out of the interrogation room as soon as Slider leads Dani away, and turn to head back to my office, when Raze's voice cuts through the room.

"Hero! Get your ass into Church. Now!" he bellows.

Fuck. I knew this was coming after my shit show performance in there. It's better to just get this over with.

I trudge to the room and step inside, slamming the door behind me. Raze doesn't wait to start in on my actions.

"What the fuck, Hero? I thought we agreed to play stupid with her. You basically just laid out the fact that we think she's a fucking spy for the double T's."

Running my hand through my hair and down my neck, I think about what I want to say. He has to know I've met her before, but he's going to go into DEFCON One when he realizes he's seen her before, too.

"I couldn't help it, Raze. She rubbed me the wrong way."

"I have to ask. Do you know her? Because as soon as you saw each other, shit went weird."

He's not going to like what I'm about to tell him. I hope he's ready for the big reveal.

"Remember that night at Red's a few weeks back, when Maj got shit-faced, and you had to take her home? She was there. I just about had her seduced, when the blonde blew chunks all over her, and she disappeared. Red told me before we left that the blonde works for him, and is Ricky's bitch."

"You've got to be shitting me, right? Red knew about the blonde being tied to Twisted Tribe, and he fucking hired her? Send Tyson down there to get more information about her and the roommate."

I pull my cell phone out of my pocket and send off a quick text to Ty, instructing him to pay a visit to Red. He quickly texts back, confirming my request. Soon, we will have more answers. Raze is right about the situation. Red Rocket's may not be a sanctioned club bar, but we visit there often. Our patronage alone should be incentive enough to keep the Tribe out of there. Yet Red hired one of their girls. And not just a lower member's girl, but the goddamn leader's son. Just the thought brings more and more questions.

Was she planted to spy on the club? Was it a coincidence? The lines between reality and fantasy are blurring. When things line up just a little too perfectly to be coincidence, at what point do you call it what it really is? A sure-fucking-thing.

"Sure thing, but, Prez, what if she's really innocent?"

Raze stills. His face grows serious, considering the implications of having a woman with no ties to the club in our clubhouse in the midst of war. She has no allegiance to us, and that makes her a liability. If she really is innocent, it's an enormous risk.

"Shit," he utters. "Hadn't gotten that far."

I turn on my heel, side-stepping around him.

"It's something we should probably consider sooner rather than later, Prez. She's going to see and hear things around here, even if we confine her to her room. This is the worst possible time to have any outsider here."

"No shit," he retorts. "My wife has shit timing."

My mind goes over the options. None of them are particularly good, except for one. Death would be the easiest. Dead girls can't talk. On the other hand, if she is innocent, my feelings towards her could drastically change. I'd be a fucking dumbass if I didn't admit to myself that I wanted her. It was clear enough that Raze even picked up on that. If Voodoo could clear her name, she wouldn't be off the fuck-able option table anymore. A myriad of ideas float through my mind, but I shake them away. It was a big if, and I wasn't about to get my hopes up on screwing her, until I knew for sure which way her pendulum would swing.

"Maj might be the short-term solution, you know?" I offer. "She seems to trust her. What if we let Dani work with Maj, once the repairs are finished on the salon? Give her a purpose, and maybe another avenue to divulge a little information. Girl talk and all that shit."

Raze grins. "You know, it's scary how your mind works sometimes."

"And that's why you keep me around."

Chapter 11

DANI

IT TAKES NEARLY three weeks for my house arrest from my room to be lifted. I feel like such an outsider here, and honestly, I guess I should. I had no idea what to expect with club life, outside the stories I've heard about outlaw biker gangs leaving chaos and murder in their wakes. Were these men like the horror stories I had heard growing up? Maybe, but there isn't anything I can do to change my predicament or my immediate future. My only option is to deal with this situation the best I can and follow their rules.

Stay out of the way.

Stay out of club business.

Do what you are told.

Simple enough. I'm sure there are other rules, but at this point, they don't apply to the prisoner that I am. The less they see of me, the better. A cloak of invisibility is my best option, as I try to figure a way out of this mess.

My first night exploring the main room and kitchen was met with complete silence and stares from everyone. I refused to let them get me down. Every day, I walk out into the dining and lounge areas, like I own the place. I park my ass at the table or on the couch. Of course, they all come up with excuses to leave or fall silent, but I want to prove to Raze and Hero that I want to make the best of my confinement. In the meantime, I do what I can to pass the time. Movies, books, and television have become my friends. Slider tries to be friendly, but I saw through his motives from day one.

I'll admit, every single time the news comes on, my heart stops. These guys aren't exactly CNN, or local news kind of guys, so the TV never stays on those channels long enough, but I have a deep-seated fear that my face will be plastered on the scene, alerting them to my past predicament in Ohio. The longer I'm exposed to this caliber of people, the more likely I will be hauled away in cuffs. I coach myself in the mirror every morning to just keep biding my time and to keep my nose clean. The sooner they trust me, the sooner I can escape.

Hero has been true to his word and watches my every move when I'm out in the public rooms. There are times, even at night, that I can smell his cologne wafting beneath my door before his footsteps fade down the hallway. I was such a fool to think that he'd realize the error of his ways, and treat me like he did the first time I'd met him.

Raze pulled me aside after dinner about a week ago, to tell me I would be venturing outside the clubhouse and starting a new job at Maj's salon. The work to rebuild the charred parts of the building is finally finished, and Maj is ready to re-open. It took me two days to convince Maj that I'm not cut out for being a hair stylist, before she set me up to work as their cleaner. Sure, sweeping up discarded hair on the floor, and cleaning the bathrooms isn't a luxurious job, but it's better than staying in the clubhouse. The conversations with them aren't exactly mind-blowingly insightful either, but I listen intently, just for the noise.

Every single morning is always the same. Get up, get cleaned up, then head out of the door for breakfast.

I went to bed early last night to ease my aching ribs. They've been healing over the last few weeks. The club doctor has been to see me several times, and informs me they are healing nicely, but they still hurt from time to time. At best, I still have a few weeks to go, before I will feel one-hundred percent. It isn't ideal to stick around that long, but again, there isn't exactly a Plan B in place.

Slider meets me, as usual, by the breakfast nook with a coffee in hand, ready to escort me to work. I've noticed Maj spends most of her time away from the clubhouse, ever since her fight with Raze about bringing me here. Yes, I had heard them. They were loud as fuck. Plus, it worries me that my benefactor and protector isn't here with me, but at least Slider seems to care about me.

"Ready to go, sweet cheeks?" Slider asks, thrusting the steaming cup of caramel-flavored coffee into my hands. "We better get you to work before Maj hacks my balls off. She warned me the last time we were late that she was going to take possession of them the next time."

The visual of Maj hacking off his balls and keeping them in a jar on her desk at the salon brings a smile to my face. That crazy bitch would actually do it, too, which is why it's so funny. Purposefully walking out of the door at a turtle's pace, Slider literally shoves me towards the waiting SUV. I can't help but to laugh at him. He knows my game, which is why he throws the car into gear and peels out of the dirt driveway, onto the curvy mountain road. I just smile and laugh, watching the time ticks closer to us being late yet again.

"It's not fucking funny, Dani. It's not your balls on the line!" he snaps, as we fly through a yellow light on Mountain Avenue. He drifts the SUV around the corner and barely squeezes into the parking space in front of the salon a few minutes later. He laughs as I hop out of the passenger side of the SUV. Together, we burst through the door, and Maj smacks him upside the head.

"You're late, Slider. When I tell you I want her here

promptly at nine thirty, I mean nine thirty. Not nine thirty-eight," she says, poking a fine-toothed comb into his chest. "If you want to make it in this club as a prospect, I'd suggest getting my ward here on time. Now, scoot on back to the office. I need you to take a look at the computer. It's doing weird shit again."

"You know that's Voodoo's area of expertise, right?"

"You're here. He's not."

Smiling at him, I watch as he flips me off, and shuffles back to the office. Slider told me he sucks at anything with computers, so he will have to sneak Voodoo in the back to fix it. If she only knew half the shit he did back there while he's on babysitting duty, she'd lose her mind. I caught him once, watching porn and jerking off. That is something I will never be able to erase from my memory. Trust me, I've tried.

The shop is busy today, so of course, I have plenty of work to do. Maj keeps insisting that she's going to teach me how to cut hair, but she's delusional. Giving a suspected spy scissors isn't exactly the brightest idea, even if I'm innocent of their alleged crimes. An hour before closing, the office phone rings, and Slider rushes out.

"Maj, I need to run back to the clubhouse. Can you watch Dani for me?" he asks, his eyes pleading that she'll agree.

"Like I have a choice. Just go," she orders, and he runs out the door.

"Men," she mutters. "Whether they're bikers or metros, they're always dramatic over the littlest things. You'd think my husband called to tell him that his baby is about to pop out any second, from the way he went running. The little shit can't be on time bringing you to work, but he'll be five minutes early when my husband calls."

She lets out a hearty laugh that echoes off the salon walls. She's about to finish up her second to last client for the night when the phone rings again. I'm usually not permitted to answer the phones, but Maj sends me back to get it before it drives her crazy.

"Blazing Beauty Salon," I answer.

"What the fuck are you doing answering the phones, Dani?" Hero yells into the receiver. "You know that's one of the rules for being permitted to work there." Oh joy. My best friend is calling. Why me?

"Yes, Hero. I'm well aware of the rules, but Maj is busy, and I'm the only one here. Is there something I can help you with, or did you call just to be a dick?"

"You need to cancel her last appointment and get out of the salon. I'm sending someone to get you. We're locking down the clubhouse. I know you have no clue what that means, but tell Maj. She'll know what to do," he barks. Before I can reply, he abruptly hangs up on me.

He's such as asshole.

Walking back out to the workstations, Maj is just about to start cutting her client's hair. "Who was it?" she asks, snipping a piece a hair from the woman's bangs.

"It was Hero. He said we needed to close up shop. Something about a lockdown."

As soon as the word 'lockdown' exits my lips, panic flourishes in Maj's eyes. Ripping away the cloth draped around her client's neck, she informs the lady that there's been a family emergency, and she needs to cut their appointment short. As she shoves the woman out of the door, she yells that her next cut is on the house for the inconvenience. Turning back to the door, she locks it and pulls down the blinds.

"I need you to go to the back door and make sure it's locked. Turn off all the lights, and close the rest of the blinds. We need to make sure it looks like no one's here until one of the guys gets here. Do you understand me, Dani?"

Nodding my head, I bolt for the back and throw the dead bolt on the door. Flicking the lights as I move toward the office, I catch Maj pulling a gun from the safe and tucking it into the waistband of her jeans. She drags me back to the front and watches the street from a slit in the blinds. My heart races with every minute we wait for our pickup. A bike rumbles down the street and screeches to a stop out front. Banging comes from the door, and Maj cautiously opens it. Voodoo stands on the other side, and shock registers on his face when he sees me standing behind Maj.

"Fuck. I thought it was just you, Maj. I don't have room for her on my bike," he says, pointing at me. "Dani, you're going to have to stay behind until I can send someone else to come get you."

Maj looks bewildered and tries to stop Voodoo from pulling her out of the building. "We've got to go now, Maj. I'll send someone for her. You're our priority. I promise I'll send someone back. Please, just get on the bike," he pleads. Looking back at me, she steps towards Voodoo and issues more orders.

"Someone comes back for Dani, V. I won't leave her here like a sitting duck, just because my husband is a fucking idiot."

Voodoo motions for her to get on the bike before returning his attention to me.

"Dani, you stay inside with the doors locked. Do not step one fucking foot outside until you see one of us coming back to get you. Do you understand me?"

"I'll stay inside," I say.

He runs away from the door, and I hastily slide the deadbolt back into place. Time slows to a screeching halt the minute they pull away from the salon. My eyes are glued to the traffic outside, begging for the rumble of a motorcycle getting close. Fifteen minutes pass with no sign of rescue. Just as I decide this may be my chance to leave, a silver Harley Davidson pulls up with a helmeted rider. He stalks up to the door, and just as I'm about to open it for my rescuer, I realize his cut isn't in Heaven's Rejects colors.

Fuck! It's Twisted Tribe. What do I do?

Hide. I have to hide. Sliding to the floor, I crawl towards the back door just as the doorknob begins to jiggle. I quickly crouch behind a stack of boxes in the back room when he kicks the front door in. Loud bangs come from the front, and it sounds like the man is throwing around anything he can get his hands on. Each bang makes me jump in fear. If he finds me, he'll take me back to their clubhouse. Glass breaks and a chair scrapes across the floor. His phone rings then, just as he gets to the office door.

"Fernando," he answers. "No, boss. No sign of the head bitch. Looks like she cleared out before I could get here."

Slinking towards the back door, I reach up and try to quietly click the lock open. Just as it clicks into position, I stumble, knocking over the boxes that were hiding me.

Fuck! I have to run.

I start to run, but I don't make it far before the man grabs me around the waist, jerking me back into the salon. I try to break away from his grasp, but fall to the ground, still in his grip. He plants his feet on either side of my waist, falling to his knees, pinning me to the ground with his weight.

"What do we have here?" he says, pinning me harder. "It's the little puta who escaped from the car. Ricky will be very glad to see you."

Chapter 12

HERO

HAVING her here is my own personal nightmare. Dani tempts me without even knowing it. It takes every ounce of willpower I have not to bust into her room and fuck her every time I walk past, knowing that perfect body and smart mouth is lying in bed alone. She's the siren calling me ashore, and I'm about to crash and burn from her silent presence.

It was easy to avoid her while she was hidden away in her room, but Raze had lifted her restriction last week. I'm sure my brothers have noticed my sudden absence, but it's best for me until I figure shit out. She is a problem on top of so many other problems already on my plate. I'd be a fool to think that the proverbial shit isn't about to hit the fan with the Tribe. We've given them too much time to prepare. They'll likely out-man us, and out-gun us, because of our inability to act promptly. Raze is a smart man, but he's been too fucking cautious since they'd murdered Jagger. He needs to find his balls again, and seek the revenge we are owed. It's a price we all might pay in the end.

Tyson's discussion with Red didn't illicit any mind-blowing details about Dani, or her roommate. Red said the blonde has worked there for several years, and that she brings in more tips than any piece of eye candy he'd ever hired before her. Our prisoner had only worked there a few weeks, and she kept to herself. She wanted to be paid under the table, which raised red flags, but Red couldn't elaborate on the reason for it.

Raze stalks into the office just as I'm about to shut down the computer for the day. I've been reviewing the financial figures Tyson had laid on my desk from our security firm for the previous month. With all the shit going on now, we can't exactly accept any work. But we've made quite a bit of new money in the last few months, with our protection details to keep us comfortable. We've even had to go so far as to recruit more than the usual number of prospects this year, just to cover our bases. We can't go to work on protection detail jobs and leave our home unprotected. The security work gives the prospects experience and teaches them the skills they need to survive in this world.

"Any particular reason you're hiding out back here

and not out with the guys?" Raze asks from the doorway.

"Just getting shit done," I reply. "Someone has to look out for our best interests."

It doesn't take him long to realize I'm taking a dig at his decisions lately. I'm not about to apologize for not sugar coating my feelings. I think he's dragging his feet, and he needs to know. It's part of my job as VP to keep track of our side businesses and financial reports of the club, even if they aren't the same ideals of my president. I don't always agree with the stubborn asshole, but you just have to know how to approach it without painting a target on your head.

"That mean what I think it's supposed to?" he asks, sliding farther into the room and plopping down in the chair that sits in front of the desk.

Propping his feet up on my desk, he kicks dust on the papers lying there.

"You know it's close, Hero. I can feel it in the air. Shit's about to happen."

"I can feel it, too. Have you heard from any of the clubs up north?"

"All, but one. I had to send Trax up to Chico to check on Ace's clubhouse, since he's gone dark. He's supposed to report in soon. Hopefully, Ace just has malfunctioning technology in that shithole clubhouse. You'd think with the cash they're bringing in since starting their weed extract business, they'd upgrade the place."

His eyes peer down to his cut when the buzz of a vibrating phone penetrates the conversation. He slides his iPhone from the inside pocket and brings it to his ear.

"Raze," he barks. Unable to hear his conversation, a sober look settles onto his face. "Call a lockdown and get your asses back here. Start your guys on calling the other chapters."

Hanging up the phone, he slams his fists on the desk, shattering his phone into pieces that scatter across the tile floor.

"They hit Ace's clubhouse. It's been reduced to ashes. Trax counted twenty burned bodies inside the rubble. Those fuckers burned them all alive."

"Jesus, Raze. What about the old ladies and the club girls? Any sign of them?"

"Nothing. They've either run off, or they've been taken hostage. Call the guys, and have them bring their families back here. We're going dark."

Tyson comes skidding into the room. His chest heaves from the exertion.

"We've got a situation, Prez. One of our civilian contacts just called. Twisted Tribe is rolling into town from the south," he declares.

"Fuck!" Raze exclaims. "Get on the horn and call all

the chapters home. It's time to take these fuckers out once and for all."

I make the necessary calls as Raze and my brothers circle the wagons. Hearing Dani's voice over the phone when I called Maj's salon was shocking at first, but at the same time, it meant they were okay. Soon, both of them would be back in the safe confines of the clubhouse.

Not soon enough. They were sitting ducks out there, and every second they're away is a second too long.

I hear the familiar sound of a Harley engine pulling into the parking lot. I start out of the room, down the hallway, and out the back door to find the source. Maj finally arrives on the back of Voodoo's bike. Seeing her safe brings me relief, but it's short-lived.

Dani is nowhere to be found.

"Where's Dani?" I yell over the roar of his engine.

"She's still at the salon. She's secured in the building. I'm about to go back for her."

How could he be so stupid? She could be dead by now. That bastard should have called as soon as he realized Dani was going to be left behind.

"There's no time. Tribe's already rolling in. You get Maj inside and lock shit down. I'll go after her. Get the bikes out back, and the outbuildings locked down. Have the girls get the basement rooms ready. We've got a lot of brothers on their way."

I jump into one of the club's SUVs and tear down the

drive. Breaking just about every traffic law on the books, I make it to the salon within five minutes. Broken glass litters the sidewalk, and several of the chairs that used to be in the waiting area are lying busted next to a Silver Harley.

Fuck, I'm too late. They've been here.

Circling around back, I barely get the vehicle in park before I jump from it, hitting the ground running. I hope she's either hidden well enough to avoid discovery, or she's gotten away. I'd rather she be back on the run than dead. Her death would be on all of our hands, because we failed to keep her safe. I don't care if she may be a traitor. She's our responsibility. I round the corner of the door with my gun drawn when Dani runs into me. Her shirt and arms are covered in blood, but it doesn't seem to be hers.

Thank fuck, she's alive. "Are you okay?" I ask, holding her out to get a better look at her.

"The man—," she stutters. "He tried to..."

"Tried to what?" I growl.

"To rape me," she blurts out.

I hear a groan coming from the back door.

"Stay here."

Shoving her aside, I rush inside. I'm shocked as I take in the scene in front of me. A Hispanic man lies on the ground, bleeding profusely from his face. He writhes and moans in pain. *Jesus, Dani put up a fight and took the bastard down herself. Fuck, he's three times her size. How did she take him down?*

Kicking a toolbox out of the way, I move closer, my gun still drawn. His cut tells me all I need to know. He's a Tribe officer. Everything inside me wants to kill him for what his club did to my brother, and for what he tried to do to Dani. Had she not been a stronger woman, this might not even be a possibility. She could be dead. Something I don't even want to think about right now, because it will make it harder not to pull the trigger. "Who are you?" I snarl, pulling him up from the ground, and stowing my gun in the waistband of my jeans.

He's no threat now. He likely can't even see from the coagulated blood and embedded glass in his face. He mutters something in unintelligible Spanish. Dani must have broken his jaw with the bottle. He's useless to us if he can't talk. I pull my handgun back out and cock the hammer back, putting the barrel of the gun to his forehead. Just before I pull the trigger, my eyes catch the patch on his cut. He's the fucking vice president of Twisted Tribe. Looks like it's his lucky day. Raze will want him alive, to use as a bargaining chip. Replacing the gun back into my jeans, I pull some wire ties from the open toolbox by the back door, securing his hands together.

I grab Dani roughly as I walk out the door and forcibly shove her into the SUV. She begs me for answers about what's going on, but I'm not in the right headspace for this conversation. Going back for the bastard, I haul his ass out of the salon, taking the time to drag him through the broken glass and wreckage he'd caused, then shove him into the backseat of the SUV, making sure the fucker lands on his injured face. I'm not about to be careful with the man who likely ordered the deaths of over twenty of our men in Chico. His club will pay for every drop of Heaven's Reject blood they've spilled. I speed off towards the clubhouse, with Dani safe and the break we needed to go after the Tribe. Two birds, one big fucking stone.

Pulling into the clubhouse, I park the SUV in the back lot.

"Go get Raze," I order Dani. "Then go straight to your room and lock the door. Do not come out unless Raze or I come to get you. There's other chapters here, and it isn't safe for you."

She nods and slides from the SUV without an argument. She's shaken, and for a good reason, but I can't focus on that now.

While she runs into the building, I drag our prisoner into the shed. Right where they had strung up Jagger. His blood will replace Jagger's on the floor, wiping that murder clean. Dani had listened to me about giving Raze my message, because he stalks out of the clubhouse.

"Brought you a gift, Prez. The VP of Twisted Tribe

attacked Dani, but by the time I got there, she used his face as a bottle opener. Pretty sure his jaw is jacked, but figured you'd want him in our possession instead of dead on the salon's back room floor."

"Dani did this to his face?" Nodding, I kick our prisoner into the dirt. Raze takes one look at the man and trudges into the side room of the shed, returning with a rope. Wrapping it around his bound wrists, he throws the other end over the ceiling brace, and hauls him from the ground until he's left dangling in the air. His blood streaks the ground as he's dragged. His body swings as Raze ties the rope onto one of the support beams along the far wall. He walks up to face the man, then spits in his face and sucker punches him in the jaw.

"Your club killed my brother. Your death will be the first of many."

Raze continues to hit the man, again and again, until he's completely unrecognizable. It's a surprise he's still alive after taking such a beating. Wiping his bloodied knuckles with a rag, Raze steps out of the shed and closes the doors. I take one look at the sad sack of shit strung up like piñata before me, and it brings a smile to my face.

One down. Several more to go.

His blood drips in thick drops to the ground at my feet. I watch him sputtering and begging in broken

Spanish for a few minutes longer until a welcome sound deafens his groans.

Ratchet appears in the doorway as the rumble of a large group of motorcycles. His gaze immediately goes to the man strung up.

"Starting the party without me, Prez?"

"Something like that," Raze mutters before shoving past me and moving towards the door. Following him, Ratchet and I step out from the shed as the hoard of Harleys pulls into our drive, shaking the ground beneath our feet like an earthquake. *Our brothers are here.* Raze stands just outside, watching as they pour into the parking lot in droves. More will be coming soon enough, and with them, the end of the Tribe.

"Ratchet, he's yours. Just don't let kill the fucker."

"With pleasure, Prez," Ratchet smiles wide. "With fucking pleasure."

"We hit Twisted Tribe tomorrow. Get what you can out of him. As soon as that's done, you will finish this motherfucker when we get back," Raze orders.

"Whatever you say, Prez."

He stops and looks back at the shed before we leave Ratchet to his work and head back to the clubhouse.

"Their bloodlines ends tomorrow."

Chapter 13

DANI

HOURS PASS with no signs of Raze or Hero coming to get me. Maybe it was a little presumptuous on my part to think they would care enough to check on me, considering what happened at the salon. The memory of that man coming after me sends shivers down my spine.

No. Not now. Please.

The memories come, despite my pleas to will them away.

The sound of his fly unzipping.

His hands on me.

The fear coursing through my body as I fought to get away.

Then it happened. A glass bottle of sterilization solution glittered behind him. He smirked down at me and licked his lips, excited for what he had planned. But my split-second decision to head butt him and break the bottle over his head became my saving grace. My survival mode kicked in, and the rest of it was a blur. And then Hero showed up.

I had been relieved to see him, because his appearance meant I was safe. The relief on his own face was comforting, but now it's clear that maybe I mistook his relief for something else. Maybe I was just holding out, hoping that inside his coldness was the man I saw at the club that first night. The man who warmed me with his touch and made me feel like things could actually be okay again.

Fool. You're asking for the moon, with no means to lasso it. Just fucking move on before you get yourself any deeper into this world.

"Dani?" a soft feminine voice calls out.

"Yes?"

"It's Bubbles. Can I come in?"

What the hell does she want?

Slowly opening the door, I see Bubbles impatiently waiting, wearing only a blue rhinestone-covered bikini.

"What do you need, Bubbles?" I ask, eyeing her apparel. That outfit doesn't exactly cover much. I can see her nipples through the flimsy material.

"Can you come help me at the bar? Ruby was helping me, but some guy dragged her off somewhere."

"No, Bubbles. You know I'm not supposed to leave this room," I say, shaking my head.

Her smile fades from her excessively made-up face. "Raze said you could help out."

My eyes narrow at that. Hero told me to not leave, unless it was him or Raze coming to get me. Something about this doesn't seem right.

"Are you sure Raze said it was okay?"

Her dimpled smile returns, and she vigorously shakes her head.

"Please, Dani. I really need the help. The guys have probably already overrun the bar while I'm back here talking to you."

"Fine, I'll help, but you better not be lying to me about Raze's reprieve."

She attacks me with a hug and giggles, like a teenage girl at a boy band show. "Thank you, thank you, thank you," she cries, dragging me down the hall, into the heart of the party. I don't recognize any of the old ladies in the bevy of women littering the room. Every single man here has a pretty woman draped across him.

Moving behind the bar, I notice a blonde quaff of hair bobbing up and down in Slider's lap, while the men surround him, watching with beers in their hands.

Jesus. Is this the side of the club I have been spared from? Does shit like this happen all the time?

I try to drown out the sight now burned into my eyes by getting to work and keeping the drinks flowing. Bubbles and I take command over the bar, catching up on the backlog of orders in about thirty minutes. An older man steps forward and plops down on the stool next to where I'm pouring buttery nipple shots. His face is worn from years of riding his motorcycle in the California sun. It almost reminds me of leather.

"What can I get you to drink?" I ask, as I turn to get the bar rag off the back counter. He yanks me by the arm, attempting to pull me across the bar and into his lap. Jerking my arm from his grip, I move myself farther away from the front counter. "What the fuck do you think you're doing?" I yell.

He jumps up from his stool and slides across the bar. His tattooed, leathery arms pin me against the wood. "You've been flaunting those beautiful tits and perfect ass around here, yet not a single man has touched you. I want to know why. You property? I don't see a patch on you." His whiskey-laced breath burns my nostrils. He pulls me in tighter, and I squirm, trying to escape his grasp. "Name's Trax. What's yours?"

"Not interested, pal."

"Come on, baby girl. Give this old man some of your sweet pussy," he whispers into my ear, his lips descending closer to mine.

"No means no, asshole," I declare, fidgeting in an attempt to get away.

"I'll touch you any way I want, bitch," he seethes. "Get on your knees."

I do the only thing I can think of in this kind of situation. I improvise. Slamming my head against his face, he stumbles back, releasing me. My vision goes blurry from the collision, but I force myself to shake it off. His eyes are wild with rage.

Fuck. I need to run. I dart out from behind the bar. He follows me as I attempt to make my way back to the safety of my room. I should have never left it in the first place. I'm so goddamn stupid to think Raze's men would protect me.

Get back to the room and lock the door. You'll be safe.

It was a fleeting thought. Just as I reach the hallway, he reaches me. I try to dodge him, but he catches me again. This time with a much harder grip.

"Now, darlin'. You didn't think I'd just let you walk away after that? I was going to be nice to you, but now I think I'm going to fuck you raw, right in front of everyone in this club. No club whore strikes a patched member," my attacker growls.

The fat, old bastard obviously isn't the type of man who takes no for an answer. I turn to walk away, and he grabs my right arm. I use the momentum from his pull and rear back, throwing the hardest haymaker I can manage. I feel the cartilage and bone snap from the force of my fist connecting with his nose. His hand comes to his face, covering the source of pain and bleeding.

"You stupid bitch," he screams, lunging for me.

"You'll pay for this. No two-bit whore strikes a member of this club."

His hands grab my waist, just as my knee connects with his balls. He falls to the ground, screaming in agony. I kick him in the ribs twice to make sure he not only stays down, but to make my point crystal clear.

"I told you, you fucking piece of shit, not to touch me. You think just because I'm a woman, I can't stand up for myself? It's fucking bastards like you that make women weak. Well, that's not the woman I am. I will put a bullet between your eyes if you ever get close to me again."

The club stands in silence as the final word slips from my mouth. I know that threatening a club member will probably land me on the street, or worse, dead and buried in an unmarked grave, but I'm not about to be raped for their continued protection. Heavy footfalls reverberate from behind me, and I tense, waiting for the next attack. I will not go down without a fight. Not with the fucking bastards who kidnapped me. Not the bastard back at the salon. And sure as fuck not with this fat son of a bitch. Every ounce of fight inside me courses through my veins, and I turn on my heels, my balled fists ready to strike. But what I find isn't the fight I was expecting. I momentarily sigh when I find Hero behind me.

Hero's eyes are unreadable as his gaze locks onto

mine. Leaning down, he extends his hand to Trax to help him stand. He is helping up the man who would have raped me had I not struck first. I guess I know where I stand in the pecking order of his life. Brothers first.

Trax uprights himself and immediately turns his sights back on me, ignoring Hero at my side.

"You think because this club is protecting you, you've got the right to strike a patched member? I need to teach you some manners."

Before anyone can react, he has me by the throat, choking the life out of me.

"You'll wish you were dead once I'm done with you."

His grip tightens, and I squirm to break free. Hero moves to pull him away from me. Moving my hands from his, I maneuver my arms into a triangle shape and push against Trax's arms. His hands break away from my neck, as Hero decks him, sending him to the ground.

I quickly recover, moving towards him.

"Never. Fucking. Touch. Me. Again," I say, stomping my heel into his balls with every word. Hero pulls me off him and shoves me away. This fight may be over, but I have one last thing I need to do. Shoving past Hero, I spit on the bastard writhing on the floor and walk out of the still silent room. Slamming the door of my room behind me, I slide to the floor with heavy tears streaking down my face. My heart is racing, and then I hear heavy foot-steps thumping down the hall in my direction.

In a flash, I jump up and lock the door, then run straight for the bathroom. There's a window I might be just small enough to fit through, so I can get the hell out of here before they break into the room and drag me out. The door to my bedroom rattles as I pry open the window. It will be a tight squeeze, but I think I can make it through. I hop up onto the counter and start pushing my head and arms through the space when I hear wood splitting.

Fuck! He's in here. What the hell is with the men in this club breaking down doors? That must be part of their initiation ceremony.

Panicking, I push farther into the window. Then two hands grab my waist, pulling me back inside. I fall hard onto the sink, my elbow connecting with the porcelain, causing me to fall to my knees on the dirty tile floor. Black leather boots stand over me.

"Where the hell do you think you're going?" Hero hauls me to my feet and pushes me against the wall. He stands far enough away that I can't reach him with my knee. Lifting my eyes to face him, I can feel the rage returning.

"Away from you and your fucking psycho club."

"Doubt that," he says, his lip quirking up just a little on one side. "You beat one of my brothers."

"I'm glad I did. If you knew what he was planning to do, you'd have done it, too." I snarl.

"If you'd have done what you were told, you wouldn't have found yourself in that situation."

"Fuck you."

His face moves towards mine, his grip on my chin rough. "You're fair game. He had every right to proposition you. You have no patch to claim you, but he should have never laid a finger on you after you said no."

"What the fuck does a patch have to do with this?"

"I know you don't understand, but it's our way of marking women who are off-limits to other members."

"I thought Maj's decree would have been enough. He touched me in plain sight of the entire club, and no one stopped him."

"Slider came to get me when he saw him bothering you. Had I heard or seen what he did to you, I would have taken care of it before you ever had to defend yourself."

His eyes soften momentarily, and then the cocky asshole side of him flares to life again.

"Why did you leave your room?"

"Bubbles came to get me because she needed help at the bar. I didn't realize that serving a few drinks would land me in rape territory. Raze told her to get me to help."

Shock crosses his face at Raze's name. His hand releases my chin, and his body slowly releases the tension set into his bones.

"I've been with him all night. Raze didn't say shit about you helping out Bubbles."

"But I thought…" I stammer. "She said he did."

"He didn't. I promise you that. I think I need to have a discussion with Bubbles about disobeying orders."

"All you fucking care about is that Bubbles lied to me? Jesus, Hero. Your priorities are seriously messed up if you're more worried about a lying whore than an attempted rape, but I guess brothers first, right?"

I shove against his chest, but he locks me even tighter in his grasp.

"It would have never gotten that far, Dani. I told you once, and I will tell you again, nothing will ever happen to you while you're under our roof and protection. How badly did he hurt you?" I try to push away from him, but his arm stays firm, keeping me pinned to the bathroom wall. "I asked you a question, Dani. How badly did he hurt you?"

Still attempting to shake him away, I push harder. "Hero, just let me go. You don't care that I'm hurt. It's not like you plan on keeping me around much longer."

With one final push, I break free.

Charging past him as fast as I can, I reach the bathroom doorway before he pulls me against him, then pushes my back against the door frame. His lips collide with mine before I can get away. The heat from his lips devouring mine sends fire through my veins. My core feels as if it's about to explode from his touch. His tongue forces my lips to part, then his lips caress mine. He continues to pull me closer as his tongue explores my mouth. My body hums louder with each passing second. Suddenly, he breaks away from me and stares into my eyes. My rage is replaced by confusion and need. The man who has treated me worse than any man in this club just kissed me like he would never see me again.

What the fuck just happened?

I stare blankly at him, frozen in shock.

"I've wanted to do that since the first moment you walked into my club and ripped the place apart like an F-5 tornado. Your fight out there only made this problem fucking worse."

His hands press against my neck as he claims my mouth once more. He only breaks away when I wince in pain.

"Shit, are you okay?"

"I think I'm fine. You were just squeezing me a little too tightly. I think Trax bruised my throat. It's tender."

The mention of Trax's name sends the rage flying back into him. He releases me and stalks towards the shattered door. He turns back before walking through the mess of wood on the floor.

"He'll pay for touching you, Dani. I'll make damn sure of it." He pokes his head out in the hall and yells for Slider. A few seconds later, Slider's head pops through the door frame, taking in the scene, a knowing smile on his face.

Fucking men.

"What's up? You need something?" His eyes scan the scene before him. "You okay, sweetheart?"

I nod my head, but Hero cuts me short before I can answer.

"I need you to move Dani's shit into my room. Put a guard at the door. I don't want Trax, or any of the charter members, fucking with her. You got it?"

A smile lights up Slider's face. "Sure, Hero. I'll watch her tonight. The pussy is otherwise entertained tonight, and I'm not into sloppy seconds from another charter." I laugh to myself thinking about the show I just witnessed. Blondie might have broken his dick if he's not chasing after more than a blowjob.

Slider walks into the room and plops himself on my bed, waiting on orders from me on what to move.

"Get off her fucking bed," Hero growls.

He heads out the door without even asking me if I'm okay with moving into his room. I'm not about to just up and move on his command.

"I'm not moving into your fucking room, Hero. Just get me a new door. I'm sure the club has a shed full of them at the rate you all go through them, or is that just reserved for me?"

His eyes flash with intense anger. "You'd rather stay

in a room without a door, where any of these bastards can sneak into your bed or watch you dress, than stay in my room, where you'll be safe? You're fucking kidding me, right?"

I hadn't thought about that. There's no way the door can be replaced in the middle of the night.

Sharing a room with him will only make my attraction and need for his touch grow. I can't let him break down these walls and discover the truth about why I left Cleveland. As much as my body wants his, I have to resist him.

"I'll stay with one of the girls. I won't hole up in your room like some club whore. I'm better than that."

Ignoring Slider, he seizes me by the arm. "You aren't a club whore, Dani. Get that out of your fucking head right now. Your ass better be in my room by the time I get back, or I'll drag you in there myself."

He doesn't even give me a chance to argue before he walks out of the door.

I punch the door frame. "Fucking bastard," I mutter to myself, forgetting that Slider is perched on my bed.

He chuckles to himself, then says, "He might be a bastard, sweetheart, but he's your problem now."

I shove Slider off of the bed and onto the floor. He jumps to his feet and helps me pack what little clothes and toiletries I have into laundry baskets. Then he starts to haul them into Hero's room down the hall. His room is so much bigger than my tiny one. A king-sized bed with a black comforter and sheets sits against the wall. A couch, dresser, and TV line the other side of the room. A typical man cave.

I stake claim to an empty drawer in his dresser and deposit my clothes into it. He probably won't like that, but tough shit because it just happened. He forced me into this arrangement, so it's only fair I get what I want out of this.

Slider walks in with the last load of my things and deposits them on Hero's bed.

"Sweetheart, I can see how much he's pissed you off with the new digs. I understand why he did it, but all I can say is that you need to make him pay for this order. I love to watch him squirm, so hit him where it hurts." He laughs to himself as he walks out the door, closing it behind him.

Hero may think he knows the type of girl I am, but he doesn't know the real me. I know I'm in the worst possible place to keep my secrets, especially with his assumption of my suspicion and guilt, but I need to stay strong and keep my composure. I hope he enjoys sleeping on the couch, because he's just lost the privilege of the bed. I like to spread out, and I'll make damn sure I'm taking up as much room as I can when he gets back. I flip on the TV and hide the remote. I hope he likes lifetime movies, because that's all he'll be able to watch while I'm in here.

Payback is a bitch.

Waiting for Hero to return becomes pure torture. It's been over an hour since he ordered me to move in here.

I've sat on his soft bed and nervously counted the seconds since he busted through the door and chewed me out for my attack on Trax. I don't know what came over me when he touched me, but the feel of his skin on mine had sent me into a blind rage. Anything and everything in my way would have been destroyed if I hadn't walked away. My escape attempt wasn't exactly my brightest idea, but it was the only viable option my brain presented to me in a moment of sheer panic. I had assumed I had limited time left breathing on this earth, and I wouldn't go silently.

My eyes begin to droop, and I know I won't be able to stay awake much longer. Sliding under the silky covers of his bed, I lay on my side, absently watching the movie on TV. Sleep threatens to pull me under, and I know that I'm losing my battle against sleeping before Hero comes back.

Stay awake. You have to stay awake.

But my eyes only become heavier. Just as I feel myself slipping past the dark veil of exhaustion, I hear the door open.

He's back.

Chapter 14

HERO

I DON'T KNOW what I was thinking when I ordered her to move into my room. It was either watching her nearly castrate one of my unruly brothers in the middle of the clubhouse bar, or that kiss.

Who the fuck am I kidding? It was both.

The feel of her lips against mine made me nearly cum in my jeans. I've wondered so many times how soft her skin would feel under my fingers, and about the taste of those plump lips, but now I know. Somehow, this woman has gotten under my skin. She has to be part hell-cat, and that pisses me off and turns me on all at once. The kiss was a mistake. One that moving her into my room will only complicate further, because I don't trust myself to not do it again.

That mistake is currently taking up residence in my room, and in my fucking bed, while I'm out here on the main floor mopping up Trax's blood and holding back from murdering him myself. I'll deal with him after we settle our business with Twisted Tribe, but my self-inflicted problem remains.

Returning the mop and bucket to the kitchen, I slide back into my normal seat by Raze, kicking my feet up on the beer bottle covered coffee table.

"I hear you have a new roommate," he states.

"Yeah, figured it would be easier watch her if she's locked in my room. Well, that, and I kicked her door in to have a little chat with her about our brother's obliterated balls. I caught the bitch trying to squeeze out the bathroom window."

Raze shakes his head. "Must have been desperate to leave if she was going to risk a two-story fall into a pile of cacti," he quips. "You know Trax will want her punished after she crushed his balls in front of everyone."

"Yeah, that's not surprising, but he crossed the line. We both know he'll try to save face by spouting some bullshit about her not having a property patch, but I'll take care of him."

The thought of that rat bastard losing his family jewels brings a smile to my face.

"Doc's checking him out now. He's holed up in one of the rooms downstairs. He passed out from the pain as his guys were dragging his ass down the stairs."

A thought crosses my mind that will likely piss Raze off, but I can't help myself. "You could always let Maj take care of it. She is technically in charge of the girl."

"You know full well that Maj would only cause more problems if we give her the power to punish Trax. I already had to send her back to our house. She keeps trying to tell me how we should attack the bastards. It's like she gets off on pissing me off now."

The truth behind his words really surprises me. Maj used to be this calm, cool, and collected old lady when she first married Raze, but lately she's been far too inter-ested in club business. I hope Raze flips the kill switch on Maj's curiosity soon, before she lands herself in even more trouble. We can't have the club president's old lady stirring shit up and poking her nose too far into our busi-ness. If he doesn't rein her in, someone else will, and he won't like it.

"All the more reason to stay unattached if you ask me."

Raze just stares at me with a smirk on his face.

"What, old man? Just because you fell for Maj's love-me-forever bullshit doesn't mean I will."

He lets out a hearty laugh and shakes his head. "You're already there, brother. That woman has caught you hook, line, and sinker. Don't think I haven't caught on that you watch her every time she walks into the room. Your bullshit may fool everyone else, but not me.

will solve all of our problems tomorrow, when we wipe Twisted Tribe off the planet, soothing the entire club's ache caused by Jagger's murder. He wasn't a fan of condoning violence, but in some cases, the old adage of an eye for an eye fits better than a slap on the wrist. Our goals are simple in the attack. Take them out and make it back home. I'm not foolish enough to believe we won't end up with casualties. Even if things work perfectly, they'll fire on us just as quickly as we will on them. If the military taught me anything, it was kill them before they kill you.

Locking up behind me, I walk out to the front gate. A couple of Trax's prospects are manning the gate, while a few of ours are lying low on the roofs of the buildings. Ratchet waves to me from the roof of the clubhouse, his rifle in hand. Bastard is nuts, but he's a crack shot. I'd rather have him with me than against me any day.

Giving the guys their orders for the night, I return to the clubhouse. The party is finally dying down when I make it back to a thinning crowd in the main room. Only a few guys are lounging in the sitting area, while a couple of the girls clean up empty bottles and cigarette butts. How they can party like this the night before they'll be dealing out justice doesn't make sense to me, but as long as the results are the same, who the fuck cares?

Ruby walks out of the kitchen with a trash bag in her

hand, just as I round the corner to head to my room and to Dani. She rushes to me and wraps her arms around my neck.

"Are you sure you need to go tomorrow, Hero?" she asks, poking her lip out in a sexy pout. "I don't want you to get hurt… or worse."

Pulling her arms from me, I step back just enough to put space between our bodies. I know where this is headed, and I'm not in the mood for whining and fake emotions. Maybe before this shit went down, I would fall for her song and dance of worrying for my safety, but not anymore. I know her game, even if it has a well-ended meaning behind it. What feelings I had for Ruby blinked out of existence the instant Dani came barreling into my life. She's nothing more to me than a past lover who refuses to walk away.

"I'll be fine, so don't worry your pretty little head over nothing."

I try to move away from her, but she grabs me by the arm, pulling my attention back to her. "Can I stay with you tonight?"

"I want to be alone tonight," I lie. "Silence helps me focus on the mission ahead. The place I have to go to prepare doesn't make me fit for company. Why don't you take the night off? You and the girls have been busy keeping the clubhouse clean and the guys happy. You need a break."

Stopping short of my door, I hesitate before opening it. I know as soon as I step foot into the room, it will go one of two ways. She'll hurl something at my head, or I'll climb in bed next to her. Each possibility comes with its own set of consequences. I weigh my options before I turn the knob. The room is dark, except for the flickering lights of the TV screen.

Trying to find the remote to switch it off, I notice a bare shoulder sticking out from under the covers. I abandon my search when the thought of her possible nakedness makes my blood pump straight from my brain to my dick. I need to stow my aching cock for at least one night. I don't want to scare her away the very first night she's in my bed.

Stripping down to my boxer briefs, I step to the unoccupied side of the bed. Calling the sliver of space she's left unoccupied is nonsense. She's lying literally in the middle of the bed, with her arms and legs outstretched as far as she can reach them. Fuck, seeing her laid out so openly makes the predicament in my pants grow harder.

Delicately picking up one of her arms, I slide into my apportioned piece of the bed. The smell of her freshly washed hair and skin settles over me, soothing my nerves about being alone in the same room with her, let alone a bed. Her scent is a mixture of honey and lavender, and makes me speculate what she may taste like.

You know she'll taste like heaven. Why deny it?

I force myself not to just reach out and touch her, coaching myself that, until I know for sure she's cleared of all accusations, she will remain a prisoner. After the things I've said to her, I doubt her legs will fall open easily for me. She might not even be worth the trouble anyway, but I can't shake this unending desire to hold her, and feel her beautiful body under me.

Settling on my pillow, I close my eyes and beg for sleep to come easily.

Her voice stirs me just as I'm drifting into oblivion. "Why did you move me in here?" she asks, without turning to face me. "I thought you hated me."

She thinks I hate her? That's far from how I feel about her, but it's better for us both if she believes I do. That way, only one of us gets hurt if this blows to fucking bits.

Hate isn't exactly the word I would use to describe my trepidation about her. Skeptical or cautious would be more like it, but not hate. How could you hate the one woman on the planet that makes you question every decision you've ever made, or the way you process your thoughts? She tempts me like no one else has before, but this isn't about my feelings. My club and my brothers will always come first. Even if she is innocent, she'll never outrank them. My life isn't exactly white picket fences with two point five kids like you see in the movies. It's dark and dangerous.

"After the show you put on earlier with Trax's ball sack, it's safer for you to be in here with me."

"He attacked me first, you know. It's sweet how you protect a potential rapist, just because he wears the same patch you do." She turns onto her side to face me.

Her face is beautifully illuminated by the glow of the TV. Her deep brown eyes contrast with her soft, feminine features. She was right about being bruised from Trax's choking. Deep purple bruises encircle her throat. Seeing his marks on her brings the asshole inside me flooding back to the surface.

"If you had listened to me, you'd have never been in that situation. Next time I issue you an order, fucking listen to it."

The intensity of her stare shatters the willpower I'm desperately clinging to. Her eyes could unman the staunchest warrior from his post.

"What happened to the man I met at Red's that night? The asshole façade you put on for the club doesn't feel like it's the real you. You care about the people here."

"Don't, Dani. I'm not the man you seem to think I am. There's not a heart of gold buried underneath my black heart."

"I don't think that's true at all," she whispers.

"Then you don't really know me."

"I would if you'd give me the chance," she whispers. Her words nearly stop my heart. She's here, lying in my bed, and I can't bring myself to touch her. Not until I know for sure. It's fucking torture having her next to me. So close, yet so far away.

Not yet. A few more hours until you know. A few more hours until you can be absolutely fucking certain she's not one of them.

"Go back to sleep."

"Done talking, huh?"

"I'd advise you not to leave this room until we get back. You'll be safer in here after your little stunt tonight."

I roll away from her and settle into the pillow. Darkness begins to take hold, then she whispers one last thing into the blackness of the room. I can barely hear her words as I fall asleep, but they resonate in my mind as sleep pulls me under.

"Your heart may be black, Hero, but it still beats in your chest, just like everyone else's."

Chapter 15

DANI

SOFT SNORES VIBRATE from his body just as the last word leaves my lips. He probably didn't hear me at all, and I sigh in relief that my confession may have fallen on deaf ears. It's true that he can be a black-hearted son-of-a-bitch when the club is around, but the man I met that first night has feelings buried in that thick skull of his somewhere, despite him trying like hell to hide them. And honestly, I don't blame him. The pull between us is obvious, at least to me, but why would he want a girl like me? My past is shrouded in darkness, and my present isn't exactly any better. If he knew what laid back in Ohio, he'd be gone in a flash. It's better for us both that my past stays exactly there.

Sleep completely evades me, my mind unable to come to terms with my present situation. Why move me into his room? It makes no sense. He's spent all this time avoiding me, only to bring me closer. It's as if he cares about me, but his behavior since I got here says otherwise. I'm a burden to them all. A threat. Guys like him normally take threats out without a second thought.

So why am I still here?

Why am I sharing a bed with a man who loathes me?

Is his cool demeanor finally cracking?

Probably not, because let's face it, he's moody and unpredictable at best. This could be nothing more than a power play I hadn't figured out yet. He's calculating, but I don't think he realizes just how calculating I can be. If he thought his closeness would lower my guards, he's dumber than I thought. My guard is the only power I have left, and I will die before I let it go. Everything I ran from in Cleveland should have killed me, and I will not let a good-looking guy do what my past couldn't.

Hero doesn't stir as I resettle beside him. I stow a fleeting thought to reach out and touch his sleeping form. Getting attached isn't a part of the plan. The kiss was treacherous enough, but it can't happen again. I stiffen as I watch him shift closer to me in his sleep. He throws his arm over me, pulling me to his side. I try to move away, but his weight and his strength trap me beneath it.

If I move away, he'll wake up.

If I stay here, I will probably fall asleep and pretend

this didn't happen. I will also deny I liked the feeling of him wrapping himself around me.

I opt for the latter and quickly find myself asleep in his arms. My dreams flitter from my past to his face, each one cascading behind the other, before the sense of overwhelming pressures surmounts to my breaking point. My eyes flutter open just as the sound of Harleys firing up outside fills the room. I'm completely encompassing his pillow. The smell of his cologne lightly covers the soft fabric. I press my face into the pillow, inhaling the intoxicating scent.

Why do guys like him always smell so good?

It's just not fair.

Sliding out of bed, I walk to the window and watch bike after bike drive away. The clubhouse is eerily quiet as I watch the last Harley leave the premises. A pin could drop downstairs, and I'd probably hear it striking the ground. Did they really leave me here alone? Are the other club girls still around? Is Trax? The thought of having no one else here, but him, sends a shiver down my spine. I'd held my own against him last night because he wasn't expecting me to fight back. It would be a different story this time. Hero's words echo in my head.

He told you to stay here. Maybe this time you should listen.

Betrayed by my own conscience, but I know the voice

inside my head is right. All the men who can protect me are gone, and with them, my safety. Leaving this room would be a mistake. I just need to bide my time until Hero comes back.

Shuffling to the bathroom, I quickly shower. The hot water eases the aches from my fight with Trax, though my head still pounds from the head-butt. That was one move I would be moving farther down on my defense list. It may have been effective, but it came with a cost. As the water runs cold, I step from the shower. My eyes catch my reflection in the foggy glass, and I wipe away the misty fog and peer into the mirror. My heart pounds as my fingers trace Trax's fingers bruised into my throat.

He could have killed me. All he had to do was squeeze just a little tighter, and my fight would have been over. It was the simplest solution to the club's problem, yet Hero stopped him. His bullshit reason why was just that. Bullshit.

Realizing I forgot my toothbrush back in my room, I decide just to use his. He probably wouldn't notice, anyway. I smile as I rub the coarse bristles of his toothbrush on my teeth and picture his reaction. Once I'm done, I wrap a towel around my wet hair, throw on clean clothes, and head out of the bathroom. I settle onto the small sofa and waste the day watching TV until my stomach grumbles a few hours later.

Maybe sneaking down to the kitchen will be innocent enough. A girl has to eat.

Cracking the door, I peer out into the hallway and find it empty. I tiptoe down the stairs and sneak into the kitchen. The refrigerator is a goldmine of snacks, sandwiches, and drinks. I peruse my options before I find a plate of prepared sandwiches. The girls must have been busy last night in preparation for their triumphant return. Picking a ham and Swiss hoagie, I gather up my sandwich and a can of soda before closing the door and starting back to my room.

Just as I turn the corner, Daisy and Ruby walk into the main room.

Shit. What if they report back that I left the room, or worse, send Trax my way?

I slide quietly back into the kitchen and peer at the two women from a slit between the door and its frame.

I watch as Daisy stares absentmindedly out of the window, while Ruby plops down on the couch, flicking on the TV.

"Do you think they'll be back soon?" Daisy asks, still watching outside. "It's been hours since they left. Shouldn't they be back now?"

"It's fine, Daisy. Quit worrying. Either they come back or they don't. Let the old ladies worry." Ruby doesn't once look at Daisy while she speaks, continuing to stay focused on the TV.

"I thought I would be an old lady now," Daisy pouts. "Hero seemed to like me well enough before Dani showed up. I was hoping he'd patch me."

"You're delusional. He'll always be a player. Even the little bitch holed up in his room right now won't change a man like him. He'll get tired of her and come crawling back into our beds soon enough."

"I know. I just don't understand why he moved her into his room. He doesn't care about her. Not the way he cares about us, right?"

"Sometimes men don't see what they have, even if it's staring them in the face."

I feel my heart shatter inside of my chest. He'd been with these women. I think a part of me knew he had, but their confirmation of it stabs at me like an arrow to the heart. I slip back to the room with fresh tears trickling down my face, the food long forgotten out there with them.

Did he see me like that? Like one of those girls? Just another notch on his bedpost?

My heart aches in mourning for something I never knew I wanted and could never have.

Him.

Chapter 16

HERO

LEAVING Dani in my bed is one of the hardest things I have ever done. I woke up in the middle of the night with her arm over my chest and one of her legs intertwined with mine. I'm not sure whether she was using me for the warmth, or if her body naturally gravitated to me once her mind just shut down for the night, but whatever the reason was, I liked it. The feel of her body against mine soothed me. I gently stroked her back as she peacefully slept beside me, her hair fanned around her head like a dark crown. Tonight was the first night in weeks I didn't relive my brothers in arms being blown to fucking bits. The barrage of death and darkness hit every single night without fail, so I can only assume she is the reason for their MIA status. It's a welcome relief.

Her body formed a barrier from the darkness that haunts me and blocked my ghosts from emerging. The rhythm of her heartbeat pressed against me regulates mine.

To call this woman beautiful is the understatement of the year. She's every man's dream girl, and here she is, in bed with a man like me. The higher powers in the universe must be getting a good laugh at my expense on this one. I know I'm not the right man for her. She deserves the American dream kind of life, with a rich husband, kids, a Labrador, and a house with a white picket fence and a front porch swing. Not some fucked up, rough around the edges, biker. She's not meant to live the life of a biker. I lay there holding her until a soft knock raps on my door. *It's time.*

I carefully lift her limbs from mine and slide away from her body.

Why does it feel like I'm leaving a part of me in that bed with her?

I shouldn't feel this way about her in the least. She could still be a fucking spy, and here I am skirting around the rules, trying to get to know her. I'm not made for loving a woman like her, and I need to make myself believe that. Even if she moves into the lover category, she'll never be more than that. I watch her chest rise and fall with each breath for a few minutes, savoring the moment. The vision before me will forever be present in my mind.

Is she always this beautiful in the morning?

I shake the thought from my head.

Not the time to be thinking about this, assface. Later. After you end this.

I get dressed quickly, retrieving a black leather pouch of knives, along with two loaded handguns I keep hidden in a false shelf in the dresser. I pull each shining blade from their sheath, ensuring they're all deathly sharp. If I was to be disarmed, these knives may determine whether I live or die today.

Grabbing my cut from the back of the couch, I gather my weapons and head for the door. Stopping for just a moment, I stare at Dani's sleeping form one last time.

It's now or never. She'll either be mine, or she'll be dead after today.

I shake those thoughts from my head and step into the hallway, nearly walking straight into Voodoo and Tyson.

"Walk of shame, VP?" Voodoo teases.

"Fuck off," I fire back. He smiles and starts walking away. Tyson falls in beside me, and together, we walk in tension-filled silence.

The things our club is going to do today will not be easy to deal with. Anyone with a soul will be stained for life after we execute our attack. Good thing for me, my soul was shattered in Iraq. There's nothing left of it to break.

Making our way outside to the line of bikes in the

drive, I walk to my Harley and pull my bullet-proof vest from my saddlebag. The sun has to yet to rise, and it probably won't begin to shine until after we make it back home.

Well, if we even make it back to the clubhouse.

I shrug off my cut and wrap the heavy vest around me, velcroing it tightly in place. As I pull my cut back over my shoulders, Raze walks past me and begins the suiting up process. His face is cold and unreadable. He's ready for this, just as I am. I glance around at my brothers and notice the same look on their faces. We're all ready to end this.

For Jagger, and for our club.

I strap my knife holsters around my thighs and fill each slot with a razor-sharp blade. As a precautionary measure, I shove two of the blades into my riding boots. My bike shifts as I mount it. Then I wait for Raze to signal us to leave.

The ride to their hidden clubhouse will only take about fifteen to twenty minutes, but we want to sneak in as quietly as we can. The plan is to kill the engines on the bikes and hide them in a wooded section about a quarter of a mile away. We will use the woods as our cover for the longer-range weaponry. If they can't see us, they can't target us once the melee begins. We will use any option to our advantage if it means everyone comes home breathing.

Raze waves his hand in the air, and we fire up our bikes. He leads the pack as we cruise away side by side, heading south. I let the chilled desert night breeze wrap around my body as we ride into the night. Our amigo's intel proves truthful so far, and the wooded area comes into view on the left side of the road fifteen minutes into our ride. Cutting the lights on our bikes, we ease into the woods and kill the engines. I listen for any noise as I slide off my bike, but all I hear are insects chirping.

Raze stands at the edge of the woods, watching the darkened clubhouse up the road. Had our amigo not given us the address, we'd have never known it was an active residence. One of Trax's men took one of our club's cages and drove by yesterday morning to do a little recon for us. He reported back that the bikes were well-hidden, and that very few people were visible on the grounds. The element of surprise isn't with us, but the numbers are. We have the men, and we have the location. The fight is in our favor for once.

I move to stand next to Raze, surveying the area around us. There's not a single building for miles around their compound, which is good news for us. We won't have to deal with nosy neighbors calling the local police department. Raze quietly instructs the men to fan out. Leaving the cover of the woods, we form a line and quietly walk towards the building. Ratchet and a few of the others stay in the woods with sniper rifles. They can pick off the men from a distance, if necessary. We get to within one hundred feet of the house when Raze raises his hand to halt us.

"This is it. I need four guys to get close enough to break the windows and throw in tear gas. They should run outside, and we'll pick them off as they exit. Leave the women and children alone. They could have some of Ace's women in that building, and I don't want them harmed. If you find Ricky, or any of the other officers, I want them brought to me alive," he orders.

Pulling my guns from their holsters, I click off the safety on each one, and watch the four men stealthily walk towards the building. The sound of shattering glass echoes off the surrounding mountains, just before the tear gas begins to pour out of the buildings. The gas falls like a fog around the building, as bangs and screams spill from the inside.

People bolt from the smell of the gas, pouring out into the night from both sides of the building. Raze fires the first shot, and we unleash a firestorm of bullets raining down around them. Man after man screams, as our lead tears through their bodies. Men fall to the ground in piles, writhing in agony. Blood spurts from each shot, spraying into the air.

Several minutes pass after the last man stumbles from the building. Raze signals for us to move forward. The tear gas fog dissipates by the time we make it to the building. Twenty or so men lay dead or dying on the earth around us.

"Check them," Raze bellows. "If they aren't wearing an officer's patch, shoot them in the head."

His order brings back memories of my tour in Iraq. Insurgents would target convoys with officers and hold them hostage, while killing the other men to make a statement. Raze motions for me to follow him into the building to search for Ricky. As we step through the doorway, I keep my gun drawn. We search each room, only finding two women inside, none of them ours.

We move to clear the building when a scuffing sound comes from behind a dresser. Shoving it aside, we find Ricky huddling behind it in fear. His eyes are wild as he realizes Raze is standing before him. He scrambles to move farther away, but Raze pistol whips him in the head. Ricky falls to the ground, unconscious. Raze grabs him and drags him out of the room. Something just doesn't sit well with me about this room. The vibe coming off this place rattles me, and I know I need to sweep it one more time before I leave.

I'm completely missing something here.

Searching under the bed and behind the other furniture doesn't dig up anything. I'm about to give up when I see a tiny light shining beneath a hidden door. Prying it open, it reveals an old rickety staircase going underground.

"Raze!" I yell out the door. "You might want to come see this."

He quickly joins me, along with Ratchet, Voodoo, and Tyson. We descend single-file down the dimly lit stairs and make our way underground. I find a swinging light switch and pull the metal cord. As the light clicks on and illuminates the room, we find twelve dirty women shackled together along one wall. A few of them look to be dead already, but a few of them move. Holy shit, we found Ace's women. Voodoo and Tyson break away from us, anxious to free them from their bonds, while Raze, Ratchet, and I move farther into the room.

"Jesus Christ," Ratchet exclaims, as we make our way through the next doorway.

A wooden table is centered in the room, and a naked woman is shackled by the legs on top. She's covered in dirt and blood. Walking next to her body, I check her pulse. It's faint, but she's still alive. The blonde woman appears to have been brutally beaten and gang-raped. I'm not even sure Doc could save her in this condition, but we'll have to try. As Ratchet moves to release her wrists, she stirs and moans in pain. Good, she's still got fight left in her. That might save her life in the end. He quickens his pace and finally frees her. Gingerly lifting her into his arms, he starts for the door, then her hair shifts from her face.

"Holy shit," Ratchet says. "It's Ricca."

Hearing the name makes me freeze.

"Ricca? As in Dani's missing roommate?"

"Yeah, man. This is her. We've got to get her back to the clubhouse."

"Take her in the cage and take Slider back with you. We're going to need a couple vans to transport these women back," I order.

Ratchet leaves with Ricca in his arms. The thought of finding Dani like this makes my blood run cold. Ricca was Ricky's fucking girlfriend, and he let his men gang-rape her in his basement. No woman deserves that kind of treatment, and for that alone, I will take pleasure in ending him. I hope Doc can fix her before I have to tell Dani her roommate was tortured at the hands of her attempted kidnapper.

Leaving the room, I follow Raze outside. Trax has Twisted Tribe's President and Road Captain kneeling side by side in the dirt. Raze stalks towards Ricky and lands several blows to his face. Rage and fury pour from him as lifts his gun and, without hesitation, fires a shot at his dick. Ricky screams out in agony, his eyes wide as he stares down at his femoral arteries spurting blood on the ground around him. Raze shifts without pause, and puts the barrel of his gun to the Road Captain's head and pulls the trigger. Blood and pieces of his brain rocket out behind him and fall to the ground like hailstones. Ricky continues to scream as Trax pulls him up into a seated position.

"This is for Jagger," Raze says, putting the gun to his head.

"Wait, Raze," I say, stopping him from pulling the trigger and ending it all. "I need to ask him about Dani."

Crouching down to Ricky's eye level, I stare into his agony-stricken eyes.

"Dani. Tell me how you know her," I demand. My fists grip the collar of his cut, pulling him closer to me.

"Dani who?" he sputters out. He moans and bellows, leaving me unanswered.

"Answer me, motherfucker. Who is Dani to your club?"

"Who the fuck is Dani?" he screams.

"The woman you kidnapped," I seethe. All I can see are the bruises on Dani's rib cage. The cuts on her face. All because of him. "What is she to your club?"

"Took her as collateral when my bitch tried to leave with my drugs."

Satisfied with his answer, I nod to Raze and move away from him. Raze puts one in the chamber and presses the barrel back against his temple.

"I'll see you in hell, motherfucker," Raze declares, and then he pulls the trigger. The bullet enters Ricky's head and explodes brain matter on all of us within close range.

It's finally done. Jagger's death is avenged. His soul is free to rest in peace.

Looking over the remains of the men that surround us, my memories of the war flood back to me. Sadness and guilt threaten to pull me under as the vision of my fallen men settles onto the cocksuckers kneeling around me. The nameless faces of these men become my fallen unit, and their clubhouse is replaced with the sand-brick homes of Iraq. Walking around their bodies brings me back to checking my brothers for signs of life, just as one of Trax's men pumps a bullet into a man's head, silencing his moans. I have to force myself not to kneel beside them and press my fingers to their necks, searching for a pulse. These aren't my men, and they do not deserve to take another breath on this earth. The gunfire shocks me back to the present. We killed in the name of revenge, but deep down, I question what kind of blowback we'll get from this. We may have won the battle, but was the war really over for our club, and for me?

Slider pulls in with a work van minutes later and helps Tyson and Voodoo load the rescued women into it. He walks over to me to tell me that Doc is already at the compound and doctoring Ricca.

"Dani doesn't need to know about her. Not until we know for sure she's gonna pull through. Do you understand me?"

Slider nods and walks back to the van. As he pulls away with the brutalized women, Dani enters the forefront of my mind again. She could have been one of them in their basement of pain, and I wouldn't have even cared about her when we rescued her because she would have been just another nameless woman in my life. The decisions I've made lately could have turned this situation completely around had I not pulled my head out of my ass about her. On the other hand, my head up Dani's ass sounds like a good fucking time. Jesus, I'm a fucked-up man.

We clear the scene as the sun begins to rise. Raze orders the building and the bodies to be torched, and then we walk back to the woods to retrieve our bikes. As I mount my Harley, orange and red flames rise from the remains of Twisted Tribe. Watching their clubhouse burn against the sunrise harbors a disturbing peace inside of me. Justice was served, and in it, we've secured safety for the club.

Raze's gaze catches mine, and I can tell the darkness that was swirling inside of him has subsided for now, although I catch a small glimmer of sadness before he turns on his bike and takes off. I do the same and ride beside him.

The entire ride home, I think about what we did. It was war, no matter what way you looked at it. Lives were taken, revenge was reaped, and at the end of the day, only one side could stand as the victor. Today it was us, but tomorrow could be a completely different story. It's something that should be celebrated, but this feels wrong to me. Like this is only scratching the surface of our problems to come.

I waste no time and run up the stairs to my room when we return to the clubhouse. I need to be alone with my thoughts. Bursting into my room, I forget about Dani being in here. I can't verbalize words to apologize to her for the things I've said and done over the last few weeks. Stalking past her and into the bathroom, I slam the door and throw myself, clothes and all, into the shower. I turn the water as hot as it will go, and sit under the hot spray, attempting to wash away the guilt and pain of everything we did today, and the painful memories of my past. Tears soon fall, and as I weep into my knees, I beg for mercy for my transgressions as a man. Justice was served today to a murdering club that had killed my friend, but what about the women they tortured? The thought of finding Dani like that reemerges, and I can't shake it off. I did what I had to do for the sake and pride of my club, but I'm not proud of the things I've seen today. We failed to protect those women, just as we failed to project Jagger in his retirement.

That kind of guilt just doesn't wash away, and it will haunt me for the rest of my life.

I don't know how long I sit in the shower, but when

the water finally runs cold, I make myself get up off the floor. Stripping off my soaking wet clothes, I reach for a towel on the shelf and wrap it around my waist. I still see the blood on my skin, even though it's been washed away. I feel unclean, and uncertain of myself as a man. Dani's eyes lift to mine when I step from the bathroom. She jumps from the couch and runs towards me, wrapping her thin, delicate arms around my neck and holds me close.

Her reaction to my return surprises me.

Is this pity or compassion? Whatever it is, I don't care. I need to feel something. I need to feel her.

Holding her against my cold, damp body, she begins to shiver.

Shit, I'm freezing her to death.

I bend down and pick her up into my arms. Carrying her to the bed, I lay her down gently and slide the covers over her hips. She trembles and shakes the entire time it takes me to move to the other side of the bed. I remove my towel and slide in next to her, pulling her shivering body against mine. Her ass nestles against my aching groin, and my arms encompass her slim waist.

We lay melded together for hours, just comforting each other with our presence and warmth. Her heart beats in rhythm with my own. She stays quiet, likely knowing I'm not ready to talk about what happened. The quiet was fine for a while, but I need to hear her voice. I need her to understand everything.

"Dani?"

"Mmhmm," she hums.

"I'm sorry," I whisper.

"For what?"

"Everything," I admit.

She stretches and rolls to face me.

"You did what you thought was necessary."

I can't hold back any longer. Pulling her closer to me, I press my lips against hers. The softness of her lips feels like kissing pure silk. She fully awakens under my touch and wraps her arms around my neck, kissing me in return. Our lips meld together, and I slip my tongue into her mouth, caressing hers. She moans and wraps her legs around mine. Rolling her onto her back, I lean over her and kiss her again. Her lips are intoxicating.

I trail kisses down her neck, my hands roaming underneath her shirt. Her breasts fit perfectly in my hands. This woman seems to have been made just for me. Everything I love about a woman has been tightly bundled in a Dani-sized package. She's perfect, and wanting her this badly, knowing everything about our history, makes me feel guilty for pushing her away. The sudden realization that I need Dani like I need oxygen in my lungs scares me. I'm not built to love, nor do I want to. My purpose in life is to kill when commanded, and fuck when I need release.

Pulling up her shirt, I place tender kisses along the contours of her exposed belly. She moans and watches me as I trail below her navel. My hands trace the path of my kisses, and my finger brushes against her apex. Slowly moving her shorts to the side, I lightly stroke against her pussy. My touch sends shivers up her body as I push my finger into her wetness. Her breath hitches as I stroke a circle around her clit, and soft moans fall from her lips as her eyes lock onto mine. She watches me intently as I circle her clit again. She moans louder with each rotation I make around her throbbing nub. Watching her enjoy my touch stiffens my cock even harder. I want to bury myself in this woman so badly, but I don't want to rush with her.

"Does your pussy like that, Dani?" I ask as I press harder. "Does she like the feel of my hands on her?"

"Yes," Dani breathes.

"Does my girl have a greedy pussy? Do you need a release so bad you'll beg me for it?"

"Yes," she cries, as I rub tight circles over her clit.

"Your wish is my command."

Lowering myself deeper onto the bed, I pull her soaked shorts away from her body and toss them on the floor. Jesus, her pussy is so wet, it's glistening. My dick throbs harder, knowing I've done this to her. I hover my face over her pussy, pressing my tongue against her, letting my hot breath fall against her folds. My hands grip her waist and pull her soaking wet pussy against my face. Dani quakes at the new sensation and moans with each lick as goosebumps race along her smooth skin.

"You taste like heaven, Dani."

My tongue continues to dance around her clit as she grinds herself into my face, pressing as hard as she can against me. She rubs herself against my tongue, increasing the friction as I roughly grip her gyrating hips, applying more pressure to lock her in place.

"Fuck!" she screams, as I nip her little bud with my teeth, pulling her legs over my shoulders.

"This pussy is mine, angel. Only mine. Do you understand me?" I circle once more. "The only man that will ever see this pussy is me."

"Yes, Hero. Only yours. Please, I'm so close," she pleads. "Fuck, right there! Just like that." She directs me, as if I've never gone down on a girl before.

Her pussy contracts in anticipation of the impending orgasm, just seconds before she screams out. She vibrates against my face as I tease her entrance, plunging just one finger inside, massaging her sweet spot as she rides out her orgasm. She gyrates against me, her moans like music to my ears.

"Jesus, Dani. I've never seen someone come that hard before. Did I hurt you?"

"Shut the fuck up, Hero," she giggles, an infectious smile on her face. "Just let me enjoy the afterglow before you say something fucking stupid."

Letting her rest for a few minutes, I trace the curves of her body. She's driving me insane with her satiated smile. I rocked her fucking world, and I've wasted enough time contemplating what her pussy feels like. I need to bury myself inside her before the darkness takes over again.

"I need you, Dani. I need you like I've never needed a woman before," I declare with longing. Admitting that out loud surprises both her and me. She is the only one who kept the ghosts at bay after what I saw today. Pleasing her had helped me chase them away, but even I know it's a temporary fix. I need to feel something other than pain and hatred. Dani is the only one who can save me from myself.

A flash of seriousness crosses her face, and she suddenly sits up and tries to scoot away from me.

"I can't do this, Hero. I can't be the woman you drown your sorrows in and forget about the next morning," she says, looking away. Shame on her face.

"That's not what this is."

I know she has every reason to question my actions, especially after everything she's witnessed here, but I'm still not thinking clearly. I pushed her too far. Too soon. I've fucking hurt her again, and she's shutting back down.

"What happens when I give it up to you? Will I go back to being nothing in the morning? I need to know I'm not just another notch on your bedpost."

"Is that what you think this is, Dani?"

"I have no idea what this is. One second, you hate me. The next, here I am. I'm getting whiplash from you and your personalities, Hero. I know that I didn't end up her under great circumstances, but I'm trying. I'm trying to fit in. I'm trying to find my place. I'm trying for *you*."

"If that's what I wanted, you wouldn't be in my room under my protection."

"That's another part of the problem. Why me? Why now? When there's all those girls out there waiting for you to come back to them." She gazes towards the door. Towards the noise of my brothers and the club girls celebrating our victory.

"Those girls mean nothing to me. If wanted them, all I would have to do is snap my fingers and they'd get on their knees." I try to move closer to her, but she stiffens, throwing up her walls again.

Dani's face falls. Sadness and anger clouding her beautiful eyes "Then maybe you should."

"Maybe I should what?"

"Snap your fingers. I can't do this, Hero. I can't be that girl."

"I'm not asking you to be like them, Dani. I just want you."

"You can't have me. Not really."

"The fuck does that mean?"

She slides from the bed and pulls her shorts back on. Walking to the door, she stops and stares at me.

"Dani," I growl, sliding from my bed. "Talk to me, angel. Don't leave like this." I reach down for my jeans, stumbling trying to stop her from leaving.

She says nothing else, but the sound of the slamming door as she leaves our room says enough for her silence.

Chapter 17

DANI

"ALL I HAVE to do is snap my fingers."

His stark reminder of just how many of the women living in this clubhouse have done just that for him. A reminder that I'm nothing special. Running away the safest option for us both. I was just about to surrender everything to him when my brain finally kicked back in after a mind-blowing orgasm. Jesus, I didn't know I could feel that way with anyone but my battery-operated boyfriend. Hero had officially skyrocketed to the best sexual experience of my life with just his tongue and a single finger. The thought of adding of his dick into the mix makes me quiver all over again. *Stop thinking about it, Dani. He's not ready for what you have to give yet.*

It isn't a matter of want in our situation. Want is already there. It's more about need, and his intentions for after we've fulfilled that need. Watching him break down in the shower must have affected my brain to give in as far as I did. I need space from him, and time to think. His one-eighty turn from I hate you to I need you, has put me into a tail-spin of confusion. If I had stayed, I would have slept with him and taken the risk of losing it all in one night of sexual conquest. The odds are against me, and until I know for sure this is what he wants, I can't put myself through that again.

Walking down the hall to my old room, I notice it remains unoccupied. The door still needs to be replaced, but I'm so damn tired I just don't care if anyone walks in on me. I step inside and fall onto my old bed, quickly falling asleep.

The feeling of I'm being watched awakens me several hours later. Seeing two bright blue eyes in the dark shadow of the room startles me, and I fall out of the bed.

"Shit, Bubbles. You scared the shit out of me," I gasp, panting with the adrenaline coursing through my veins. "What time is it?"

"Evening, why?"

"I slept longer than I thought."

Bubbles giggles uncontrollably as I try to pick myself up off the floor.

"Did you need something, or were you just in the vicinity and wanted to make me pee my pants?"

She continues to laugh until she's nearly in tears. "Sorry," she says between breaths. "I didn't expect you to react like that. I thought you were just pretending to be asleep. Why are you in your old room?"

Narrowing my eyes, I think about what happened earlier.

Knock that shit off, Dani. Do not think about Hero's face buried between your legs. That's a no-go. Yes, he knows how to use his tongue like the devil sweet talking a saint, but he's not the guy for you.

"I don't want to talk about it. I would like to know what warranted this odd wake-up call. Did you need help with something? Another bar fight you'd like me to start?"

Bubbles' smile fades at the mention of the bar fight with Trax. I still partially blame her for lying to me and getting me into that mess. She knew better than to bring a woman without a patch into a club party. Deep down, I think maybe she did it on purpose to win favor with Hero. Nothing screams 'pick me over her' than watching me heel stomp a man's balls. Just thinking about Trax screaming in pain brings a sick smile to my face.

Jesus, what has this club done to me? I used to be a good girl.

"I'm sorry about that, Dani. That was entirely my fault. Will you forgive me?"

"Yeah, it's water under the bridge. Hopefully, Trax's balls will heal okay. I'd hate to have left a lasting heel impression in his crown jewels."

Bubbles looks almost relieved, before she says, "I was wondering…"

"Out with it, Bubbles. I'd like to go back to sleep before dawn."

"I was wondering if you wanted to join the old ladies and us in a girls' night out party. We want to go out and celebrate."

She can't be serious. A night out at a bar? There's no way in hell that even remotely sounds like a good idea.

Knowing how they acted at Red's the night I met Hero, I can only imagine what they would do without male supervision.

"No thanks. I think I'm going to pass and catch up on my sleep. Thanks for the invite, though."

"If you stay here, you might want to know that Raze hired some strippers to entertain the guys while we are out. I'm sure you don't want to see that spectacle."

Shit, she had me at strippers. I don't need to see what those men would do with women that were paid to like them, after seeing how they acted with the regular girls. Why do I always get talked into this shit?

"Sure, I guess. How long do I have to get ready?"

"Oh, don't worry. I brought something with me in case you said yes. Come on. Let's get you dolled up and ready to party!" Bubbles squeals with joy and grabs my hand, nearly dragging me into the bathroom.

The room fills with a cloud of hairspray, and the

fumes nearly choke me. There's also a thick layer of stage make-up plastered on my face. Between her and Ruby, they paint my face, style my hair, and stuff me into a dress two sizes too small and about six inches too short. Add in the six-inch death traps strapped to my feet, and I'm modeling the look to interview for the newest club girl at Heaven's Rejects.

I practically sneak out of my room, tugging at the short hemline of the dress the entire time I walk to the main room. It's enough of a distraction that I don't even see Voodoo crossing into my path.

"Whoa there, Dani baby. Looking good, doll face. You sure you want to go out looking like that? You could always stay here with me and have a little fun," he cat-calls.

Hero walks into the room just as Voodoo finishes hitting on me.

I'm in trouble. I was hoping to avoid an awkward exchange with him tonight.

Anger fills his face as he stalks over to me and hauls my ass outside. Pressing me against the closed door, he stops me from escaping.

"Who dressed you like this?"

"Bubbles and Ruby," I admit. "Don't you like it?"

"No. I don't like you dressed up like one of the club whores. Can we talk?"

"No, sorry. I'm a little busy right now."

He pulls me back inside and down the hallway, away from the groups of people now intently watching us.

"I was trying to pour my heart out to you, and you fucking used me and left," he remarks.

Oh my, I pressed his buttons by leaving. There's a shocker.

"Pouring your heart out to me? You weren't even in your own head," I say. "I was saving myself from making the biggest mistake of my life."

"Last night wasn't a mistake."

"It was, and it will never happen again."

My fists ball at my sides as I fight the urge to throat punch him. He doesn't have the right to treat me like an unruly child after tasting my pussy.

He doesn't fucking own me.

"Jesus, Dani. What do you want me to say? I suck at apologies. The best I can say is go un-fuck yourself or whatever. What the hell can I do to make you believe me? I'm fucking sorry."

"Can I go now? I've had just about my fill of fun with you the last twenty-four hours."

Shoving him off of me, I stalk outside to the waiting car. The ladies cheer and clap as I slam the door. Hero follows me out, but doesn't protest my leaving. He just watches as we pull away. That fight went down far too easily. He's up to something.

Pulling up to the club, I realize how much of a monumentally bad idea this was. If it wasn't for the nearly naked women standing in line outside tipping me off, the thunder from down under poster certainly screams bad fucking idea. We file out of the car, and the bouncers wave us in without checking our IDs, which is a good thing because I don't have one. I really need to figure out a way to get a fake one before something like this happens again. I'm sure someone at the club could help me if I come up with a good enough lie to cover my ass. A hostess escorts us back to a private booth near the stage.

"Let's do shots!" Daisy screams. One round of shots turns into three, and before I know it, I'm walking the fine line of sobriety. My vision wavers with each shot I sling back. I need to drown Hero out tonight and let loose. Without him here, I don't have to be on guard. Thankfully, the male revue ended just before we arrived, so at least I won't be subjected to that. I don't know how I feel about being fake-fucked by a stranger in front of a crowd. Sure, they're nice to look at, but I doubt what they have downstairs is as big as they make it seem. They might as well have the stickers plastered all over them saying 'peckers may appear larger than they are'.

The next thing I know, the girls drag me out onto the dance floor. We shake our asses for hours as our drinks continue to be magically re-filled. A well-dressed man pulls me against him as we sway to the beat of the music. He grabs my hips and holds me tight. I can feel his erection growing against my ass as we move. His hands roam from my hips and cup my breasts, his face nuzzling into the side of my neck. He's not bad looking, but he's certainly not Hero.

Jesus, I can't even enjoy a night out without him penetrating my mind. What do I need to do to drown out his presence?

Chapter 18

HERO

WATCHING Dani leave with the girls nearly killed me. I wanted to go after her, but maybe she was right. I did come on a little too strong after treating her like shit. She is trying to teach me a lesson, and I will give it to her. For a little while, anyway.

I fall into the seat next to Raze. Just as the girls left, the two strippers had arrived. Their fake tits wave and bounce in my face, but I'm not interested. I have the real fucking deal, and she's the only thing that will do for me tonight.

Shoving one of the girls off my lap, I stalk away from the others. Raze is the only one that notices I've left since blondie-fake-tits moved onto someone more interested and willing to pay for her services. I have to admit, I had imagined Dani coming in here and going off on the stripper for touching me. Now, that would have been a show. The visual of it happening has my dick screaming to go find her and fix this shit between us.

When the evil little minion inside her takes over, she's hot as fuck with that smart mouth.

I don't exactly like my women submissive, but watching her verbally tear me limb from limb when she's angry is the hottest thing I've ever seen. My girl doesn't take shit off of anyone, even me. Tonight is proof of that.

Fuck, I keep calling Dani my girl.

She's far from that right now. Instead of staying here with me after I tried to fucking apologize to her, she ran off with the girls. That's a dangerous combination. The more I think about it, the more I hate that she's with them right now. Maybe I should go see what they're up to. Hell, maybe I'll get lucky, and drunk Dani will actually want to have a conversation with me, instead of trying to verbally hack off my balls.

I know she'll be mad either way. So what's stopping me from showing up?

Absolutely fucking nothing.

Raze must have the same idea, because as soon as I'm out of the door and starting my Harley, he's next to me on his.

"You thinking this girl's night out bullshit was a bad idea?" he asks.

"I know it was a bad idea. Maj and the girls at a club with no supervision. Of course, nothing could go wrong there," I say with more than a hint of sarcasm. "Do you know where they were headed?"

"Ruby said something about Tallywackers, or some shit like that. The only place I could think of was that new male strip club off of the ten."

A male strip club. They took Dani to a fucking strip club. Just what I fucking need. A bunch of overcompensating ripped fuckers trying to rub their shit all over her while she is drunk. No way in hell am I going to let that happen.

I haul ass out of the parking lot without even waiting for Raze. This shit ends now. Dani is coming home with me tonight or not at all. I can't stand having her within arm's reach and not being able to feel her body writhing and moaning beneath me. That little stunt she pulled last night with her 'thanks for the orgasm, but I'd rather not fuck you' bullshit has had my blood pumping all day. Who fucking does that? Well, me, I guess. I've done that before. But fucking hell, it feels completely different experiencing it from the other side. I'm trying so fucking hard to make her see that I can change for her.

Pulling up to the club, I know I'm about to walk into a shit storm. The line of ladies waiting to go in so close to closing time tells me that this was a bad fucking idea. No woman waits in line all night if the show is bad.

Holding back my control is one thing, but to not kill someone for touching what's mine will be fucking impossible. I'd likely kill him before even saying a word to the guy.

Luckily for us, a friend of the club is working the door.

"Evening, gentleman. You might find what you're looking for in the private booth on the left-hand side of the stage. Should I call the ambulance now, or after you leave?" He unhooks the red velvet rope and allows us inside.

"How bad is it, Bubba?" Raze asks.

"Bad enough that you might want to take those cuts off before I have to call the police. Maj disappeared into the back about an hour ago."

Raze stares at Bubba Ray for a solid thirty seconds before bolting into the club. If Maj is in the back room with a male stripper, Raze is going to lose his shit. I actually feel sorry for the guy if Raze finds him grinding on his wife. He'll be leaving this club on a fucking stretcher and singing soprano.

Would Maj even pull shit like that?

Maybe. It would make sense with the issues between them lately. Her string of rash decisions, and his outward frustration with her actions. Maybe they aren't living in marital bliss anymore.

The thought crosses my mind that maybe I should call a couple of the guys away from their entertainment. They may need to help me restrain him. He'll go full on beast mode, and I doubt I'll be able to hold his shit together on my own.

Thanking Bubba for the information, I step into the club. Thank fuck there are no dancers on the stage right now. I don't exactly want to see a male prima donna with a tube sock stuffed in his shorts, gyrating on the stage to some shitty pop song.

I scan the room and find my targets in the booth, just like Bubba said. Making my way over, I find it nearly empty. Only a couple of the old ladies are still sitting there, sipping glasses of wine and watching the crowd.

"I'm impressed, Hero. It only took you two hours to crash the party. That must be a new record," Dixie chirps. "If you're looking for Dani, you might want to check the dance floor."

Turning towards the floor, the crowd parts, and Dani comes into view. Her curves sway beautifully to the beat of the song, sending out its siren call to me. I start to walk out to her, deciding that pulling her against me and letting her grind out her frustration on me seems like the best-case scenario for both of us. I come within ten feet when a man grabs her and pulls her against him. Watching his hands roam over her body sends shock waves of anger through me.

This fucker is going to die if he doesn't move back.

His hands lock onto her tits, and he leans down into her neck.

Oh yeah. He's dead. If this motherfucker thinks for one second that she's about to warm his bed tonight, he's in for a rude awakening. The only thing he's going to have in his bed is an ice pack on his missing dick.

I charge forward, but pause when Dani pulls away from him and leaves the dance floor.

Good girl.

Now is my chance to corner her and get her to fucking talk to me like an adult. I just hope she's not too drunk to reason with. We need to talk, and it's going to happen tonight.

Shoving my way into the crowd, I stand right in her exit path.

Come on, angel face. Walk right into my trap.

Her body slams into mine, and apologies fly from her lips. She hasn't figured out that it's me she's plowed into. Maybe she is too drunk to function. Shit, this isn't going to work if she's going to pass out as soon as I get her out of here. Moving to block her exit, my little spitfire comes to life.

"Seriously, dude. Just let me pass. I want to go back to my table."

"Enjoying yourself, angel? You and I need to talk," I say, motioning between us with a finger. Shock registers in her eyes, and she knows she's been caught like a little kid with their hand in a cookie jar.

The big bad wolf has come to get you.

"I have nothing to say to you, asshole," she says, trying to push past me.

"You're not getting away from me that easy, angel. Not until we have that little talk."

Her anger intensifies, knowing the consequences of blowing me off. Maybe I shouldn't have pushed her too far, but she needs to know how fucking serious I am about this.

"What the fuck do you want to know? Or is this your sick and twisted way of wanting feedback about your oral skills? I can answer that right here. Solid C plus. Can I go now?"

"Oh, angel face," I say with a chuckle. "A C-plus? Now who's lying their ass off? Your body came so hard, you nearly snapped my tongue off when you wrapped those pretty little legs around my head and rode my face."

"Oh, go fuck yourself, Hero. I may have had a few drinks, but I'm nowhere near drunk enough to want anything to do with you."

Before I can respond, Ruby and the girls exit the dance floor and drag her away from me. They throw themselves back into the booth and order another round. *Will nothing tonight go my way?*

I trudge back to the booth. This ends now, whether she leaves with me, or I carry her out over my shoulder. The games are over.

"You're going home with me, Dani. Get your ass out of the booth," I order.

"I'd rather go home with the guy on the dance floor than you, Hero. At least he had the decency to ask me to fuck him instead of just telling me."

That's fucking it.

Ripping her out of the booth, I throw her over my shoulder and haul ass outside. I'm done being the fucking nice guy. She is going to sit and listen to what I have to fucking say, whether she likes it or not. I toss her on the back of my bike and retrieve a helmet from the saddlebags.

"Put this on," I order, as I slide over the seat of my Harley and turn the key. Revving the engine up, I check to make sure Raze's bike is still here, but I find it absent. It's not like him to leave without telling me, but I'd have known if he were being arrested for killing a mother-fucker by now. I make a mental note to call him in the morning to check how things went down.

"Put your arms around my waist, Dani. Try not to fall off."

"I'm only on this fucking thing because I'm ready to go home," she yells over the rumble of the engine.

Popping the kickstand, I ride from the club and head straight for my house. She'll try to run if I take her back to the clubhouse, so my civilian home is the best bet I have for actually getting her to talk to me. Her tits press against my back as we ride into town. Feeling them makes me shiver in anticipation. What I could do with those perfect tits.

Visualizing my dick rubbing between them, and my cum coating her chest, sends heat straight to my cock. The forward lurch of the bike at a stop light makes her pussy rub against the seat and me. If she and I can have an actual adult conversation for once, I'm hoping the night ends with that tiny dress wadded up on my floor, and her mouth wrapped around my aching cock. If I don't get off soon, my balls will likely shrivel up and die of misuse.

Pulling into the cement drive of my house, I kill the engine, pop the kickstand, and lean the bike against it. She slides from the seat before I swing my legs over and hop off. I help her take off her helmet and scoop her into my arms.

Carrying her over my shoulder, I can feel her head move as she takes in the house. I know she's confused, but even bikers have a real house. We all need our own space to think and figure shit out from time to time. I may prefer my room at the clubhouse now that she occupies it with me, but I like my solitude at times. Punching in the security code with my free hand, I open the door and walk her straight to the couch, depositing her there roughly.

"Take me back to the clubhouse," she demands.

"That's not how this is going to work, Dani. You and I need to clear the air about a few things. Afterwards, I'll take you back there if you still want to go."

"What exactly do we need to talk about? I assumed I was crystal clear that I don't want anything to do with you. Thanks for saving me and all, but I'd like to pass on whatever else you have planned for tonight."

I walk into the kitchen without answering, and return with a glass of ice water and two aspirin. Handing her the glass and the tablets, I walk back to the front door to secure it. When I return to the living room, she's stretched out on the couch with wide eyes.

Play time can start later. Focus. Stay on task.

Sitting on the unoccupied end of the couch, I pull her up in a sitting position. I can't fucking talk to her if she's presenting herself like a prized Thanksgiving turkey on a platter. My brain won't function long enough to accomplish what I need done. *Oh no, angel. You aren't going to brush me off that easily. I know your tricks all too well now. Deflection and distraction won't work in your favor tonight.*

"Before you ask, it's mine," I say, waiting for her smart mouth to strike again.

"I see. What does Raze have? A Mansion?" Sarcasm drips from every word.

"No, he doesn't," I answer. "I had this house long before I ever prospected for Heaven's Rejects."

"Oh," she mutters. "I didn't realize bikers could afford such big places."

"Just because I'm a biker doesn't mean I didn't work my ass off for this house."

"I just…" She pauses for a minute before trying again. "I didn't mean to sound like a bitch. I just assumed you all lived together at the clubhouse."

"Had you asked and not just fucking assumed, I would have told you I receive retirement pay from the Army."

"I'm sorry, okay?" she mutters. "I've only ever seen you at the club, and you haven't really been all that forthcoming with information. This is really the first conversation we've had where you aren't accusing me of being a traitor, tried getting in my pants, or just being a complete asshole to me."

"And I'm sorry for that, Dani. I am. The club had to come first. Why don't we start over? I'm Hero. Occasional asshole extraordinaire."

I outstretch my hand, and she lightly grasps it with a smile lifting up the corners of that sweet mouth.

"So, Army?"

"Yeah," I say. "Served in Iraq, but was medically discharged."

She takes a sip of her water, keeping her eyes on me at all times, like I'm a dangerous predator about to pounce on my prey. And she's not wrong.

"Tell me more about yourself," I say, focusing the topic back on her. "I'm Dani. Former traitor, current prisoner, and slightly confused," she says, playing along with the charade. "That's about it."

"Nice try, but there's more to your story."

"Like what?"

"Like, for instance, what the hell is your last name? I want to get to know you better, Dani. What's your story?"

As soon as I lay down what I want to know, she freezes in place. What the fuck is in her past that has her panicking at the slightest question about it? Does she have an abusive ex back home, or hell, is she still married and on the run? Nothing about her clouded past has been easy to decipher. She's hiding something from the club, and from me. I just hope the skeletons in her closet aren't bigger than what we can deal with.

"You want to know my last name? What for? Need to know what you should write down in your little black book of conquests?"

"Jesus, Dani. I just want to get to know you. Is that so bad? You've spent weeks in my club, and I want to figure out what's going on in that head of yours."

She quietly stares at me for several minutes, sending me into panic that I might have lost her again, but then she finally speaks. "Espinoza."

Dani Espinoza. God, her name is beautiful, just like she is.

"Espinoza, huh? That makes you…"

"My dad was Latino, but my mom was Greek. I know. It's a weird combination." She sighs.

"No, that's not weird. It explains your beautiful olive skin and dark features. I know you said you were from the Midwest, but what part?"

Panic flashes in her eyes again.

Why is it every time I mention her family, or where she's from, she panics or goes silent? The only reason someone would have that reaction to such normal questions is if they are hiding something about their past. It makes me wonder what the fuck happened there, and why does it make her nervous? I can't shake the feeling that there's something she isn't telling me.

"I'm from Ohio."

"What about your family? Are they still back there, or are they here?"

"I don't have any family. They're all dead," she replies, her voice cold.

"Dead?"

"My dad died when I was fourteen. He was a cop, and was killed in the line of duty, during a routine domestic violence call." She closes her eyes for a few silent moments.

"Jesus, Dani. I'm sorry. What about your mom?"

"My mom died a few months ago."

"Shit, angel. You haven't exactly had it easy, have you?"

She stays silent. I consider reaching out to touch her, but she's vulnerable. More vulnerable and open than she has been since I met her. Doing anything to make her panic will set this back. Whatever this is.

"Do you miss them?"

"Every single day," she whispers. "It's not fair that they're gone."

"It never is, angel. Life is funny like that. You can do all the right things and still come up short. Did you have a happy childhood, at least?"

"It was happy until Dad died. He and I were two peas in a pod. My first childhood memory was my dad taking me to the station and the shooting range with his partner, Bob. Ironically enough, Mom married Bob when I turned sixteen. It never felt right that she had forsaken my dad's memory with someone he trusted with his life. Don't get me wrong. My step-dad was nice and all, but my life from that day forward went to hell in a hand basket, until I bolted from Ohio. I ended up here, and well, you know the rest. Bat shit crazy roommate goes missing, I end up homeless, and now I'm living in a club-house with bikers. Sounds like the basis for a reality TV show, or a horrible made for TV movie." She tries to laugh off her situation, but even I can see the pain in her eyes. It's the same pain I have seen staring back from my own reflection every single day. The kind of pain that never goes away.

"My turn," she says, changing it back to me. "What's your real name?"

"Tyler Tobias."

"You don't look like a Tyler," she says, her brows furrowing just a little. "Maybe a Brad, or something more manly like Robert, but definitely not a Tyler."

I chuckle. "Not sure how I should take that. But remember, that information stays between you and me. I prefer my road name."

"Yes, sir," she says with a salute. "Family?"

"Dead. My parents were both killed during an armed bank robbery, just after I turned eighteen. My dad had gone in to cash out their savings account, so they could put me through college. Two guys came in and put a bullet between both of my parents' eyes."

I know she thinks talking about this shit will break me down like it does her, but I've told this story so many times, it's like reciting the *Pledge of Allegiance*.

"Is that why you joined the Army?" The sadness in her eyes is clear as day.

"Yeah. Joined a month after it happened and landed my ass in Iraq, just after 9/11. I did my duty there until a roadside bomb killed my entire unit and left me fucked up." I pull up the leg of my jeans to show her my scars. I'm sure she's seen them before, but was too afraid to ask. It's easier just to get this part out of the way.

"I took shrapnel to my knee, and was sent home with a medical discharge and a shiny Medal of Honor. It took six surgeries to repair the damage before I could finally walk again."

Dani crawls over to me and wraps her arms around me. I know she thinks this is comforting to me, but it only feels like pity. No one knows how to respond to the wounded soldier part of my story.

"How many did you lose in your unit?"

"Twenty-one." Pulling my shirt over my head, I turn to expose the tattoo on my back. A pair of metal dog tags lies on my left shoulder. Below it is a list of each of their names.

"I may never get to see my men again, but they'll always be with me," I say, as her fingers trace the tattoo. Her touch stills me.

"What about your other tattoos? Do they mean anything?" Her fingertips don't leave my back.

"Most are just pieces of my past. I needed a way of remembering all the fucked-up memories in my head. The cross on my sternum is the cross I bear for my brotherhood, and for the things I've seen and done in my past. Of course, you know the one on my stomach is for the club. It was supposed to be on my back, but I refused to let Raze cover up my brothers' names. Took me two years to convince them to ink me somewhere else."

"Why did you join the club?"

"I joined because I needed an outlet. I was a fucking train wreck when I got home, and then I met Jagger in a bar one night. Bars were the only place I felt normal. I'd drink myself fucking stupid, and start a fight just so I could feel something. I was hollow, and pain was the only thing that filled the void. He made me realize I needed some sort of order in my life. I joined at twenty-three and never looked back. It was the best decision of my life until I decided I wanted to dance with you at Red's that night."

She doesn't make a sound as I pull her back into my lap.

"There's something about you, Dani. I think it's taken me until today to realize what that is. I never wanted the bullshit of being with just one person until you."

"The pull I feel between us scares me."

Her admission sends my heart racing, and my blood ferociously pumping through my veins. She feels the attraction, or whatever the hell you could call this pull between us, just as much as I do. She needs to know I want her to the point I'd kill for her. I can't keep dancing around the idea that she'll just fuck me and be gone the next morning. I need her with me, or just fucking gone.

"It scares me too, angel. When you left last night, I

realized how much of an ass I'd been. You didn't deserve my anger being redirected at you from Jagger's death. You didn't put the knife in him."

"I shouldn't have pushed your buttons. I wanted you to hurt, because I was dying inside, not being able to have what I desperately wanted."

Her words seize my chest. I've wasted so much goddamn time trying to figure out club shit, and where she fell into this life, I ignored the signs. I'm the biggest fucking idiot on the entire planet.

"You want me?" I ask.

"It was torture to push you away last night, but you weren't in the right frame of mind. I didn't want to sleep with you and live to regret it when you shoved me away the next morning. I could see the nothingness in your eyes."

"Shit, angel. I was hurting last night, but it wasn't just from the past creeping back over me. I was in agony. The way you were looking at me—like I was about to shatter apart—broke something inside me." He pauses, rubbing his hand over his chest. "I've done a lot of bad shit in my life. Things I'm not proud to admit. But with you? It's different. I've never needed someone as much as I fucking need you in my life."

Her eyes fill with shock and lust as she realizes I've just opened myself up for her disposal.

"Take me to bed, Hero." I never thought this day

would come. She stands up abruptly, pulling me by the hand. Without hesitation, I scoop her into my arms and carry her up the stairs to my bedroom. Clicking on the light as we pass, I lay her on the bed. She moves to sit on the edge of the bed and stares at me, waiting for me to make my move.

"Are you sure about this, Dani? This is your last chance to leave, because as soon as I sink my dick into you, you're mine. No more running. No more hiding. You're mine, or you're gone. There's no middle ground."

"Please, Hero. I need you. Make me feel happy again," she pleads.

Chapter 19

"ONCE WE CROSS THIS LINE, there's no going back to the way things were. I won't give you a bunch of bullshit forever promises. It's just you and me, as long as this ride lasts."

"I want you for as long as we have together."

The truth behind those words is meaningless to him, but I know that at any moment, this life could be ripped away from me. I'm tired of denying what I want. I want Hero, and all the fucked-up baggage he brings with him. He'll break my heart in the end, but I don't care right now. Life is short, and I want to take it for what it's worth, until the end comes.

"One more time. You sure?" he asks.

"Make me yours."

Hero cocks an eyebrow and just observes me. Maybe he's waiting for me to bolt and run, or hell, maybe he's calculating his next move, but I can't wait anymore.

I fly off the bed and collide with his body, crashing my lips to his. His hands grasp my ass, hoisting me into the air. We stumble backwards, landing hard against the wall. I wrap my legs around his waist, my dress riding up past my hips in the process. Hero's tongue slips between my parted lips.

"Jesus, Dani. You go from zero to sixty in less than a second."

"Just shut up and fuck me, Hero."

"My girl wants to be bad? Well now, if you get on your knees like a good girl, I'll fuck you like a bad one. I need to see those luscious, swollen lips of yours wrapped around my cock," he rumbles, running his thumb across them.

Unwrapping my legs, I slide down his body and kneel before him. I run my hands down his tight abs, tracing his club tattoo as I hook a finger inside the waist of his jeans. I lick a trail down from his navel to the button of his jeans. I pull the button free, unzipping his jeans with my teeth. His breath hitches, and he laces his fingers in my hair. Pulling his jeans free from his waist, I find his cock hard and straining against the thin fabric of his boxers.

"Dani," he moans. I tease him, dragging his boxers down inch by painstaking inch over his hips. His cock springs out in front of me. He's longer, thicker, and wider than I could have ever imagined. A drop of pre-cum glistens on the tip of his dick. Rubbing my finger across it, I stick my finger in my mouth, savoring his salty taste.

"You taste so good, Hero," I moan, removing my finger from my mouth. He watches me through hooded eyes as I lick his dick, flicking my tongue against the tip. I graze my mouth against his throbbing cock while rubbing my hand up and down his shaft, lubricating it with his pre-come and my saliva. Wrapping my hand around his base, I stroke him upward and pull his engorged cock into my mouth.

"Fuck, Dani. I've never seen anything more fucking amazing than your mouth around me. Suck me, baby."

He grips my hair and uses it to pull me closer to him as my mouth bobs over his dick. With each thrust he delivers into my mouth, I circle his shaft with my tongue. Opening wider, I fit his entire length into my mouth, letting my tongue lick up to the tiny place at the tip that I know will drive him wild. Switching up the rhythm, I lick a circle around the head before putting it completely back in my mouth again, adding my teeth just a little, lightly grazing his sensitive skin.

"Angel, if you keep this up, I'll be blowing my load in your mouth. As much as I would love to see my cum staining your lips, I need to taste you."

Pulling away, I grin and rise from the ground. I kiss him then, mingling the taste of him in my mouth with his. His hands trail down to the hem of my dress, and he pulls the fabric over my head. He cocks an eyebrow when he discovers I wore nothing underneath.

"The only time you walk out in public with an exposed pussy will be with me, Dani. You've been a very bad girl, flaunting what's mine to other men."

"Hero, I didn't—"

He presses his fingers to my lips, shushing me. "Get on the bed on all fours, Dani, and part your legs."

Happy to do what I'm told, I crawl onto the bed with my ass in the air. He moves behind me, rubbing his hands over my skin. I feel his tongue licking up my inner thigh and down to the other, completely skipping my soaking wet pussy. My fingers trail down my stomach to touch myself, when Hero slaps my hand away.

"This pussy is mine. You are not to touch yourself unless I order you to touch it. Your orgasms belong to me now," he says. And then his mouth is on me.

His tongue teases my clit, his hands pulling my ass against his face. His hot breath fans against my sensitive flesh. Shock waves of pleasure rip through me as his nose brushes against my entrance.

"I could spend hours between your legs. Just teasing, sucking, biting, and tasting you on my tongue."

"More," I demand with a lusty tone. "I need more."

"Do you know what really pissed me off after eating your pussy last night, Dani? It wasn't that you left me high and dry. It was the fact that I could still taste you on my lips hours later, and I couldn't get another taste."

"If I say I'm sorry, will you lick me again?" I ask, my voice barely a whisper.

And then he licks me. Spreading my lips with his fingers, he licks the hood surrounding my clit, teasing it. He flicks the tip of his tongue against my sensitive nub, sending shooting waves of intense pleasure radiating throughout my body. His tongue circles my clit in a slow and steady rhythm. And then he presses a finger inside me.

"Just like that. Fuck! Just like that. I'm close," I scream. I'm so fucking close that, if he ran his finger down my pussy, I'd light up like a firework on the Fourth of July.

"Do you want to come, Dani?"

"Mmhmm," I whimper.

He sucks roughly on my clit, as his finger slides into me, slowly thrusting inside my slick entrance. My core is throbbing now, but Hero isn't about to let me cum. No, he wants me to break apart.

"Please," I beg him, my whole body trembling now. "Please, I need to cum."

Breaking contact with my core, Hero rises from his knees and pulls my ass against his dick.

"The only way you're coming tonight is around my cock. Are you ready for me, baby? Do you want to feel my cock stretching that pretty pussy?"

I can hardly breathe he has me so worked up. "Please, Hero. I need it so fucking bad."

Flipping me over on my back, he positions himself at my entrance and thrusts into me in one quick motion. His girth pushes the limits of pleasure and pain. It hurts, but fuck does it feel amazing.

"Fuck, Dani. You feel so fucking good," he says. "Your pussy is clamped around me like a fucking vice."

"Move, Hero. Please move," I cry out. "I'm so close it fucking hurts."

He thrusts harder and harder into my pussy, each thrust stretching me farther. He pulls my legs over his shoulders, making his cock drive deeper into me. His hands move to cup my breasts, playfully rolling my nipples between two fingers. His steady rhythm increases again, and I can feel my orgasm building.

"I can feel you pulsating, Dani. Let go, angel."

Circling his hips as his cock plows into me, he brushes against my G-spot. The sensation pushes me over the edge. Bucking wildly against him, my vision goes blurry and my body quivers with a thousand tingling sensations like me entire body is on fire. Delicious, pleasurable fire. I moan and writhe with uncontrollable pulsations as Hero watches me come apart around him.

"Eyes on me, Dani. I need to see your fucking eyes," he orders, his pace increasing.

Forcing my eyes open, I watch him thrust into me again and again, and then finally, he finds his own release. He trembles on top of me, his cock spasming inside me. Our chests heave in unison as we enjoy the aftershocks of release, our hearts rapidly beating in satiated synchronization. Smiles beam from both of our faces as Hero rolls off of my body and onto his side. He pulls me against him, molding my body to his, his face nuzzling into my neck.

"You have exactly ten minutes to rest. I want round two, Dani. The next time, there will be no breaks. I want to see how many times I can make you cum tonight. We've got lost time to make up for." I can already feel his dick hardening against my ass.

Two rounds later, we fall into an exhausted heap without a word. I've never felt this blissfully happy before, but with Hero, I want this feeling every fucking day.

Chapter 20

HERO

AS I WATCH DANI SLEEP, I realize I want to make her this happy for as long as we have each other. Even as she skimmed the surface of her family life in our tense, yet eye-opening conversation earlier, I saw the pain in her eyes. She may not have come right out and said it, but she was robbed of a real childhood, and denied everything a beautiful girl should have been given by her family.

Do I want to be the person to give her that happiness? Am I ready to make that kind of commitment after just one night? The answer is leaning towards yes, but the lingering suspicion that there are still skeletons in her closet weighs heavily on me. What if there is someone back home she's running from? Is that something I'm willing to deal with if it comes crashing down around us? I need more time with her to decide whether this is what I want. Time away from the hustle of the clubhouse, and just us, like we are now, laying in my bed. She and I here, together. It's fucking perfect. No one beating down the door, waiting to shoot the shit. No club girls. Just Dani and Hero.

My mind races with ideas I could easily put into motion to make this olive-skinned beauty next to me smile today. Shifting her arms and body off mine, I gingerly crawl out of bed and make my way to the living room. Grabbing my phone, I dial Slider's number. The phone rings three times before he picks up.

"Slider," he says on a ragged breath.

"Hey, man. Can you bring over the truck I store at the clubhouse? I need it in an hour."

"Sure, Hero. Let me finish up here, and I'll be right over."

I can hear a woman's muffled moan and creaks of a bed as he speaks.

"You sure about that? Sounds like you're a little busy," I say with a chuckle.

I know damn well he has to do whatever I tell him to do. He's a prospect. He has very limited reasons to say no, and when it comes from Raze or me, it must be an instant yes, but I like to make him feel as if he has an option to say no.

"Nah, it's fine. Let me blow my load, and I'll be there."

The moans get louder, and the sound of flesh slapping together grows more obvious. Suddenly, the background noise goes silent.

"You done?"

"Yup. Anything else, VP?"

"I want you to take my bike back to the clubhouse. It needs a nice wash and polish. Ratchet should have that new chrome I ordered in the shop. Ask him if he has time to shine her up for me while I'm off today."

"Yes, sir. Anything for you, sir. Would you like me to spit polish the chrome, sir?"

The boy's got a good sense of humor, but until his cut has a real patch, he needs to learn to keep it to a minimum.

"Just do what you're told. Oh, and grab some of Dani's clothes from my room."

"Oh, man. Permission to rummage through her underwear drawer. Nice!"

"Don't you even fucking think about it, prospect. You lay one hand on any of her underwear, and you can kiss your chance at a patch goodbye," I growl.

Slider laughs into the phone.

"Laugh it up, prospect."

"You got it, VP," he says, still laughing as he hangs up. *He does listen to orders from time to time. Shocking.*

I grab my laptop and plop into my black leather recliner, pulling up my secret plan for the day. It's not exactly my idea of fun, but I know Dani will love it. After gathering the intel, I close my laptop and head back into the bedroom.

I check to make sure Dani is okay, only to find her patting her hands on the exact spot where I was lying in the bed. Even in her sleep, she searches for me. That thought alone puts a smile on my face and a zap of arousal to my already throbbing dick. That woman gave me everything last night. Today, I will give her something in return. Needing to get a start on today's events, I plant a kiss on her tousled black hair and walk into the bathroom.

The shower is hot and steamy by the time I finish shaving. Shedding my blue jersey pajama pants, I step into the hot spray. I lather soap in my hands and begin to rub it down my stomach and onto my legs. My dick is rock hard as my mind plays over the night before. I had no idea that making love to a woman would be so different from just normal fucking. She had been bare before me, and damn, did I take the chance.

After I came, I felt like Dani took possession of a piece of my soul. I hope to fuck she doesn't try to give it back. I want more nights with her beautiful curves and filthy mouth in my bed. My dick throbs at the memory of her spread legs and perfect fucking tits. My hand moves back down my stomach, grasping my dick in my hand. I know

I could walk back into my room and solve this growing problem with Dani, but I want her to rest. Pumping my hand up and down, I work my dick like a madman, squeezing tighter and tighter, the warm water lubricating the motions. The door to the shower opens then, and in walks Dani, just as I'm about to blow my load in my hand.

Without saying a word, she pulls my hand away from my dick and replaces it with her own. She uses her other hand to pull my face closer to hers, bringing me to her lips. Her tongue parts my lips and forces its way into my mouth. I back us into the wet tile wall of my shower. She continues to squeeze and pump until she pulls herself away from my mouth and falls to her knees. She takes my pulsating dick into her mouth, and I nearly lose the paper-thin grip I have on my control.

"Fuck, Dani," I hiss.

A laugh escapes her lips as they close around my dick. That laugh rumbles against the sensitive skin, making my dick even harder. Her tongue rolls around my head as she slides her lips farther down my length.

I grasp her soaking wet head and pull her closer to me. Sensing I'm close by some sheer magic skill, she moves her hands from my thighs and grabs my balls. She rolls them between her fingers, causing me to moan in painful pleasure. The intensity of her mouth and hands overloads my system. My balls clench, and I know I'm about ready to cum like a sixteen-year-old getting his first blowjob.

What the fuck is this woman doing to me? I don't blow my load like a sixty-second assassin, but she unhinges me.

Her mouth is a damn godsend, but I don't want to cum in her mouth. Not yet anyway. I want my cock balls deep in her sweet little pussy.

Pulling her and that magnificent mouth away, I bring her back to her feet, hoisting her up the wall against me. My mouth goes to her neck, planting kisses and licks along it. With her in my arms, I bend down and take her dark nipple into my mouth. She moans as I bite down on it, massaging the dark bud with my tongue. I watch her as I lightly bite again, and her head falls back in ecstasy. Her eyes lock on to me, and she watches me tease her nipple.

"I need to feel you inside me," she moans.

Releasing her nipple, I pull her against me and slide my aching dick between her wet folds. Stilling to allow her to adjust to my size, I kiss her deeply with a few choice words escaping my lips, my tongue dancing with hers.

"Please fucking move. I need you," she pants, pulling away from my mouth.

"I'm not going to last long, so just fucking let go when you feel it," I say, and then I thrust into her.

Her hands move to my neck, and I move faster,

pounding into her pussy like my life depends on it. The water streaming down on us heightens the sensation. I continue my movements, reveling in the way her body fits around me like a glove, and then I feel her body tense. She's close.

"Fuck. Fuck. Fuck!" she cries with each thrust, her sweet pussy gripping me harder. Her pussy clenches and releases in a mind-blowing rhythm as each wave of her release carries her away. Unable to last another second, I pound into her three more times, and then I cum. I feel my release pouring into her as she shudders against me. Taking her mouth with mine, I kiss her deeply as the high begins to slowly fall.

Finally, after our trembles slow, I pull her closer and ease her off my cock, placing her back onto her own two feet. She opens her eyes, the water from the shower now growing cold, and she smiles at me. That fucking smile will be my undoing.

She giggles. "Good morning."

"That's one hell of a good morning, angel," I say with a laugh. "I didn't even hear you get up."

She just grins and turns to face the water. It glistens down her body, caressing her every curve. She returns to face me, reaching behind me to grab the soap. While she lathers her body, my dick rebounds for round two, but we have shit to do today, so he's going to have to wait.

"I heard you turn on the shower, and I wanted to join

you. I didn't expect to find you jacking off, though. Not when I'm perfectly willing to help you out with that."

She stuns me. "I know, baby, but I wanted you to get some sleep. You were tossing and turning all night long."

Moving back into the chilled spray of water, she rinses off the soap. *Shit. Even my dick likes that she's going to spend the day smelling like me.*

"I'm never too tired for you, Hero. I may not be as experienced as those club girls, but I don't want to leave you unsatisfied."

Her words instantly piss me off. I push into her and pin her against the wall.

"Don't you ever fucking compare yourself to those women. If I wanted a woman like that, I would have any one of those club sluts in my bed. I fucking want you, and only you. Do you understand me, Dani?"

Her eyes grow large in what I can only assume is a combination of fear and lust.

"Yes, Hero. I understand," she says meekly.

I know I've scared her, and that's the last fucking thing I want to do today. I need her smiling and not crying, because I don't know how to handle my feelings for her.

"I don't mean to be such a dick. They meant nothing to me then, and they mean nothing to me now."

That goddamn smile blossoms on her face again, and I can only hope I've made her see how I feel. I'm not ready to tell her that I love her yet, but I care about this woman far greater than I have cared about anything in my life.

"Now, you finish up and get ready. I have a big day planned for you. Wear something comfortable and meet me out in the garage when you're ready."

I slap her ass on the way out of the shower, and then she pokes her head out the door.

"Where are you taking me?"

I'm not exactly ready to show her my hand yet, so instead, I tease her. She needs to be surprised, because I'm fucking sure if she protested, we'd spend the entire fucking day in bed, and that would defeat the damn purpose of giving her a happy memory. My cock driving into her for hours would sure as fuck be burned into my head as a goddamn happy memory, but that's not the point of today. It's about her. I just have to convince my dick that he needs to take a vacation day until later. As she waits for my answer, I can see her frustration plainly across her face.

"I'm taking you to a place where all your dreams will come true, Dani."

Confusion fills her eyes, but I just walk out of the room. She needs to get ready, and so do I. I just hope deep down she likes what I have planned, because her pussy is mine, as soon as we get back to my house.

Chapter 21

DANI

EVERYTHING ABOUT HERO makes me feel as if he can see into my soul. I'm honestly glad he can't, because I never want him to know about my past, and the details I've deliberately hidden from him. I've given him all he needs to know about my family and my past. The rest needs to stay buried back in Cleveland, not only for my sake and his, but for the club's as well. They wouldn't want a woman hiding from the police in their midst. I know they aren't angels themselves, but this could be one step too far over the bad shit meter for them to want to deal with. Especially now that Twisted Tribe is no longer an issue for them. I just need to keep my guard up around him until I know it's safe to reveal my secrets, if that day ever comes.

I hurry, trying to get ready to meet Hero in the garage, but it doesn't take me long to realize that the only clothes I have here is the dress from last night. Opening the bedroom door to yell down to him about my lack of decent apparel, I find a bag of clothes hanging on the doorknob. I unzip it to find some of my clothes from the clubhouse. *How in the hell did he manage to get clothes here for me that quickly?* Rummaging through the bag, I find a pair of jean shorts, a simple pink and black tank top, a pair of my flip-flops, and a bra.

He didn't get me underwear.

Walking out into the garage, I see that Hero's black Harley is gone, and in its place is a black Ford F150 pickup truck. He's out in the driveway talking to Slider when he sees me. Hero and Slider both flash me mischievous smiles.

What the hell are they up to?

Slider then revs the engine of Hero's Harley and pulls away, leaving a cloud of dust with his departure.

Hero doesn't have his cut on. He never takes it off. He's so attached to that thing, I bet he'd rather die than have an emergency room cut it off. I mean, come on, he didn't even take it off the first time we had sex. Not that I was complaining, but it's like another appendage to him. His cut, bike, and dick are all his favorite toys. What the hell is going on?

"Where's your cut?" I ask, giving him a suspicious look.

He simply shrugs at my question and opens up the truck door.

"Your chariot awaits," he says with a sweeping bow.

Crossing my arms, I look at his grand gesture with skepticism.

"You're acting weird. What is going on? You're not wearing your cut, and we both know you'd rather die than take it off. Plus, not only did you let Slider ride off into the sunset with your gas-powered second favorite appendage, but now we're riding in a four-wheeled vehicle. So, I'm going to ask again, where the fuck are we going?"

My irritation and suspicions about his secretive plan must amuse him, because he's nearly doubled over laughing at me.

"Dani, just get in the damn truck. You need to wipe that frown off your face, princess, because I'm taking you out today, and you will enjoy it."

"I'm not a fucking princess, Hero. Never fucking call me a princess ever again. I hate that word."

"Princess is off the nickname roster. That came out of nowhere," he says, hands raised in surrender. Pulling me with him, he ushers me into the truck and shuts the passenger door. He deposits himself into the driver's seat and starts it up before pulling out of the driveway, heading south on CA 57.

An intense silence falls over the car. I hate that things

from my past keep creeping into the present. He used to call me his princess, and I loathe the word. That name needs to stay buried in the past and far away from being associated with Hero. He isn't him, and I can't let something like that fucking nickname brand him an enemy in my mind. Settling into staring out of the window, I watch as the buildings and cars zoom past us.

"You can keep watching the road signs to figure out where we're going, or you can scoot your sexy ass over here and snuggle up with me. Hell, I wouldn't mind some road head at this point. Can't do that on the bike, so I guess driving a cage does have its perks."

"Maybe I like it over here. No one keeps secrets on this side of the truck."

As soon as the lies spill from my mouth, I instantly regret it. I have more secrets than I care to admit, and continually lying to him hurts more and more each day. He must sense a change in the mood, because he reaches over and pulls me closer. Smashed up against him in the driver's seat, I start to feel a little better about my lies. It's for his own good. He won't want me once he finds out.

"Not sure what just crossed your mind, Dani, but that shit needs to stop now. Smiles only today. No tears, sadness, or shitty moods. You got it?"

"Yes, Hero. I'll be a good little girl," I say, teasing him.

He smiles and reaches over to the stereo, cranking up

Theory of Deadman. As the driving rock beat pounds from the speakers, I drift in and out of consciousness. The swaying of the drive soon rocks me to sleep against Hero's shoulder. Why is it that I can't seem to relax unless I'm with Hero? It's like my body senses him nearby and flips the relaxation switch. No one has ever done this to me before, and I'm not sure I like it.

I don't wake up again until the truck comes to a stop.

"Time to wake up, Dani."

Hero grins and scoots himself out of the truck, pulling me along with him. Once my eyes focus on my surroundings, I realize we are in a parking garage. He laces his fingers with mine, and it seems so normal that it's almost weird. I'm not used to normal relationships, or hell, a real relationship where I wasn't being used. We continue to walk to an escalator that ferries use to the ground floor of the parking structure. As soon as my feet hit the ground, I realize where I am. My face is frozen in shock. Hero brought me to Disneyland.

"Is this…" I stutter.

"Surprise, angel."

My eyes grow wide. The sights and sounds of my childhood dream are literally in front of me for the first time. "You did this for me?" I ask, not knowing what else to say.

"It's just you and me today. No fucking rules or regulations. No club brothers watching us. Just you and me.

Dani and Tyler. I might lose my man card for doing this, but fuck it. I want my girl to be happy."

I'm still too shocked to speak. This badass biker brought me to Disneyland. He's willingly given me a slice of normal happiness, even if he's not exactly the hearts and flowers kind of guy. I guess this explains why his cut remained at home. It might have had security on our ass the entire day.

"Hero, you have no idea what you've done." I jump into his arms, hugging him tightly and kissing him feverishly. His lips return my gratitude, before we notice we're being stared at by the young families entering the park beside us. He lowers me back to the ground and reaches into his pockets, retrieving a sparkly silver headband.

"I couldn't fit a tiara in my pocket, so I got you this instead," he says, gently pushing it into my hair. "You might not be able to go through the Disney Princess experience, but you are a queen in your own right today."

I squeal as he puts the headband into my hair. Reaching up to his neck, I pull him into another impassioned kiss. "Thank you, Hero."

"I'm not Hero today. I'm simply Tyler."

Stepping onto the tram, we ride into the park. We wind around the beautiful sections of plants and flowers as the tram's speaker system relays park information. A few minutes later, the tram comes to a stop in front of a line of buildings. Disney themed shops and restaurants line the tram stop with lights swinging from the tree branches. Family after family exits and runs for the entrance of the park. *God, I'd love to bring my kids here someday. To see their smiling faces as we pull up would be well worth the expensive price. A pang of sadness hits me. I may never get the chance to have kids.*

Hero snaps me out of my depressed haze. Taking me by the hand, he leads me to the ticket counter. He gets two all-day passes for us, and we walk into the park. The hustle and bustle of the various families reminds me that I never got to experience this kind of magic as a kid. My heart aches that I was never given the chance to dress up like my favorite Disney princess and walk the park like royalty. My mom could never afford to do anything like this after my dad died. Even after she married Bob, money was always tight. Yet this man is attempting to give me the experience I deserved as a kid. I don't fucking deserve him. Watching the children run into the park, giggling and screaming in excitement, brings a smile to my face and fills my heart with hope. I want this life so badly. It's so simple and happy. There's nothing complicated about it all. No running or hiding, just blissfully happy smiles and fun.

"So, what do you want to ride first?" he asks. "It's a bit different from the last time I was here, but I've heard a couple of the guys say their kids liked the Pirates of the Caribbean and the Indiana Jones rides."

"I don't even know where to start."

"Well, I grabbed a map for you. Pick a land and we'll go."

Scanning the colorful map, I notice the various lands and their corresponding rides. I know I'll never be able to pick, so I close my eyes and point to a random place on the map. "Well, it looks like we're going to Fantasyland. You ready to ride It's A Small World?"

"Fuck, you had to pick that one first," he laughs. "Just don't tell the guys we rode it. Please."

His admission makes me snort and my pussy clench all at the same time. He's still the badass biker and club VP that could melt my panties off with just one glance, even without the cut and the Harley. "Your secret is safe with me, biker boy. Hell, maybe you'll like it so much, you'll ditch the leather for a Mickey Mouse costume."

He throws his head back and laughs, shaking his head at my response. "Biker boy? Baby, you know damn well my cock can do things to you that no boy would ever be able to do. I'm all man, angel. Don't forget that."

He trails his fingers down my neck and grazes my erect nipples.

"You remember how much I filled your mouth and pussy up this morning? Try thinking about me bending you over, ripping your panties off, and fucking you in one of those boats from that goddamn ride. I would be pounding into your tight little pussy to the beat of the music."

"Jesus, Tyler. I think I just came from that visual. I mean, my panties would be soaked if you'd have gotten me some this morning." I flash a smile at him. "I guess that's one less barrier for you, if that's what you have in mind for later."

Hero cocks an eyebrow, a sly smile forming on his lips.

"Are you the reason I didn't get panties?"

The asshole smiles with a shrug. "Do you think I'd let any other man, my brothers included, touch your fucking panties, angel? No one touches what's mine, and you, angel, fall into that category."

Heat flushes into my face. His hands slide to the zipper of his jeans as he adjusts himself. "We have to quit talking about this shit. I'm half-cocked as it is. Let's get the most annoying ride on the fucking planet over with, before I drag you off to the darkest corner I can find and fuck you while Mickey Mouse watches and beats off."

The thought makes me shiver, and although I'm excited at the idea—well, not the Mickey Mouse part—I can't let him know that the idea turns me on, or we'll end up in Disney Jail for indecent exposure.

Wait! Is there a Disney Jail?

The thought of Mickey Mouse slapping a set of handcuffs on Tyler sends me into a fit of internal giggles. He'd never live the moment down. He watches me for a moment, gauging my reaction at his proposal, before dragging me off towards the princess castle. I bet he was hoping for a quickie rather than going on the first ride I picked. Too bad. I want to experience everything I can while we're here. Living for the moment, and not letting tomorrow take away from the experience, is my motto for today.

We spend the entire day riding the rides and taking in the various parades. It took some convincing, but Tyler finally agreed to get his picture taken with Ariel and me. I kept trying to tell him he was going to be between two hot chicks, but he still dragged his feet before finally relenting to my will. I might have bribed him with sucking his cock on the way home to do it, but it still worked. He ordered that I only get one copy of the photo, but what he doesn't know is, I bought a second one when he had stalked off to the bathroom. One for me, and one for club blackmail. I wonder what Raze and the guys would think about their VP canoodling with a Disney Princess. You'd probably be able to hear them laughing all the way to Anaheim.

Tyler insisted we watch the fireworks, much to my anguish and need for him to act on his previous promise after teasing me the entire day. Every time we stood in line for a ride, his hands found their way to my ass, his lips assaulting me. I thought for sure that security would be waiting for us after he tried to finger me on Pirates of the Caribbean. Even the cannon fire couldn't hide my moans when his fingers brushed against my core. The fucker plays dirty, but I love that about him. He doesn't care who's watching, and honestly, that excites me a little. It's so forbidden, but it's a sinful pleasure I think I'd like to try someday. Thinking about his attempts, I honestly would have slid onto his lap and fulfilled both of our wishes if our boat hadn't been filled with a dozen little kids. After I swatted his hand away a few times, he gave up, but even I know that was just a time-out for what he likely has planned later, or at least, I'm hopeful for later.

With just fifteen minutes left before the fireworks, he finds a spot near the front of the castle and pulls me into his arms. Tinkerbell flies across the sky as the fireworks boom behind the castle. Tyler places his chin on the top of my shoulder, watching them with me. Just as the finale springs to life, he twirls me around and brings his lips to mine. He kisses me like no one is watching, running his fingers through my hair, as colorful bombs burst in the air over us. It's the perfect moment for such an impassioned embrace. The only thing that would have made it better is if we were climaxing during the finale's booms, but we'd have to explain to Disney Jail why two grown adults fucked to the beat of the fireworks on Main Street, USA. At least, it would have made a great story for later.

He pulls away from my wanting lips just before the last firework explodes in the sky.

"You look beautiful under the fireworks," he says with a smile. "I never knew I could want something like this, but for you, angel, I'd walk through fire just to kiss you one more time." His words cut through me, but before I can speak, the crowd begins to push against us, and the lights illuminate Main Street again. "Let's get you home," he whispers into my ear.

"Home?"

"Where you belong, Dani. With me, and my head between those beautiful thighs of yours."

We ride the tram back to the parking garage.

Sliding into the truck, I snuggle up against Tyler and begin to doze on the ride home. He's true to his word as he carries my exhausted body into the house. We make quick, passionate love before falling asleep in each other's arms.

As my eyes succumb to exhaustion, I wish every day could be like this, but even I know that hell will be constantly looming in the distance.

Chapter 22

HERO

WAKING up to Dani straddling me and riding my cock is the best damn wake-up call a man could ever dream of. I don't know how she managed to get me at attention without even stirring me from sleep, but fuck, I love it. Feeling her slide herself over me while I'm still groggy made it feel like a dream coming to reality. It wasn't until her fingernails skimmed my stomach, leaving red trails along my flesh, that I realized it wasn't a fucking dream.

"Ride me, angel," I say, guiding her by her hips and slamming her down harder. "Use my cock to find your release."

She pants with each sway of her pelvis, grinding against my hips. Her eyes remain closed as she rides me, and then she comes apart, throwing her head back in ecstasy as her orgasm takes over. She smiles then, and I continue to rock her hips.

"Mmmm," she moans. "Good morning."

"Good morning. Was someone feeling a bit horned up this morning, and couldn't wait for me to wake up?" I tease, running my fingers over her pebbled nipples. She squeals from the touch. Damn, she's sensitive after she gets off. I need to make a mental note of that to use to my advantage later. I wonder if I could lick her into another orgasm with just her nipples.

"You could say that."

She giggles as she tries to remove herself from my dick. "I thought for sure you'd wake up sooner."

I quickly reverse our positions, rolling her onto her back, never pulling my dick from her still clenching pussy.

"Well, I seem to have this insatiable angel that wakes me up at all hours of the night. It makes it hard for a man to get some sleep."

"I guess I'll have to seek attention elsewhere if you can't keep up. A girl has needs, you know."

Seriousness crosses my face. Pinning her arms to the bed above her head, I claim her mouth while thrusting into her.

"I thought you understood, angel. This pussy belongs to me. If you think for one second that another man, or that vibrator you have hidden in your drawer, can fuck you into submission like me, you've got another think coming."

"Someone thinks highly of himself," she teases.

"Damn right I do. If I have to hogtie you to this bed, Dani, I will. Not a bad idea now that I think about it."

The thought of her bound by ropes in my bed turns me the fuck on. Her wanton body lying frozen in the sheets, begging me for more. Jesus, that would be a sight.

"Ever tried a little bondage? Rope would look so fucking sexy against your skin."

Her smile is laced with a mixture of fear and excitement. "I don't know if I'd like being tied up, but if you want to try it, I'd be willing to give it a shot. Under some conditions, of course."

"All in good time, angel. I have a few more things higher on my 'do to Dani list' that I want to try first," I say, leaning down and taking her taut nipple into my mouth.

"Like what?" she moans.

"Claiming your perfect ass, for one. The thought of claiming it as mine has crossed my mind more than once, but it will take some practice, and a trip to the local adult toy store. Maybe we'll take a ride out there soon."

"My ass?" she asks with trepidation.

"I'll be careful with you, angel. I won't force you into anything you aren't comfortable with, but at least give it some thought."

"Okay, but no promises," she says, pointing her finger into my chest. "So, are you going to lie here all day with your dick in me, or are you going to fuck me already?"

"So demanding. I guess you'll have to wait and see what I have in mind for today."

I roughly thrust into her, cupping her ass and hoisting it off the bed, increasing the depth of each thrust. She arches her back more, grinding harder against me. My girl has a greedy fucking pussy, and I fucking love it.

"Touch your clit. Rub it for me, angel. Make yourself come around my dick. I want to feel you lose control."

She licks two of her fingers and slides them between her legs. I watch as she spreads her lips apart and rubs a circle around her clit, flicking it with each thrust I pound into her. Pulling her finger from her wetness, she slides it into my mouth, followed by her own, before returning them to her swollen nub.

Her body spasms around me as another orgasm builds. Sliding a finger farther down to her entrance, she touches my cock, as it plunges in and out of her, pushing back on the finger on her clit.

"Come for me, baby. I want to feel your pussy milking my cock for every last ounce."

She rubs her clit between two of her fingers before finding her release. Her body trembles beneath me as my own orgasm strikes. She swirls her hips, and my dick pulses inside her. We've never talked about birth control, so I assume she's on some sort of contraception. Even if she wasn't, if an accident happened, deep down I think I'd be okay with it. It's only been a week, but having a child would mean she would be tied to me for the rest of her life. I may not have wanted forever before, but Dani is making me want more than I ever have, despite my reservations about her past.

Sliding out of her, I lean down and kiss her swollen lips. I pull her from the bed and lead her to the shower, turning on the water. Sliding in together, I wash her luscious body clean, knowing full well in just a few hours, it will only be dirty again. I think she half expected another round in the shower, but today I have another surprise in mind. Her pussy needs a break before I set the wheels in motion for tonight.

Exiting the shower, we both quickly dry off and get dressed. She looks perfect in a pair of cut-off jean shorts and a club t-shirt. The shorts hug every single fucking curve on her body, and they are nearly to the point of being indecent. I'm tempted to tell her to put something with a little more coverage on, but I know it will only start a fight. Today's not the day for fighting. Seeing my club's colors on her excites me more than I ever thought possible. Pushing the thought from my mind, I walk to the door, and we head down to have breakfast.

Dani hops up on one of the bar stools at the kitchen

island and watches me rummage through the refrigerator. I can feel her eyes on my ass.

"Are you eye-fucking me, angel?" I ask, not turning around. "I figured you'd be tiring of my old ass by now."

"Oh, there's nothing tiresome or old about your ass, Hero," she quips.

"Damn straight."

Setting a carton of eggs and a package of bacon on the counter, I pull out a pan from under the stove and flip on the burner.

"What will it be, angel face? Scrambled eggs and bacon, or a bacon omelet?"

She smiles before answering. "I'll take a double order of you on this counter, followed by a bacon omelet, please." I drop the carton of eggs onto the counter. They hit the frying pan I had set on the stove and send it flying. "Oops," she laughs.

"Fuck, Dani. You can't say shit like that while I'm standing over a hot stove. Christ, woman, are you ever satisfied?"

There's that fucking smile again. She could bend me to her will just by smiling at me. Her lips form this almost evil and sexy grin when my girl is being playful. God, I fucking love it.

"Every word you say or move you make is dripping with this come over here and fuck me, Dani call. You're intoxicating. I thought you'd have figured that out by now."

"Is that a yes?"

"You have no idea how much I'd like to take you on this counter, but we've got shit to do today. So, park that sexy ass of yours down, and be prepared to be amazed."

She sighs as I turn around and get to work on our breakfast. Five minutes later, two bacon omelets are steaming on the plates I had set on the island, along with two glasses of orange juice. Sliding onto the bar stool next to her, I hook my arm around her waist and haul her into my lap. Taking my time, I feed Dani her omelet bite by bite before devouring mine. Sitting here eating like a fucking normal couple makes me happy. I never expected to like civilian life so much, but with Dani, I love it.

Easing her off my lap, I dump the dirty dishes into the sink, making a mental note to get them cleaned up later. I'm ready to take my girl on our adventure. The weather is finally decent enough that she won't freeze or melt on the back of the bike as we take a long ride down the Pacific Coast Highway. It is the perfect stretch for a day trip, with views I know she'll love.

Grabbing my cut and keys, Dani and I walk out hand in hand to the bike. I help her get on the back, before sliding on myself. She wraps her arms around my waist as I start the engine. Pulling out of the driveway, I head towards the freeway. Just as we pull off to get some gas, my cell phone vibrates in my pocket. Raze's name pops up on the screen.

"This better be a fucking emergency," I bark into the phone.

"I need you to come by the clubhouse. There's some shit you may want to see. Bring Dani with you," he orders.

"Sure thing. Anything I need to worry about? It's not like you to request Dani's presence any other time," I say with a frown.

"We'll talk about it when you get here," he says, before hanging up.

Putting my phone back into my pocket, I let Dani know we've been ordered to appear at the clubhouse, and that we have to postpone our plans for a few hours at least. Making a U-Turn, I head north towards the clubhouse.

Pulling into the parking lot, I spy a large SUV with Federal Marshals lettered on the side parked by the main entrance. Raze and a couple of the guys are standing outside next to the SUV. As soon as I kill the engine, Dani hops off and waits for me to follow. Raze meets us halfway between the clubhouse and my bike.

"Why are the federal marshals here?" I question.

"Been asking that since they arrived."

"And you just let them in?"

"Didn't have a choice. They burst through the gate like a fucking wrecking ball, with a warrant to search the property." I eye him carefully. Had they found something to link us to the TT extermination? Ratchet was good at his job. He'd never fucked up before, so the likelihood of that happening this time would be slim to none. Especially with so much on the line for us.

"This about our old friends?" I ask quietly.

"No. They haven't said a word about it, but I couldn't chance it." Raze's face slackens before seriousness sets back in. "They came asking about Dani."

"What do you mean, they're asking about Dani?"

"You might want to ask her," Raze says, turning to look at her. Dani's face is pale.

"Angel?"

"I…" she stammers, just as two uniformed officers exit the clubhouse, spotting Dani. Walking up to her, one of the officers removes his cuffs, while the other officer directs his gun on her. Shoving me aside, the officer with the cuffs grabs her as she tries to run away. He reaches out, grabbing hold of her arm and shoving her to the ground. She kicks and rails against him, but he manages to drag her up from the ground by her hair.

"What the hell are you doing?" I scream at the larger of the two marshals, charging towards him. "Don't fucking touch her."

"Get the fuck back," the armed marshal orders,

pointing his handgun at me. "You make a single step in our direction, and I will not hesitate to fire."

The smaller one slaps the cuffs on Dani, shoving her against the squad car. Her head slams against the metal of the roof roughly, breaking open her skin and letting blood flow over her face. I fight, trying to get away from Raze and get to her, but the larger marshal aiming for me moves quickly, gun still raised.

"Stay where you are," he orders.

"Or what?" I challenge back. "You fucking busted up my girl, asshole. Don't think for a second I am going to let it slide."

His body stiffens at my threat. "She's not your problem anymore." Then the bastard smiles at me. His partner nods and returns to his grip on Dani.

Smiling the entire time as he speaks, he says, "Dani Espinoza. You are under arrest for the murders of Bob and Diana Williams."

Chapter 23

DANI

"HERO, I DIDN'T DO THIS," I scream as the marshal shoves me into the back of the car. "Please, you have to believe me. I'm innocent, goddammit. I didn't kill them. Please, Tyler. You know me."

He charges for the car. The two men put themselves between us, and I hit the window and the door with my body, praying it will open up. I peer up, tears streaming down my face. "I didn't do it," I repeat over and over again.

His face is nearly unreadable. So much like he was when I first came to the clubhouse, when he put up his walls, shutting me out again. "Why didn't you tell me?"

I told him everything I could without outing myself. He knows I'm not capable of this. Why isn't he fighting harder for me?

"I wanted to tell you," I cry. He shakes his head. "I

didn't do this. You can't let them take me."

"It's too late for that." His murmured voice cracks a little. "I thought we were being honest with each other."

"I know, and I'm sorry. I just didn't know how to explain this. Explain my past."

"You didn't even try."

"That's enough," one of the marshal's growls, then pushes him back to where Raze stands. They speak to them for several minutes before returning to the car and sliding into the front seat. I kick and scream the entire time, hoping Hero will fucking come back to real life and realize that this is wrong. The marshal starts the car and backs out. I watch Hero through the window as we pull away. His face is expressionless and cold. Then he follows Raze into the clubhouse, shutting the door and shutting me out, with no hope of being saved.

He's not going to come after me.

"Please, Hero. You know I didn't do this!" I bellow, pressing my face against the glass, attempting one last shot at rousing the man I had been with this morning. The clubhouse remains closed as we pull onto the street, and then it shrinks in the distance.

"Shut the fuck up back there," the marshal in the passenger seat orders. "None of these fuckers are going to help you. You're a fucking cop killer. They don't want anything to do with someone who has the law chasing them down."

"I didn't fucking kill my mom or Bob."

"That's up to the judge to decide."

How did they get involved in this? Sure, Bob was a cop, but he was far from the officer-of-the-year caliber that would be recognized. He and my mom were just normal people. Nothing extraordinary.

My head aches from being slammed against the car. Blood drips down the front of my face, impeding my vision. With each throb of my head, my vision clouds and I grow weak. Suddenly, the memories of that last night in Cleveland flood my brain and take over my mind.

Coming home from my kickboxing class, I walk through the door. "Anyone home?" I yell up the stairs. The house is completely pitch black and silent. It's unlike my mom and step-dad to be out so late during the week. Maybe Bob is working late, and mom went on to bed. She usually takes an Ambien when Bob's on the night shift to help her relax and sleep. Since Dad was killed in the line of duty, she never sleeps well until Bob comes home in the mornings. She is too afraid of a repeat of Dad's murder. Wait. Both of their cars were in the drive. What the hell is going on?

"Mom? Bob? Is anyone here?" Still no response.

Shrugging, I start towards the kitchen. I toss down my car keys onto the counter, flick on the light, and head to the fridge for a bottle of water. Groans from the dining room echo into the kitchen.

What the hell was that?

I walk towards the noise, only to find my mom and Bob strapped into two of the dining chairs. Bob is completely disemboweled with his mangled internal organs spilling from his stomach, down onto his lap and legs. Blood pools around him as he convulses before going still.

Who the fuck did this?

I'm motionless with fear. Who would do this? I don't even recognize my own mother's scream for me to run, but I can't leave her. I won't leave her to the same fate as her husband. Running to her side, I tear at the duct tape binding her hands and feet.

"Run, baby. Don't try to save me. Save yourself. You've got to run, baby. He wants you," my mother pleads.

I free her hands just as something comes down hard against my head, sending me crashing to the floor. A maniacal laugh echoes through my brain, and an evil, familiar face leans over me.

"You're mine now," he says. Then blackness washes over me, pulling me down into hell.

Screams rip me back to reality. My mother's words resonate with enough force to know I need to find a way to escape. Maybe if I play the innocent and stupid card, they'll be dumb enough to leave me with a chance to escape, just like Ricky did. I need to try something to break free.

"I don't understand," I cry. "Why would anyone

think I killed them? I loved them." Good girl, play innocent. Maybe they'll show me enough mercy to make my move.

A sick smile forms on the officer's face.

"You sure have a funny way of showing your love by hacking your mother and step-father to death. Your blood and fingerprints were found all over the crime scene, and on the murder weapons," he says.

"I didn't fucking do it. I'm being framed." I yell, kicking the seat with my feet.

"If you kick that seat, or open your mouth, one more fucking time, I will pull your ass out of the car and teach you how to respect an officer of the law, you fucking cunt. Sit back and shut up!"

I spit on the glass divider between us, and the driver slams on the brakes, sending my head rocketing towards the glass. "That's fucking it. Harris, shut her the fuck up, or I'm killing her now."

The man I now know as Harris bolts from his seat and flings the back-passenger door open. He crawls in to grab me as I scramble back and away from him. Wildly kicking my feet, I connect to his face, sending him falling to the ground. The other one flings open the door I'm cowering against while I'm distracted, and pulls me from the car by my hair. He throws me to the ground and kicks me in the stomach twice before hauling me to my feet. He slams my face against the back window, causing me to slump over the back fender.

"Are you sure we can't have a little fun with her before we take her in? She's a hot little number, even if she is covered in blood. We could break her jaw afterward, so she can't talk."

Who the fuck are these guys?

"You're fucking sick, Harris. You know we have strict orders to take her down to the warehouse. We weren't even supposed to bang her up this badly before he got to talk to her. He's going to be pissed she's roughed up as it is. If you fucking rape her, he'll kill you for it."

Who the hell are they talking about? Who is he?

"I know, Parsons, but fuck, I like it when they fight. Maybe the boss will let me play with her when he's done. She might not look as good, but her cunt will still be useable."

"I fucking doubt it. Get her ass back in the car," Parsons orders. "Make fucking sure she doesn't open her mouth this time."

Harris stumbles around the car and uses my hair to jerk me against him, before leaning down to my ear. "You're fucking lucky the boss ordered you to be delivered alive, or I'd have my dick pounding into that ass of yours right now, while Parsons watches," he whispers. Then he slams my face into the car, sending blackness spiraling around me.

I'm jolted back into consciousness when one of the fuckwit officers drags me out of the car again, and onto gravel. My hands try to go out and soften my hard collision with the ground, but I had forgotten about the cuffs. I fall face first to the ground, cut open and bleeding from the embedded stones. My vision is blurry, and my already aching stomach is on the brink of retching up the breakfast Hero made me.

Fuck, Hero.

He watched as these men threw me against that car as they took me into custody. He spouted all this bullshit about protecting me and needing me, but he just sat there like a fucking statue and let them haul me off. Where the fuck was the fight in him? Where was the man who eliminated an entire fucking motorcycle club as revenge for taking a member's life in cold blood? He's no one's hero. I was so stupid to believe he was the real deal. I'm a fucking idiot to believe my life could ever be sunshine and rainbows with him. It was all just a pipe dream of a romance that could not, or would not, ever happen.

"Get up, bitch," one of the marshal's order. My attempt to stand on my own is fleeting without the use of my hands. Falling back down to the ground, I flinch as the officer continues to scream at me. Finally realizing that I can't move, they drag me from the ground and carry me up the wooden steps of a building by my arms.

Swinging open the front doors, they literally throw me inside. This is not a police station at all, but an old cabin. I can smell the cedar of the wooden floorboards, and the scent of a forest trickling in from the open door.

"Where am I?" I rasp against the floorboards, my head pounding with the beginnings of a migraine.

A heavy set of footsteps walk towards me, the wooden floor creaking beneath the person's weight. Black polished dress shoes stop in front of me. Who the hell is this guy?

Craning my neck upward, I find him wearing black dress pants. His large frame is evident as my eyes scan farther up. His chest is broad, but it's his face that sends fear spiraling within me.

It can't be him. No! Please, God. Let it be anyone but him.

"Hello, Dani," his low voice says. "I've missed your pretty face, princess."

The man standing before me is my worst nightmare. He is the reason I ran. The reason I left my life in Cleveland behind and traded it for sunny California and a motorcycle club. He is the ghost from my past that made me fearful of everyone and everything around me. He is the catalyst to all the bad shit in my life.

Billy is the fucking cop that murdered my parents to get to me, but that's not the worst of it.

My step-brother has finally come for me at last, ready to finish the job he started that night.

Chapter 24

HERO

"HERO?" a soft voice calls from outside my door.

"Go the fuck away, Ruby," I yell through the door. "My answer's not going to change."

Sitting on my bed, I just sit and stare into nothingness.

Dani is wanted for murder. Even worse, the murder of her own mother. Watching the police haul her away bleeding in the back of that goddamn car nearly killed me. I wanted to reach out and save her, but I couldn't. I just stood there and watched them rough up my woman, then take her away. The police made it clear that if we interfered, we would be charged for harboring a known fugitive and possession of drugs. With the kind of rap sheets our club has, we'd be locked up for life. I had to protect my club, and in order to do that, I had to let her go.

And I fucking hate myself for it. I should have gone after her, or done something, but I couldn't. Not without sending every one of my brothers to jail along with her. I couldn't help her if I was in there with her.

Raze ushering me inside was for the best, because he could see the beast inside me rising. I would end up in jail next to her if I acted on the rage-induced acts playing in my head. Those two bastards signed their death warrants when they slammed her face into that car. Raze had to restrain me from tearing off after them. There had to be some mistake. She's not like us. She has a temper sure, and a violent streak when provoked, but she's not a killer. There's no way, but doubt creeps into my mind.

"Hero, get your fucking ass out here right now," Raze bellows from outside the door.

"Go fuck yourself, Raze. I don't need a lecture from you. I know we're fucked."

Raze barges through the door, huffing in anger. "The next time I order you to open the door, you fucking do it. I don't want to keep sending the prospects to Home Depot to get new ones every fucking day."

"What do you want from me, Raze? I know I fucked up. I trusted her too goddamn much without really knowing her."

The bed dips with Raze's added weight. His face is hard, but his eyes are gleaming with pity. I know he's trying to keep his cool, but I don't need pity. I need Dani, as much as I hate to admit it. Guilty or not, I need a chance to find out for myself.

He slaps his hand on my shoulder.

"I understand, Hero. Trust me, I do. The women in our lives royally fuck us up to the point we even doubt our own minds."

"I never thought I'd be torn like this, Raze. One minute, we were fucking happy. The next, she may have bodies lying in her wake back home. I just don't know how to process this. She was the only pure thing left in my life, and she's just as fucked up as I am. Her soul is stained just as black as mine."

"I know what you're going through. Once you lose trust in them, everything falls apart. Dani's a good girl. I know it, and you fucking well know it, too."

"You know something, don't you?" I say, lifting my gaze to meet his.

"Not yet, but Voodoo hacked into her police file from back in Cleveland and is looking through it now. If she's guilty, we'll know within the hour. I sent Slider down to the police department, to see if they'll let him talk to her. I've got you, brother. We'll find out the truth. Until we know for sure, do not give up on her on like I gave up on Maj."

"Wait. Gave up on Maj? What the hell are you talking about?"

Raze's head hangs low.

"I'm divorcing her. The night we went to the club to get them, I found two of those male strippers fucking Maj in a private room. She knew I was there watching them. She came home spouting some bullshit about how it was a mistake, and she was drunk, but I know it wasn't the first time. She slept with a guy from Trax's chapter the night before the hit on Twisted Tribe. I found them in our bed together. I'm fucking done being miserable, while she whores herself out behind my back."

Is no one happy anymore? Everything is imploding around us.

Twisted Tribe was just the beginning. We are systematically being dismantled by the fucking women in our lives.

"Fuck, Raze. I'm sorry. What about Ky and Harley? When are you going to tell them?"

"They already know. We told them yesterday. Honestly, they weren't surprised."

"How the fuck did we get here? Your woman's a cheater, and mine may be a killer."

He laughs and slaps me on the back. "Brother, I'd much rather have your problems than mine. At least, there's a chance she's innocent. I know Maj isn't."

Raze is a broken man, just like I am. These two starkly different women have ripped our lives apart. He'll get a chance to repair his life once the dust settles and Maj is gone, but for me, it's not that simple. I need proof she's innocent. I need solid evidence to tell me the woman I love is still the woman I know.

"Raze? Hero?"

Looking up at the doorway, Slider hesitantly stands staring at us both. Damn, he has perfect timing. Hopefully, he got her to talk, or at least found out something that would prove her innocence, or damn her in guilt. I need to know either way. My stomach twists and turns in knots as we wait for Slider to deliver the news. I've never felt like this before, even in the heat of combat. The dirt and sand hell I left is nothing compared to this.

"Did they let you see her?" Raze asks. I need her to be okay, even if I'll never see her again.

"She wasn't there, Prez. The cop sitting at the front desk said they didn't know what I was talking about. They didn't have a Dani Espinoza booked, nor did they know anything about her."

"Fuck," I roar. Raze and I stare at each other before jumping up from the bed and bolting down the stairs to Voodoo's tech room. He's frantically tapping away on his computer when we walk in.

"Talk to me, V. What did you find?" I ask.

He looks up from his computer before sliding over to the printer and retrieving a stack of papers.

"It's muddy, at best. Cleveland PD found her mom and step-dad gutted in the dining room of their house. DNA in the room was a match for both victims, Dani, and an unknown male related to the step-dad. According to the police report, a family member reported Dani missing the morning of the murders, and they issued an APB for her. It was a standard issue search for the Cleveland area. It was never expanded outside of Ohio. We, of course, know where she ended up, but I found something odd about her file."

Flipping through the pages, I verify everything Voodoo reported, searching the pages for the oddity. The answer doesn't immediately become apparent, but Voodoo points to the details of the APB.

"Look here. Dani was never officially listed as a suspect. They considered her a possible kidnapping victim. A missing person. Not the perp."

The pictures of her parent's mutilated bodies are amongst the reports. The DNA does confirm Dani was there, but just looking at the bodies, I know it takes a lot of rage and strength to gut someone like this. Handing the pictures to Raze, I see shock register in his eyes.

"Look at her step-dad's body in this photo," I say, pointing to the photo. "He has to be at least one hundred and fifty pounds heavier than Dani. How in the hell does a woman weighing a buck forty-five force him into that chair and restrain him? It doesn't make sense. That's Ruby versus you, Raze. There's no way a woman could do that, even if he was drugged. Not without help, anyway." Grabbing the photo back from Raze, I toss the pile back onto Voodoo's desk.

"Any information on the other set of DNA found at the scene? You said it was a relative. Maybe she had help," Raze suggests. He looks at me while speaking. His words stoke the fire of anger within me, but I know he's just trying to be thorough.

"I hacked into the criminal DNA database, and it's still searching. It could take weeks before I get a hit, or I could get nothing at all. It takes time."

Running my hands through my hair, I pace the room. I slam my fists against out of frustration, but a pair of bleeding knuckles won't help find Dani.

"We don't have that kind of time, Voodoo. Slider just got back from the police department, and she's not there. The fuckers that took her weren't real cops. Someone sent them here after her, and we just fucking let them take her."

"Shit," is all Voodoo replies as he frantically types on his computer. We wait in silence for hours as he works his magic, trying to find every lead to who the other blood had belonged to. That would lead us to who has Dani. Finally, his computer beeps loudly. We surround his desk as a report loads onto the screen.

"Obituary," he mumbles to himself, typing on the keyboard. He reads aloud until he makes to the list of family members. Billy Amos Williams. He's the son of

Dani's step-dad." He types a search for Billy into Google. News report after news report comes up in the search. Billy is a rookie cop. One that has been suspended twice for misconduct and harassing two female suspects. The last new story is dated just four days ago. Voodoo clicks on the link, and the story pops up.

"Looks like Billy boy missed his court date for a sexual assault on a female prisoner." Her photo pops up on the screen and shocks us all. She looks just like Dani.

"It's the fucking step-brother. He killed them to get to her," I snarl as everything clicks into place. She is innocent, and I just handed her over to the man who killed them. I have to fucking find her.

"You've got to track them down, Voodoo. Call in every favor we fucking have. I don't care if we have to alert the National Guard. We need to find her before he kills her."

"On it, boss. I can't promise a miracle, but I'll fucking try."

Leaving Voodoo to his work, Raze calls an emergency session of Church. My brothers come running into the room quickly, and he doesn't wait to start barking orders.

"Dani has been kidnapped by her step-brother. His name is Billy Williams, and he's a cop on the run. He killed her parents to get to her. Looks like Billy has a sick fucking obsession with Dani. He's assaulted two women that look just like her. Now, she's either already in his hands, or she's on the way to him with those fucking bastards I let take her. I need you all to contact the other chapters and get them on the road. Send them Dani's picture. I want every single fucking Heaven's Reject on the road looking."

"Of course, Prez," is the unanimous response.

"They can't be more than a couple hours away. Hot Shot, get on the horn to your cop cousin. See if he can issue an APB on Dani, or the two fuckers who took her. Check in with Voodoo to see if he can pull the license plate number off the car. Make tracks, brothers. Let's bring Dani home."

The men disperse quickly from the room, leaving just Raze and me alone. He comes to sit by me, as my head hangs in my hands. Guilt pangs me for the things I said to her.

"I should have fought for her. I shouldn't have let them take her. If that fucker touches her, I'll die taking him down. She's probably already fucking dead, and it's my fault, Raze. I won't be able to live with myself if she's dead."

"Hey, we don't know anything yet. Dani is a ball buster. She'll fight to survive. She won't go easily."

A knock comes from the door. Voodoo stands there with a piece of paper in his hands.

"I think I might have found them. There's a cabin listed for an Amos Williams up near Lake Arrowhead.

It's a long shot, but I thought you might want to check it out."

Grabbing the map from his hands, Raze and I bolt past him. As Raze calls in the cavalry, I head straight to my bike and pull the guns out of my saddlebag. Firing it up, I tear out of the parking lot before Raze or any of the others even get outside.

I need to get to Dani.

I just hope it's not too late.

Chapter 25

DANI

"DID YOU MISS ME, LITTLE PRINCESS?" he whispers in my ear, before jerking me up from the floor and into his arms. His fingers gently play with my blood-covered hair, his nose pressing against the side of my face. "You know I missed you, Dani," he says, inhaling my scent.

His ear passes my mouth as he continues to rub his face all over mine. Lashing out, I bite his ear and pull, trying to Mike Tyson his Evander Holyfield ass. Billy screams, and his blood pours into my mouth, but I don't let go. He shoves me away, his hands cupping his bleeding ear.

"You stupid bitch. I was trying to be nice to you, but you had to fuck that up like always. You'll pay for that, bitch."

Spitting his blood on the floor, I laugh. His idea of nice would be to rape me slowly, while the other two assholes watch, then let them have their turns. Billy isn't nice. He's a fucking animal that thinks no is the new yes. He gets off on torturing his victims. He may not know it, but I know all about the skeletons in his closet. I was the one who told his dad about finding him lurking in my room at night, watching me sleep. Bob had disowned him for his obsession with me.

I was the reason he lost his family, but it was his own actions that caused the split. Placing the blame solely on me, the bastard took away my family to get his revenge.

"You're so fucking delusional, Billy. If your version of nice is murdering my mother and your father because they wouldn't let you play deluded step-sister fuck time, then I'd hate to see what your version of angelic would be. Slaughtering puppies?"

He snarls at me, but I don't let the insults stop. I want him emotional. That's when he makes mistakes, and a mistake may just save my life.

"Oh, wait! I know. Sweet and innocent Billy would likely gang rape a dead woman. Am I right? Feeling a little necrophilia coming on, Billy?"

He charges towards me and slaps me across the face, sending me flying backward. He jumps on top of me, his legs straddling my stomach. I can feel his erection digging into my flesh as he holds me down. This sick fuck is getting off on this. I just need to keep him talking long enough to distract him. If I keep running my mouth, he won't be raping me. Hopefully, he'll smack me around hard enough a few times, I'll pass out from the pain before his grand finale. Knowing what's likely to come will be so much better for me, if I were unconscious or dead. Truth be told, death was looking pretty good right now. It would be easier than living with the scars and memories of what he had done and will do to me.

"Do you feel that, princess?" he sneers, grinding his erection into me. "This is what you do to me. That smart mouth of yours, and that fucking body, has driven me wild, ever since your whore of a mother married my father. I beat off every single night to the thought of you on your knees servicing me."

My stomach rolls. I knew he fantasized about me, but his words throws me off more than I had expected. The vision of what he described takes over my mind, and I can barely contain throwing up on him. Billy may be the single most fucked up person on this planet. His hyper-focused sights on me make him even more dangerous, knowing his obsession with me is stronger than ever.

"How did you find me?"

There you go, Dani. Keep him talking. Buy yourself some time.

"I'm a fucking cop, princess. You know that," he says, rubbing his hands across my face. "I'll admit, you were far more difficult to track down. But if you grease enough palms, and spin the story to say you were a cop killer, everyone takes an interest for the right price. You'll be surprised to know that it wasn't a dirty dealer or a snitch that ratted you out, but a whore living in that clubhouse of yours."

"Who?" I rasp out.

"She didn't give me her name, princess. Just that she was sick and tired of you flaunting your shit around her home, and in front of her husband," he says, sending anger flushing throughout my body. One of the fucking old ladies turned me over to this sick fucker.

My mind races to think of who it could be. Ruby? Maybe. Bubbles? Doubtful. Dixie? I'd never met her. Outside of Jagger's widow and Maj, the list of who it could be comes up short. Until my mind clears. Who would have the most to gain to turn me in? Who had all but disappeared after the strip club?

Maj. The woman who brought me into that club had signed me over to him. What did she gain from this? Why would she hate me so much that she'd do this to me?

Gritting my teeth, I decide I need to survive long enough to settle the score, because the Heaven's Rejects need to know that a snitch lives within the walls of their clubhouse. Maj will pay with her life. Even if I die in this fucking cabin in the woods, I will find a way to lead the evidence back to that traitorous bitch. As much as I hate Hero right now, I know he will eventually come looking for me. At least in my death, he will learn the truth, and will be able to protect the club, even if the price was paid in my blood.

Billy's fingers trace my face and graze down my neck, snapping my attention back to him. "Apparently, she didn't like you screwing that fucking biker, and frankly, neither do I."

His hands encircle my throat and squeeze just a little.

"You are fucking mine, Dani. How could you let another man touch you? I bet there's a bastard child growing in that belly of yours right now. If I find out he's planted something inside of you, I will kill him, and the baby, right in front of you. No one fucking touches what's mine," he roars, increasing the pressure on my throat.

"Boss, you'll kill her," Parsons warns.

Billy releases me and draws a gun from his back, then he turns, pumping two bullets each into Parsons and Harris. *I was hoping they would realize how wrong this was and try to save me, but my fucking back-up plan is gone now.* It's just me and the demonized monster alone in this cabin. My luck just keeps getting worse.

"Now, where were we? Killing the man who touched my property, and carving out anything that may be growing inside of you. Tell me, princess, did lover boy knock you up? Do I get to carve up your pretty stomach like I did your mother?"

What the hell is he talking about? My mother wasn't... oh shit. Mom was pregnant with Bob's child.

That has to be part of the reason he killed them. They were having a baby, and he saw it as his father replacing him after he was kicked out of the family.

Sweet merciful Jesus. He killed three people that day, and he's working on the fourth with me. Shock must register in my eyes, because he throws his head back and laughs.

"You didn't know dear old Mom was having another baby?" He laughs harder. "My fucking father always wanted more children, but when my mother couldn't have anymore, he dumped her ass on the curb to raise me on her own. I spent my entire life trying to please him and make him come back, but he didn't. He got a new wife, and a daughter, leaving me to fucking rot. Then my mom died, and he was forced to take me in. I hated him for what he did to my mom and me. We lived in squalor, all while Mr. Big Shot Cop lived the high life with his new family. I'll admit, though, having such a sweet piece of pussy flaunting her naked body around me was the best part of the shitty situation."

I stare at him in disbelief and disgust. He thinks I was teasing him in my own fucking home. He needs serious help, or a bullet to his brain. I'd prefer the latter, but I'm useless with my hands still cuffed behind me. Shit, there's no way I can break off these cuffs, or get out of them, unless the dead dipshits by the door have a key in their pocket. I need to scoot to the door next to their bodies. I just have to keep him distracted as I do it.

"Flaunted myself in front of you? Billy, you hid in my room and waited for me to change, or to go to sleep. You were fucking stalking me in my own home. I didn't ask for this, or for you to obsess over me, you fucking bastard. I wanted a home, and a life without death taking away everything again. I didn't want anything to do with you or your dad. I was there because of my mom. She was the last family that I had, and I wasn't going to leave her behind."

"A fucking family? I had that until your mom came along."

"It wasn't my mom's fault your parents got divorced. That was years before my dad even died, douchebag. You're grasping at sanity straws, trying to rationalize your shitty existence of a life, and placing the blame on everyone but the real problem. You are your own worst enemy, and in the end, you're the reason you're the monster you are. No one else but you."

He yanks me to my feet, forcibly holding me by the elbow as he walks to me the kitchen table.

"Get on the table, Dani."

"Fuck you!" I scream.

His open palm throttles towards my face, connecting with my cheek with a slap that stings my face and sends my head flying back. "Get on the fucking table, princess." He picks me up then, and throws me onto the table. I land on my belly, the wind knocked from my lungs.

His hands run down my ass, as he squeezes both cheeks before landing a painful slap there. "The things I have planned for you, Dani," he grumbles, more to himself than to me. His hands move up to my cuffs, and I feel him fiddling with them. "As much as I love seeing you bound in metal, I need your hands free for what I have in mind."

A click sounds, and suddenly, my hands are freed from the tight cuffs. I hear them clink to the floor, and his hands replace them as he rubs my wrists. "Your wrists are the sexist color of black and blue right now. Fuck, seeing your skin dark and broken makes me hard." His tongue runs across my wrist, then he drags my hand to the bulge in his pants. I recoil, but he presses my hand harder against him.

"See what you do to me, princess? My dick aches for you. After years of being denied the one thing I want,

I'm taking it tonight. I finally get to play with my favorite toy." I try to slide off the table as he relishes his conquests with me, but he pulls me back and pins me down with his knee. He leans forward and pulls two chained leather cuffs from a lip under the table, quickly securing them to my wrists. I scream in frustration as he pulls his knee from my back, flipping me over onto my back, and moves to the head of the table. A cranking sound clicks throughout the empty cabin, and my arms are winched forward on the table. Seeing the level of mechanical restraints he's using alerts me to the fact that he's either used this cabin before for his sick fun, or he had found me much sooner than he said. It takes time to plan and equip a cabin with this shit. There's no way in hell he had built a sick and demented kitchen of terror in just a few hours.

"There's no escaping, Dani." He runs his hands up my legs, stopping on my upper thighs. "I can smell you." His hands rub against the jean material covering me. "I can't wait to taste you. I bet you're as sweet as a freshly plucked peach." He dips between my legs, his face rubbing into me, his hands moving to grip my ass tightly. I try to kick him off, but his body is weighing down my legs.

"Please, Billy," I beg. "You don't have to do this."

He removes his face from my apex and grasps my

feet, pulling me towards him. Climbing on top of me, he uses his knees to part my legs.

"You don't understand, Dani. I have to do this. Once I have you, I can move on with my life. Find happiness. hell, maybe even have a family of my own. Your face has haunted me for years, and until I feel you wrapped around me, I'll never be able to live."

His hands cup my breasts as he grinds against me.

"You're the last thing on my list before I can be myself again. Fucking you will free my soul, Dani. Don't you see? I've done this all to have you, and then I'm going to kill you."

His hands roam to the top of my tank top, ripping the fabric in half and exposing my bra. His breathing becomes ragged as he dips to kiss me. I move my head from side to side, trying to avoid his lips. He presses his forehead against mine to stop the motion.

"You never answered me, Dani," he says, his hands roaming my exposed belly. "Is there an intruder growing in here?" His hot breath pours over my skin, sending vomit gurgling up my throat.

I have no idea if I'm pregnant or not. Hero and I weren't exactly careful, but I'm not late at all. I'm pretty sure I'm not pregnant, but would admitting it buy me time, or cut my life short? He'd focus on my stomach rather than raping me, at least for the time being. He might see it as a detriment to his sick pleasure, knowing another man's child grows inside my belly.

Shit, what do I do?

His hands encase my face, forcing me to focus on him. "Answer me, bitch. Are you pregnant?"

"Yes," I scream in panic. "Please don't hurt my baby."

His hands wrap around my throat again, pressing hard against my windpipe. "You fucking whore," he yells, squeezing my throat tighter and tighter.

"Please, just fucking kill me," I rasp, kicking at him, trying desperately to fight.

"Even death won't set you free." He releases my throat, leaving me gasping and coughing as I struggle to breathe. My chest heaves as oxygen rushes back into my lungs. My eyes catch something shining in his hands, but only in enough time to see him holding a knife over his head.

"This baby fucking dies, and then I'll fuck you to death. You will bleed out all over my cock. "

He raises the blade higher, and I scream, "Please, don't!"

I focus on Hero's face in my mind. I focus on the good times we had together as the knife plunges towards me. I pray that death comes quickly, squeezing my eyes closed as I wait.

Suddenly, an earth-shattering crash comes from the door, then two loud cracks force my eyes open. Billy is still above me, and blood is now trickling down his face. The knife falls from his hands and onto the floor, pinging like a pin dropping into silence. His lifeless body falls to the side. The room spins as my body grows weightless. Blackness takes hold, and I hear a man screaming my name. Hero's voice echoes through my mind. *He's here.*

He came back for me.

HERO

"DANI," I whisper.

Holding her in my arms just doesn't seem real. After everything I said to this woman, she's clinging to me like I'm the breath in her lungs. I squeeze her tightly, whispering into her ear, over and over, telling her that she's okay. Her tear-stained cheeks are soaking my shirt, but I just don't give a fuck.

"He's gone, baby. He'll never hurt you again. That I can promise you."

She nods her head, acknowledging my words, but she remains silent. My fingers trace down her spine in an attempt to comfort her, but she stiffens at my light touch. I've got to get her away from all of this. Especially the bloodied scene that lies behind her.

"Come on, angel," I whisper. "Let's get you home."

Using my knife to strip the leather cuffs from her

hands, I free her. The motherfucker ripped her shirt during the struggle, so pulling the shirt from my own back, I slip it over her head. I'm not about to let the guys see her like this. Her eyes are so empty, I'm not even sure she knows that I'm the person holding her. She's not really with me right now. She's retreated into the depths of her mind to block out everything that had just happened.

Shielding her eyes from the bloody, mangled mess that was her step-brother, I lead her away from her prison. She trembles as we move. My girl is in shock, and in serious need of a shower, food, and rest. She doesn't protest when I hoist her into my arms, carrying her to my truck, and depositing her on the passenger seat. She curls into a tight ball as I work the seat belt around her waist, and then she jumps at the sound of the seating belt clicking into the lock.

"Shhh, angel," I whisper. "It's just the seat belt."

Her eyes look right through me, as if she's seeing me as a ghost, instead of a flesh and blood human being standing in front of her.

Was this what I looked like when I came home from Iraq?

My beautiful daredevil is gone, and in her place lies a broken spirit afraid of her own shadow.

If I could have killed that bastard a second time, I would have fucking done it, and let her fire a few shots into his skull. If only her recovery would be so easy in the coming months. Having lived through a waking nightmare, words will not send her demons packing. She'll need someone to put the pieces back together, and that person sure as hell is going to be me. Closing the door, I walk around and slide into the driver's seat. Dani continues to stare absently out the window. The truck roars to life, and we pull away from the last bad memory my girl will ever have. I'll make damn sure of that.

Billy's hideout was about as remote as one could get in Southern California, so the trek back to the clubhouse will take a couple of hours. Without Voodoo's computer hacking skills, we'd have never found out about Billy's cabin. We'd have never found her without his help, and the thought of our failure sends chills down my spine. *She's fine*, I remind myself, or at least she will be. Dani falls asleep five minutes into the ride home, leaving me with just the thoughts in my mind. The memory of that bastard straddling her, with a knife aimed at her body, will forever be burned into my brain.

Guilt washes over me. Had I not pulled my head out of my ass, Billy would have fulfilled his sick fantasies. I would have never been able to hold my angel in my arms ever again. The only thing that brings a smile to my face is recalling how his head exploded when my shot punctured his temple. Watching his blood and brain fragments hitting the wooden floor satisfies me that I settled the score. He deserved a much slower death, but I needed to end his reign of terror before he raped Dani.

The thought of what she endured is enough to make me nauseous. A horrific vision of his hands on her helpless body makes me gag. My priority now is to just get her home and into the safety of the clubhouse. Grabbing my phone, I hit the speed dial number for the club's on-call doctor, Doc. He was never officially patched in as a member, but he's always been there to help if one of us got hurt. We kept his practice afloat a few times during the recession, when small-time medical practices were being eaten alive by the local hospitals.

"Did you find her?" Doc asks without even saying hello.

"Yes, we're on our way back now. Are you at the clubhouse? I need you to check her out."

"I came as soon as Raze called. I'm set up in your room. How badly is she injured? I might not be able to treat her here if her injuries are extensive. She might need a hospital, Hero."

How can I explain to a hospital about her situation and the reason for her condition? She may not be wanted by the police, but she's still considered a missing person. I just killed the one man who could have exonerated her from all suspicion, should she be found and questioned about their killings. I hope to hell the guys find something in his hidey hole to incriminate him and set her free, if that were to ever fucking happen. I won't be letting her out of my sights for the rest of our lives if she'll have me.

"Hero, you still there?" He asks.

"Sorry, Doc. Got lost in my own thoughts. You know she can't go to the hospital. It looks to be just cuts and bruises, but until I can get her cleaned up, I won't know for sure."

He clears his throat nervously, so I know what he's about to ask. "You know I don't want to ask this, but I need to be prepared if the answer is yes. Did he rape her?"

"As far as I know, I put a bullet into his brain before he got the chance."

Doc sighs in relief. "Thank fuck for small miracles. Just get your girl home, and I'll do my best to patch her up. I brought Nancy along, in case she has an issue with a male doctor stitching her up."

"Thanks, Doc," I say, then hang up the phone. I think he said it best. Thank fuck she's going to be okay physically. Emotionally, her healing will take much more time, but we have all the time in the world to let the emotional dust of her past settle. I turn on the radio and let Black Stone Cherry soothe my soul for the rest of the ride.

Just thirty minutes outside of Upland, my phone rings. Seeing Ratchet's name scroll across the screen, I know I need to take this call. Not wanting to wake Dani,

I pull over into a park-and-ride a few minutes later and return the call.

"Hey, boss man. Just wanted to let you know that we cleaned the place up. All's well here. Not a trace of us to be found."

"Good to hear, Ratch. Make sure that place burns to the ground, but try to avoid setting a wildfire this time," I say with a chuckle.

He doesn't laugh. Instead, he asks, "How's Dani?"

"She fell asleep as soon as the rubber hit the pavement. Hasn't woken up since. Doc's going to look at her when we get back."

"Sleep is what she needs. I'll call ahead to the clubhouse and make some of the guys hit the road for a long ride, so she isn't overwhelmed when you get back. Don't want her to bolt again."

"No shit. We need to keep her calm. Her name hasn't been cleared yet. I don't want to get her back, just for her to be shipped off to Cleveland to be questioned about her parents."

"Truth, man. Voodoo might be able to help with her missing person's report. He found a computer, and a bunch of shit you probably don't want to see stashed in the bedroom of the cabin. He's got it packed up in a cage and is already on the road. He said he'd let you know what he found later."

Relief flows over me. We might still be able to clear her name, so she can get back to living. Thank fuck.

"Sounds good, man. Have him text me instead of call. Once I get her back to the clubhouse, I want to get her checked out, fed, cleaned up, and tucked into my bed, before the crew swarms her. I know they'll mean well, but she needs to work through some shit."

"You got it, boss. I'll let you get back to driving. Good luck once the hellcat wakes up. Watch out for her claws," he says, before hanging up. Jumping back into the truck, I look over to check on my sleeping angel. Two brown eyes stare back at me.

"Hi," her faint voice whispers.

"Hey, angel face. Did you have a good nap?"

"Yes," she responds. Even though her answers are short, at least she's talking.

Turning the key in the ignition, the truck rumbles. "We're just outside Nealey's Corner. Do you need anything to eat or drink before we get back?"

She quietly ponders the question before requesting a Coke and some french fries.

"Anything you need, angel. And I mean anything. You just ask." She straightens up in her seat as I pull into the nearest McDonalds. I order Dani's food and get a sandwich combo and drink for me in the drive-thru. Once we get our food, I hand the bag to her, and she passes out our orders between us.

She pulls her legs up to her chest and rests the carton of fries on her knees. She delicately picks up each fry, studying it before putting it into her mouth. Reaching into the drink tray between us, I grab the chocolate milkshake. I thought she might want something frozen to ease her throat. Just as soon as the thought crosses my mind, I slam down the blast walls to block out the visions of her screaming my name for help. But the rage I feel cannot be contained, and I punch the steering wheel. She jumps in her seat, sending her fries scattering on the seat between us. *Fuck, why did I do that? She's scared enough as it is.* She tries to shovel them back into the box, but I offer her mine. "Sorry, baby. I didn't mean to scare you. Eat mine." She gapes at my outstretched hand, then slowly takes them from me and moves back into her corner of the truck. She polishes off the rest of my fries and finishes both drinks.

"Thank you," she mumbles. The food must satisfy her just enough, because in a few short minutes, she drifts back off to sleep.

Pulling up into the dusty dirt road of the clubhouse, I notice Ratchet was true to his word. Most of the bikes that typically line the parking lot are missing. I pull my truck around back and shut off the engine. I shoot a text off to Doc to let him know we're here, then I realize I should probably tell Dani he's going to check her over.

"Baby, Raze called the club's doctor to examine you.

Are you okay with that? He brought his nurse, Nancy, along with him, if you'd feel more comfortable with a woman present."

She meekly nods yes and starts to unbuckle her seat belt. I jump out of the driver's seat to help her, but she has the door open before I make it around the truck. I catch her by her waist as she tries to jump down. She tries to walk on her own, but as she limps along, I can't stand that she's in pain. Picking her up off of her feet, I carry her in my arms. She protests at first, trying to wiggle away, but soon gives up. Her body relaxes against mine, as I carry her inside, then up the stairs to my room.

Doc is already there, looking through his medical kit, as Nancy spreads a sheet on my bed. I carry Dani over to the bed and sit her down on the outstretched sheet. Nancy helps get her situated as I move out of the way.

"I need to examine you before you get cleaned up. We need to see what we're working with. Are you okay with that? I may need to ask you some questions as I examine you, and some of them are quite personal. Would you rather I have Nancy handle that portion of the exam?"

Dani's eyes lock onto mine, looking for reassurance before answering his questions. I nod my head to ease her nerves. "Yes," she answers, and Doc walks to the bedside, ready to begin the examination.

I move to exit the room, but she speaks again. I'm not ready to hear her answers to the questions I know Doc is going to ask, or to see the marks on her body that rat bastard inflicted on her.

"Hero?" she calls out quietly.

"Yes, angel?" I turn back toward her.

"Please stay," she pleads, silent tears falling from her eyes. Every one of those tears chip away at my heart even more. I can't deny her simple request. I need to stay calm for her.

"No one will take me away from you ever again." A tiny smile forms on her lips when I walk towards the bed and sit on the side with her.

Doc asks her to strip down to just her bra and panties so he can examine the sources of her bleeding. As she peels away each layer with Nancy's help, every bruise and cut sends rage coiling inside of me. She shouldn't have had to go through this. I fucking threw her to the wolves when those fucking fake cop bastards took her away. No, what she endured was completely my fault for not trusting her to tell me the truth. I just hope she can forgive me someday.

Dani covers her body as Nancy deposits her clothes into a paper bag I know Doc is keeping for evidence in her case. Doc gingerly examines her, noting the cuts that require stitches. Each time he touches one of them with his gloved hands, she winces from his touch and the pain. He apologizes each time, but I know he doesn't mean to hurt her.

Leaning down to examine her ankle, Dani abruptly grabs my hand.

"It's okay, baby," I whisper, as he slowly elevates her ankle.

After inspecting it, he rises to his knees and jots down more notes. Pushing his glasses back onto his face, he hands Nancy his notepad.

"Dani, I think your left ankle is severely sprained. Possibly broken. We can't exactly x-ray you, so I will have to put you in a walking cast until the swelling goes down enough to make sure it's healing properly. Nancy will help you get cleaned up here in a few minutes, and then we'll finish up, so you can rest, but I need to ask those questions I mentioned before. They're very personal, so I need to know if you are all right that Hero and I are in the room. Like I said earlier, if you want to have Nancy do this part, you're more than welcome to request it."

"Please, just ask them so we can move on," she pleads.

"Did he assault you?" Doc blurts out. Dani freezes at his question, and a hiss exits my lips before I can stop it.

"Fuck, Donny. Couldn't you have eased into that one? Nothing like pulling the fucking Band-Aid off before you clean the edges of the wound. Jesus, man." I can see the hurt in his eyes, and I know he had to ask it, but I thought he'd ask simple questions, before going to straight for the elephant in the room.

"I'm sorry, but I need to know in case I have to perform an internal exam." The thought of Doc doing that nearly makes my blood boil over, as much as what Billy may have done to her. She's been violated enough as it is, and doesn't need any further embarrassment.

"Dani, I need you to answer the question. Were you assaulted?" I can't even look at Donny right now. He won't let it go until she's ready to talk about it. Squeezing Dani's hand, I try to comfort her, and reassure her that nothing she says will ever affect how I feel. Her trembling makes the bed quiver. Her eyes stay vigilantly locked to the floor.

"He was about to… but he didn't get a chance." Her voice quivers at the admission. "He beat me, but he never… did that. He didn't rape me. He didn't get the chance to do it." I know she may be against being touched, but I need her closer to me. Hooking my hand around her slender waist, I press her against my side, my arm circling her neck. Her body tenses at first, but after a moment, she relaxes into me.

"Do you need to know anything else, Doc, or can she get cleaned up? I want my girl patched up and in bed sooner rather than later."

Dani's breath hitches at the mention of being in my bed. She must think I mean to fuck her, but that's the farthest thing from my thoughts. I doubt my dick could even get hard with Viagra coursing through my veins. This girl has been hurt, and he's not in the mood for play time. "No, angel, Sleep only," I whisper into her ear. She sighs in relief.

"That's all I need for now. Let's get you clean and stitch you up. I'm going to give you some pills to reduce the pain and to help you relax. Your number one priority is to rest and heal. I don't want you to be on your feet more than fifteen to twenty minutes at a time until you've had more time to heal."

Doc hands Nancy his clipboard and exits the room, giving Dani her privacy. She toddles to the bathroom, holding onto my arm with each labored step. She leans against the counter as Nancy all but shoves me out of the bathroom. I hear the shower turn on and the glass doors close against the tile.

The shower should help her exhausted limbs relax. I know she won't take long in the shower, so I don't have long to get something for her to eat. Judging by how fast she shoveled in the french fries earlier, I doubt she's eaten since he kidnapped her. Closing the door behind me, I run downstairs and rummage through the club-house kitchen cabinets, finally settling on a can of chicken noodle soup and crackers.

I check the laundry room for a fresh set of sheets while the soup warms in the microwave. Ruby must have been in the mood to clean, because several sheet sets are freshly laundered and sitting in the baskets for each room. Grabbing the one labeled with my name, I throw the soup in a thermos to keep it hot and head back upstairs.

Nancy lets me in when I knock softly on the door. I enter to find that Dani's dressed in one of my club shirts and a pair of the pajama pants she kept in my room. The Doc is stitching her up in the recliner in the corner of the room.

My brave girl is being sewn back together like a quilt, and not a single tear stains her face. She's been so brave through all of this, but I know the other shoe will drop soon enough.

Seeing the basket, Nancy takes it from me, pulling the sheet set out of it. She takes to re-making up the bed while I return to Dani's side. Twenty minutes later, Doc finally finishes by wrapping her ankle with an ace bandage.

"I didn't think to bring an air cast with me, but I'll make sure one arrives here tomorrow. Until it's here, you need to stay off of that foot," Doc orders. Nancy hands her two white oval pills and a glass of water.

Swallowing them down in one big gulp, she gingerly leans against her new stitches into the chair, trying to relax. Knowing the pills will kick into effect shortly, I give her the soup. She drinks it straight from the thermos in just a few swallows before returning the container to me.

A soft click of the door signals that Doc and Nancy quietly exited the room, leaving us alone for the first time since the drive here. I don't know why I feel so afraid being alone with her. Apologies have never been my strong suit, and yet I owe her the biggest apology of all. My actions nearly killed her, and I will have to live with that guilt and regret for the rest of my days. Deep down, I know it's going to take more than just pretty words to make it up to this woman. I just hope she gives me the chance to do it, but I'm not holding my breath.

Putting myself into her situation fills me with dread that once she finds her strength, I'll never see her again. I don't want to live this life without her, but because of my fucking idiocy, I may have already sealed our fates. I just need to take it a day at a time, like Dani, and see where the cards fall. That's all I can do.

"Let's get you to bed, angel. Those pills will be kicking your ass soon enough, and I want you in bed when they knock you out."

She tries to stand on her own, but I pick her up, carrying her back to the bed without a single protest from her. Her warm body feels good against my chest. It reminds me she's really here, and that her heart is still beating. It might not beat for me anymore, but it's still pumping within her chest. That's all that matters to me anymore. Laying her gently on the freshly made sheets, she snuggles into the fabric. I pull the comforter up to her hips, just like she likes it, as she settles into my bed. I click off the light and start for the door, so she can sleep in peace.

"Tyler?" she calls into the darkness. "Please, don't go. I don't want to be in here alone. Please stay with me."

I can't leave my girl now that I know she wants me close. Pulling my shirt over my head, I retrieve a pair of pajama pants from the top drawer, and trade them for my blood-stained jeans. I need a shower, but I'm not wasting any more time not holding her in my arms. I slide between the sheets, wrap my arms gently around her waist, and pull her trembling body to me. We lie there for several minutes in silence before she begins to sob.

"I'm so sorry I lied to you, Tyler. I never meant to hurt you like this," she whimpers into the pillow.

"Shhh, angel. I know you didn't, but now isn't the time for us to talk about this. I need you to sleep, angel face. We have the rest of our lives to figure shit out, but tonight is just for rest. Sleep, baby."

Dani sobs into her pillow for several minutes before her tears turn to quiet snores. Her body rattles as she sucks in air because of her crying outbursts. She blames herself for this, but I know the truth. It was me, and I'm planning to spend every single day making it up to her.

"You're safe, baby. I'll never let anything else happen to you from this day on."

Cradling her body tighter, I close my eyes and force my body to relax against hers. She may not have been awake to hear me, but I mean every damn word of it. I love her, and I will die to protect her, even if it means I have to let her go.

"I love you, Dani," I whisper into the dark night, before falling asleep myself.

Chapter 27

DANI

THE FIRST FEW days I've been back at the clubhouse have been a blur, between pain medicine induced comas and visitors. Hero banned nearly everyone from my room, but after arguing with him, he finally let Slider visit, followed by the rest of the guys. He still hovers when they're with me, to the point I had to ask Raze to keep him occupied today, so I could have a little time to myself. It's not that I don't appreciate what he did for me. He saved me and delivered death to the nightmares of my past.

For the first time in my life, I'm free from every tie that bound me to the earth. I can do everything I've ever wanted without a single person to hold me back. Well, that's not exactly true with Hero, but I like to think about the possibilities.

I knew the nightmares of my time in that cabin would

always be with me, much like Hero's nightmares of Iraq. I have to focus on the fact that I fucking survived, and he died with a bullet ricocheting around his brain. That was justice for not only myself, but for my mom, my step-dad, and my unborn sibling. He is dead, and their souls are free.

Scared and helpless Dani died that day, and like a phoenix rising from the ashes, the new fearless Dani was born. This new version of me is still trying to find her footing in this new world, but there's always going to be a constant anchor to stay.

Hero.

I've relived every single moment with Billy the past few nights, as I thrash in my sleep, but Hero wraps me in his arms and brings me back into safe reality. I know in my heart he's truly gone, but my brain can't seem to shake the thought he is still lurking around every dark corner, watching me.

Shit like this takes time, and that's what I need to give myself. I need to heal mentally, physically, and spiritually. I won't let Billy haunt me for the rest of my life. I'm determined to win this last battle with his ghostly memory.

Hero has been my saving grace throughout all of this, even though guilt and pain fill his hollow eyes after every nightmare. He blames himself for this, but in reality, the blame lies on us both. I lied to him and continued to do so the entire time I was here. Had I opened up to him, I would have been protected, but I would have been indebted to the club. I didn't want that for them, or for me. Our relationship started out of lies and convenience for me, but what we have now, as two individuals who came together in a shitty situation, is transcendent. There is nothing left in this world that can stop us.

Not Billy.

Not Twisted Tribe.

No one.

I know Hero is pissed that Raze ordered him to go on a protection run for a local celebrity, but I needed time for me, and to talk to Raze. I hadn't felt up to telling him about Maj's treachery to his club or me. I had to come to terms with the fact I would be signing the order to kill her, or in the least, she would be kicked out of the club and Raze's life.

After lying awake most of the night, internally debating about it, I decided that today would be the day. He needed to know the woman warming his bed is a fucking traitor. It would be revenge for me, but for Raze, it would be something else completely.

A soft knock raps on Hero's door, and Raze steps through the doorway.

"Hey, doll face. How are you feeling today?" he asks, carrying a vase of lilies.

That's the one thing I seem to have an abundance of

since my return. Flowers and tears. I thought for sure Hero would complain about his room becoming a showroom for a florist, but he hasn't said a word. It's nice to wake up to these delicate and beautiful blossoms, and to watch the light creep across their petals during sunrise.

Raze sits the vase next to me on the side table as he sits on the edge of the bed.

"Busted leg and an overprotective and hovering Hero. Thanks for getting me some alone time today."

His hand grasps mine, and he caresses it with a thumb. His calloused hands are rough against mine, but I just don't care. I need the feel of his touch to reassure me of what I'm about to do.

"I got rid of him for you," Raze starts. "What is it you need to talk to me about? Is that knucklehead bothering you, Dani? I can send him out on a longer run if you need me to do that."

A smile breaks across my face at the thought of Raze sending Hero out. "We both know he would defy you if you ordered that, anyway. It's not him I need to talk to you about, though, Raze. It's about something Billy said in the cabin."

He squeezes my hand at the mention of him. It's likely a knee-jerk reaction, but it's comforting.

"What about that cocksucker? You know you're safe here, doll. Voodoo took care of your missing person's report. No one is looking for you now."

"I know I am. I need to thank Voodoo properly for everything he's done. Without him, I'd be dead in that cabin."

"We'd have found you, Dani. Do not think for one second we wouldn't have torn this state apart to find you."

"I know. I just need to tell you…" I pause, unsure how to say this.

He scoots closer to me on the bed and squeezes my hand again. "Why are you hesitating with me, doll? You know you can tell me whatever it is rattling around in that brain of yours."

Tears well in my eyes as the words flow from my mouth. "I don't know how to fucking say this, Raze, because it will change everything. Everyone will be affected by it, but it will hit you the hardest."

Sighing deeply, I force myself to reveal my horrendous secret. "Billy didn't just track me down. Maj told him where I was. He had a bounty set on my head, and she called in to collect it. I was found because of your wife."

He sits silent as an icy cold fills his eyes. He looks away from me and releases my hand, then he jumps up and heads for the door.

"I don't want to cause trouble, Raze. I debated on telling you for days, but I decided it was best you knew."

Raze reaches for my hand again. It's so small in his, I

barely notice him turning away from me. "Dani, I knew what she did," he admits.

I frown. "Wait. You knew she turned me over to that bastard? Why didn't you say anything?"

"I found out after we brought you home," he says, pivoting to face me again. "She bolted the day Billy's crew came for you. I found a bank statement the day after we brought you home that had a fifty-thousand-dollar cash deposit listed. I had Voodoo track the account number, and it linked back to Billy."

"Does anyone else know besides us? Does Hero know?"

Tears streak down his face and slide down onto his shirt, one drop at a time in quick succession. Seeing a man like Raze cry sends me over the edge. I bawl into my hands, and suddenly, he scoops me into a hug, cradling me against his warm body. He holds me as we weep together before slowly pulling away.

"No one else knows. I don't want to tell you how, but Maj will never be seen again. I took care of it as soon as I realized the truth. "

"You didn't," I stutter. "Please tell me it wasn't you, Raze."

Shaking his head, he wipes away his tears.

"That's the fucked-up part about all of this, Dani. I couldn't do it. I loved that fucking woman for thirteen years, and she gave me two great kids, but when it came down to punishing her, I couldn't fucking do it. I couldn't fucking pull the trigger and kill the woman I had trusted the most."

I rub my hand across his muscled back. He jerks away from my touch instinctively, before settling against the stroking motions of my hand. He's just as broken as I am. His heart was ripped apart and left in a shattered mess around him. He deserves to be happy just as much as I do.

"You don't always have to be the strong one, Raze. You just have to be the man these men need to lead them. You damn well know this isn't a switch you can flip off and walk away from. Hell, you are preaching to the broken life parade queen right here. We just have to pick up the pieces and glue them back in a way that makes us happy again. We'll get there. It may not be today, but it sure as fuck won't last forever."

He smiles at me then and just walks away. Deep down, those words were more for me than for him, but he needed them just as much as I did. Settling back into bed, I pull my new Kindle off the nightstand and flip open the book I've been reading the for last few days. Apparently, Hero had purchased it for me during my confinement period at the clubhouse, but he had forgotten to give it to me. He even loaded his credit card onto the account, so I could one-click any books I wanted. I'm pretty sure he'll be pissed when he gets his statement next month. I've spent two hundred and fifty dollars on books the last few days. Reading has become my new relaxation technique. It helps me forget about everything, just for a few hours, and gives me a break from reality. It is a temporary fix, but it does the trick. I lie in bed reading for hours before another soft knock comes from the door.

"Dani?" a soft feminine voice calls from the door. The voice is so familiar, but I know it's not one of the club girls. Hero made sure they weren't to even step foot in my presence until I specifically asked for them. As the door slides open, my heart stops.

It's Ricca.

Her face is cut up, and her arm is in a cast. She hobbles into the room, struggling and limping with each step. Throwing the sheets from my body, I slide my casted leg out of the bed. Pulling myself up with the crutches Doc gave me, I make my way to her. As we meet in the middle of the room, I grab hold of her and pull her into a hug. Her ribs are poking out of her skin as I grip her tightly. We stand silently, embracing each other, never once letting go. She's a survivor, just as I am. I don't need to know the details of what happened to her. The anger I held against her for being homeless fades with each passing minute. Like Raze and I, the woman I'm holding in my arms was beaten, battered, and likely left for dead, judging by the looks of her.

Just like I was.

Life may have dealt us both a shitty hand, but knowing I have an entire group of people standing with me soothes my anger. Life is too short to worry about the past. It's the present and future we need to work for.

Together and with this club, we'll find our way again.

I won my freedom, and I will spend every single fucking day living my life the way I want it to be.

Chapter 28

HERO - 2 MONTHS LATER

"FOR THE LAST TIME, Hero, I said no. Just drop it," Dani yells.

"Why the fuck not, angel? You know it's inevitable."

She keeps putting me off about my question, and I'm sick of waiting. Patience has never been a virtue of mine. Who am I kidding? I have no virtues. I'm still the bastard she fell in love with that night at Red's, even if she did take her sweet ass time figuring out that she wanted me.

"Because I fucking said no, that's why. It's two letters, Hero."

God, this woman is the most frustrating person on the fucking planet. I just need a fucking answer, and she thinks this play coy shit is cute.

It's not cute.

It's the most nerve-wracking fucking game she's ever played with me.

I thought for sure that bringing her out to the beach on the bike would set the mood for her to change her mind. A beautiful view that paled in comparison to the beautiful woman lying next to me in the sand. The only thing that could make this day better was her being naked beneath me, and a fucking goddamn answer to my question.

"Just give me a reason why you won't answer. There has to be some fucking crazy ass reason you won't fucking marry me."

She stares a hole through me.

Oh shit, we've moved into pissed Dani territory. Good thing I like it when she's pissed.

Even when she frowns, she's sexy. Fuck, this woman kills me no matter what mood she's in. She already has my balls tucked neatly in her purse, but she won't fucking be mine. It took nearly a month to bring my angel back to life. I'd like to think my cock helped with that, but she did it on her own. Well, she and Ricca did. They started going to a survivor support group at the local YMCA a couple times a week. It's helping and I'm not about to stop her from finding resolution.

"How is no not enough for you? You're not ready to get married. You're letting this honeymoon phase cloud your better judgment, biker boy," she quips, rolling on her side to shut me out.

Two can play at this game, Dani.

Sliding closer to her, I roll her onto her back and climb over her. Pinning her hips into the beach towel with my own, I kiss her neck and trail my kisses down her belly. She moans with each tender kiss. She can deny me all she wants, but her body wants me. I brush my lips against the thin fabric covering her now erect nipples. She tries to pretend she doesn't like this, but she can't hide her smile.

"You can keep telling me no, angel, but you see how your body responds to me. It's screaming yes. Why don't you let your body do the talking for once, and agree to marry me?"

She tries to use her hips to buck me off, but I dig my feet into the sand, sinking her farther down into the sandy beach. She wiggles under me, a grin on her face.

Oh, angel. I know what you're doing.

"Waking up the monster cock won't get you out of answering me this time, angel. I'll get the answer I want today. I'm sure of it. In fact, I'm guessing that before we even leave this beach, you'll say yes."

She laughs in my face and wiggles again. "You're so delusional. No means no. Didn't they teach you that in school? I can say it in several languages, if you prefer."

Sliding the fabric of her bikini top to the side, I draw her taut nipple into my mouth. I tease it, licking circles around it and biting it lightly. Her head falls back as I grind against her apex. She enjoys the sensations before the sound of the waves crashing against the beach brings her back to reality.

"Hero, we're in public," she reminds me. "Someone might be watching us right now."

"Who cares if someone's watching, Dani? I want you, and your body sure as hell wants me, even if your pretty little mind is stubborn."

"You're fucking crazy. You know that, right?"

She laughs as I slide the other side of her bikini top off, licking around her nipple. It pebbles against my tongue. Dani is beautiful as it is, but when her body responds to me like this, it skyrockets her to a new dimension of beauty. Taking her nipple back into my mouth, I resume my teasing with her. She moans and rubs her pussy against me. The thin fabric I cursed for showing too much skin as we left the clubhouse this morning has now become my best friend.

"Do you want me to make you cum on this beach, angel, knowing anyone could see us?" I whisper against her nipple. Licking her once more, she moans.

"Fuck," she moans out on a breath.

"Say please."

"Fucking please, you asshole."

"Such language for my angel. Maybe you don't deserve to cum."

Anger flares in her eyes. Bingo. The reaction I wanted

is back. "Go fuck yourself," she growls. "May I remind you this was your suggestion?"

"Oh, angel. I'm about to do just that." Kissing trails down her belly, I stop just short of her pussy. My tongue dances along the skin of her inner thigh as her breath becomes ragged. I slide the damp fabric of her bikini bottom to the side, exposing her wet pussy to the world. Running a finger through her folds, I draw her taste into my mouth. She watches me intently as I moan, rubbing her excitement onto my lips and licking her taste from them.

I sink my finger into her entrance, feeling her clench against it. Sliding a second finger inside, I stroke, pulling my fingers out painstakingly slow before plunging them inside again.

"So wet for me, baby. Look at you glisten on my fingers. Your body so responsive. Anyone could come over here and see you coming apart."

"Please, Hero. I need your mouth on me. Please!" she begs, her voice low and gravely with both desire and anger.

I slide my fingers inside her again, and she grinds against them. Her pussy grazes against my face as she fucks my fingers. I pull my face away, and she sighs in frustration.

"Why won't you lick my pussy, Hero?"

Plunging a third finger inside of her, she moans loud

enough that, had anyone been close to us, they would have heard her. "Am I frustrating you, angel? How does it feel to not get what you want?"

"You're a fucking douchebag. Just lick my fucking pussy, goddammit," she demands.

"I'll lick your pussy clean, angel, if you say yes to marrying me."

"You don't play fucking fair," she cries.

I rub my thumb against her clit. "Neither do you. So, what will it be? Marry me, or leave here sexually unsatisfied? It's up to you, Dani."

I pound my fingers deeper into her wet folds. She's close. I can feel it. But she doesn't get off on just being finger fucked alone. Her sensitive little clit is the ticket to her orgasm. Her greedy pussy wants to be licked into ecstasy, but that fucking mind of hers is being stubborn. She knows she's meant for me, but she doesn't want to admit it out loud.

"Clock is ticking, Dani. I need an answer soon. The water is looking pretty enticing right now. Maybe I'll just go for a swim if you want to keep being stubborn."

She lets out an exasperated sigh.

"Say you'll marry me, Dani."

"Yes!" she yells, tired of my little game. "I'll fucking marry you."

"About fucking time," I growl, then my face dives against her.

Sucking her clit into my mouth, she bucks wildly against my face. My fingers resume their pounding rhythm as my tongue caresses and teases her sensitive nub. She moans louder as I rub my fingers against her g-spot.

Looking up from her pussy, I see her hands inside her bikini top, twirling her nipples between her fingers. Fuck, watching her pleasure herself while I lick her is so fucking hot. Flicking my tongue against her clit and sucking it one last time sends her over the edge. She rides my face as her orgasm takes hold. She slaps a hand over her mouth to muffle a scream, shaking from the intense pleasure pulsating throughout her.

Crawling up towards her face, I kiss her lips, letting her taste herself on my mouth. When I finally pull away, she beams at me.

Fixing her bikini top, I pull her against me. She seems almost shocked that I didn't plunge my dick inside of her, but I doubt she noticed the beach patrol truck driving in our direction. If I had fucked my future wife like I had planned, we'd have been arrested. Standing, I bring her with me. That's when she notices the speeding truck kicking up a cloud of sand on the beach. She grabs her bag from the sand and tosses her flip-flops and Kindle back into it. Grabbing the towels, we bolt for the bike. Sliding her onto the back, we watch the security guards search the area for us, laughing as I start it up.

"Well, my future wife, we sure do have a story to tell the grandkids someday. The day you finally agreed to marry me almost ended with us being arrested for fucking on the beach."

We laugh as I pull away from the beach parking lot. With her by my side, my future has never looked so bright. She makes me want to be a good man for her, but she embraces that I still need to be a bastard from time to time. She doesn't question my loyalty to my club, even though we both know if she'd have asked me to leave, I would do it for her. Heaven's Rejects may be my family, but Dani is my home. She made me realize that today when she finally said yes.

Epilogue

DANI - 8 WEEKS LATER

"You ready, Dani?" Ricca whispers, peeping through a crack in the door. Taking one last glance in the mirror, I smooth down my dress and walk towards her.

"Ready as I'll ever be. How do I look?" I ask, giving a little twirl that causes my dress to fan out around me.

She smiles at me warmly. "You are the most beautiful woman here today, bar none," she says with a laugh.

A soft knock at the door tells me it's time, and Ricca ushers me out into the hallway. Today marks the day I finally get my happily ever-after.

Ricca steps in front of me and leads me out of the back door of the compound, into the memorial garden the club spent the last few weeks building for the brothers-in-arms they have lost over the years. They've hung twinkling lights in the trees surrounding the garden. Thinking about bikers hanging twinkling lights brings an instant smile to my face. I wish I could have seen that. I notice Ratchet staring at Ricca with each step we take toward the aisle. His eyes never leave hers as she walks past him. I wonder what that's all about. I'll have to remember to pry a little out of the two of them after the ceremony.

Hero's song choice makes me laugh as the soft beat pours out of the speakers in the garden. What compelled him to select "Anyone But You" by Hinder as our wedding music is beyond me, but the meaning behind it nearly brings me to tears as the soft melody plays. He was reluctant in wanting to help me plan the "girly shit," as he called it, but put his foot down on the music. He made it very clear we weren't playing some sappy old music for our wedding and took over that part of the planning. As the song moves into the chorus, I see him.

Beneath the most beautiful flowering tree stands my Hero. His deep blue dress shirt shines under his cut. We argued for days about him wearing it for our wedding. He even withheld sex from me until I finally agreed he could wear it. I couldn't help but torture him during his self-proclaimed abstinence. The aftermath of that argument resulted in the best sex of my life. The cocky bastard brings it up when he wants to start a fight, hoping to top that night. He stops breathing when he sees me entering the makeshift aisle, a proud smile stretching across his face with each step I take closer to him.

Ricca settles into place behind me as I place my hand in Hero's. He mouths, "You are so beautiful," before returning his eyes to the man about to marry us in front of our club family. We are not blood-related, but these are the people who love us, regardless. Raze clears his throat, causing the muffled whispers in the crowd to quiet.

"You all know why you're here today. Let's get this shit over with, so these two can stop eye-fucking each other and just get to the good part of being married."

The men hoot and holler at Raze's words until his face hardens and the crowd quiets once more.

"Now, I understand each of you wrote your own vows. Dani?"

I pull a piece of crumpled paper out of the flower bouquet in my hand and pass the flowers off to Ricca. I'm glad she's standing next to me. We may not have had the best start to our friendship, but I'm hoping that in time, we can repair the damage. We're healing together with our support groups, but our friendship has a long way to go.

I unroll the paper slowly while Hero stares at me with impatience. I can already tell his monster cock is locked and loaded to claim his bride, but he's going to have to wait five more damned minutes. Tyler's stare bores into me, and I know I can't keep my man waiting any longer, even if I'm finding a bit of devilish pleasure in making him squirm.

My voice sounds meek as I read the words I've written.

"Tyler, I spent so many days trying to think of the words I wanted to say to you today, but in truth, no words came to me. It's not that I didn't know how to express my feelings, because I do. Simply saying your love makes me the happiest woman on the planet doesn't come close to what you've done for me. You may be Hero to everyone else, but to me, you are my Hero. You went against everything you knew to find me and seek the truth. You don't care about my past, and want to help me work through the pain that still lingers. You're more than just the man I'm marrying today in front of your brothers and my new family, but my future partner in love and in crime. I know our life may not always be perfect, but I'm okay with that. As long as you're my man, and you love me, I know nothing will tear us apart. I love you, my Hero, and will every single day for the rest of our lives."

Finally peeling my eyes away from the scrap of paper, Tyler's face tells me he understands the meaning behind my words, and that's all that matters. He was willing to sacrifice himself to save me that day, knowing I'd lied to him about my past. The love that resides in his heart is far greater than the sum of any love I've received in my entire life, with the exception of my dad. I wished so badly he could have been here to give me away. I've thought at times, while planning this whirlwind wedding, about how much he'd have hated Tyler as my future husband. He was staunchly against tattoos, and wouldn't have ever crossed the line of illegal activities. Yet at the same time, I think Dad would have liked how this man lived his life to make me happy, and to protect me. I like to think that maybe my dad would have grown to love having a biker as a son-in-law, eventually.

But Dad's gone, and Tyler is here. My heart beats for this man alone now.

Raze turns to Tyler, slapping him on the back. "Well, Hero, I have no idea why, but she still seems to like you. Let us all mourn for the butchering of vows about to be presented to us by Hero, and the removal of his balls."

His brothers erupt in boisterous laughter while Tyler moves in closer to me, grabbing my hands. The guys must know he's not in the mood for jokes, because with one look, they settle down. His hands are trembling in mine. I sweetly smile at him to reassure him. Without even reading, he speaks softly to me.

"Don't laugh at me with this. You know I don't do romance as well as those guys in the books you read. The one thing I do know how to do is to be the man you need. Dani, I knew from the first time you walked into my clubhouse that you were going to be trouble. You are the most beautiful woman I have ever seen, and with a single glance in my direction, I was yours. We both have our demons that we'll battle every fucking day of our lives. But with you by my side, we'll never lose. I know love isn't meant to be easy. I can't promise you hearts and rainbows, but know this. You are my hero, angel face. You may have turned my life upside-down like a head on collision, but I never want to live without you, or the chaos you bring, ever again."

Tears stream down my face at his words, and he gently wipes them away.

Before Raze can even resume the ceremony, Tyler jerks me towards him. His mouth devours mine like no one else is around us. Cat-calls echo off the buildings surrounding us. He laughs at his brother's cheers, making his mouth vibrate my own. Breaking away, he grabs the rings outstretched in Raze's hand. He slides the ring on my finger, and then hands me his. As soon as the metal slides into place, Hero throws me over his shoulder, sending my dress nearly over my head. Marching down the makeshift aisle, he quickly pivots back to the audience, shifting me into his arms.

"Sorry, guys, but I need to go fuck my wife now, before this romantic bullshit makes my dick soft. We can eat cake and be fucking merry in an hour. Drinks on me!"

Tyler trots back into the clubhouse and takes the stairs two at a time. Kicking the door to his room open, he deposits me on the bed before returning to the door and locking it behind him. He strips off his cut and unbuttons his dress shirt, tossing it on the chair in the corner of his room. Without a word, he crawls over me on the bed. His face freezes above mine.

"I can't believe you're mine, angel. I know you wanted the perfect wedding, but I just couldn't wait anymore. We don't need sappy bullshit to know we love each other. I need a taste of my forever pussy before we go back to the party."

He trails kisses down my neck while I reach down and attempt to unzip his pants. Realizing what I'm trying to do, he sits up and finishes the job for me. He inches the black dress pants down his muscular legs, discarding them into the pile with his shirt.

"You're overdressed. Let's take care of that, shall we?"

Tyler makes quick work of removing the poofy white wedding dress from obstructing his mission, by ripping out every single button down the back of my dress, and pulling it over my head. He grabs the white lace panties, letting his hands skim across my flesh, before ripping them from my body just as fiercely as my dress. His eyes catch the bustier Ricca basically sewed me into this morning.

"As perfect as your tits look in this, I need it gone."

He spends several minutes tugging at the strings, but it won't budge. Rolling over onto my belly, I open the bedside table and remove a knife. Handing it to him, Tyler looks at me in shock.

"Cut the damn thing off of me. I'm not waiting an hour for you to unstring this fucking thing."

"You're such a demanding little thing."

Tyler salutes me with one hand and begins to cut through the multitude of ties quickly. Pulling it away from me, he flips me onto my back, crawling towards my upper body. His warm, rough hands palm my breasts, and his mouth showers kisses down my chest onto my stomach.

"Fuck, angel. I can't believe this is all mine. Tell me it's mine."

Stopping just short of my pussy, he stares at me laid bare before him.

"Yes, Tyler. I'm forever yours."

"Fuck yes, you are."

His mouth descends on my pussy, viciously licking and nipping at my clit. Moans ripple out of me, and I can't take my eyes off him. His tongue teases the sensitive flesh before he bites down harder. The shock waves of his teeth against my sensitive nub pulsate throughout my body. He continues to caress and suck on my clit before plunging two fingers inside of me. Hooking them as he penetrates my soaking wet flesh, he presses hard against my g-spot.

"Always so wet and eager for me. I knew my beautiful bride was dripping wet for me out there, in front of everyone."

His tongue and fingers gently tease me into oblivion. Every touch and caress from him is driving me insane, to the point I can't form proper words. Only jumbled moans and garbled pleasure-laced swears are all I can manage while he explores his already-claimed territory.

"Come for me, baby. I know you're close," he pleads, as his speed increases.

Slipping a third finger into my wetness, he sends me over the edge. My body jerks and moans fly from my mouth as I pulsate around his fingers. His teeth enclose my clit one more time before he pulls away and licks my wetness from his lips.

"Sweetest fucking thing I have ever tasted," he says, as he coats my lips with my own juices before bringing his mouth to mine.

I push up against him and hook my fingers into the waist of his straining boxer briefs, shoving them down as he kisses me. He breaks away long enough to pull them from his legs, flinging them away. Taking me by the ankles, he pulls my body towards him, my wetness landing against his rock-hard erection.

"I'm sorry we rushed out of the ceremony, baby, but

monster cock couldn't be contained much longer," he growls, as I wiggle against him.

"Take me, Tyler. Please fucking take me," I plead.

He rubs the head of his cock against my already aching clit. Sliding his hands under my ass, he lifts my bottom into the air and plunges his cock into my wet folds. He hisses as he fills me, then withdraws slowly. He pushes into me harder and deeper, his girth pushing tightly against my walls with each thrust. Wrapping my legs around his waist, I draw him closer and farther into me. A primal growl escapes his lips as he pounds against my flesh. I run my fingers across his metaled nipple, caressing the smooth bar.

"Fuck, baby," he seethes. "I love it when you play with my piercing. Maybe I should get my dick pierced next."

The thought of barred metal rubbing against me sends a purely seductive smile to my face.

"Don't look at me like that. That sinister smile is enough to fucking unman me alone. This is just the warm-up. I planned for an entire week of fucking on a remote beach in Tahiti."

Pushing my parted hips against the sexy V of his abs, his hands fall to my hips, pounding me against him harder until I come undone. The heart-stopping orgasm courses through my veins, pure unbridled bliss rocking my body. My pulsating pussy sends him over the edge, right along with me.

He thrusts into me, riding out of the waves of his own orgasm, then falling on top of me with bated breath. He kisses my lips as his heart rate slows down. Our chests heave together as we try to catch our breath. He rolls onto his side, pulling me against him. Nuzzling his nose into my neck, we lay in each other's arms in sated bliss. This man has given me everything I could have ever asked for in this world. He'll never know just how much his love has saved me from all the darkness in my life.

Rolling over to face him, I study every aspect of his handsome face. Happiness shines from his eyes, like the brightest star in the sky. I snuggle in closer to him, wanting more of his body pressed to mine.

"I love you, angel. You've made me the happiest man on earth." He smiles, then kisses me on the forehead. "I never thought I could love someone as much as I love you in this very moment."

I press a soft, chaste kiss onto his lips. "You're wrong, you know. You don't love me the best."

His eyes narrow at my comment. "That's a damned lie. You're my entire world."

Giggling as he tickles me into a smile, I know I'm about to let him in on one last secret.

"Tyler, you might think you love me most right now, but our little biker baby might change your mind."

His eyes grow in shock, travelling down to my belly and returning to my face.

"Surprise, Daddy," I say with a grin.

Hero breaks out into a fit of laughter.

I frown. "What the hell is so funny about a baby?"

"Nothing," he declares, still laughing. "It's just that I fucking owe Raze two hundred bucks now."

Heaven's Rejects MC Series

Heaven Sent

Angels and Ashes

Absolution

Lies and Illusions

Resolution

Song List

"See You in Hell" by Hinder

"Drunk Enough" by Angels Fall

"Stay" by Black Stone Cherry

"Blame it on the Boom Boom" by Black Stone Cherry

"Life After You" by Daughtry

"A Place to Fall" by Emphatic

"All Around Me" by Fly Leaf

"Monster" by Skillet

"Mz. Hyde" by Halestorm

"Bad Girlfriend" by Theory of a Deadman

"Porn Star Dancing" by My Darkest Days

"Save Yourself" by My Darkest Days

"Seven Nation Army" by The White Stripes

"Give Me Love" by Ed Sheeran

"Trying Not to Love You" by Nickelback

"All The Same" by Sick Puppies

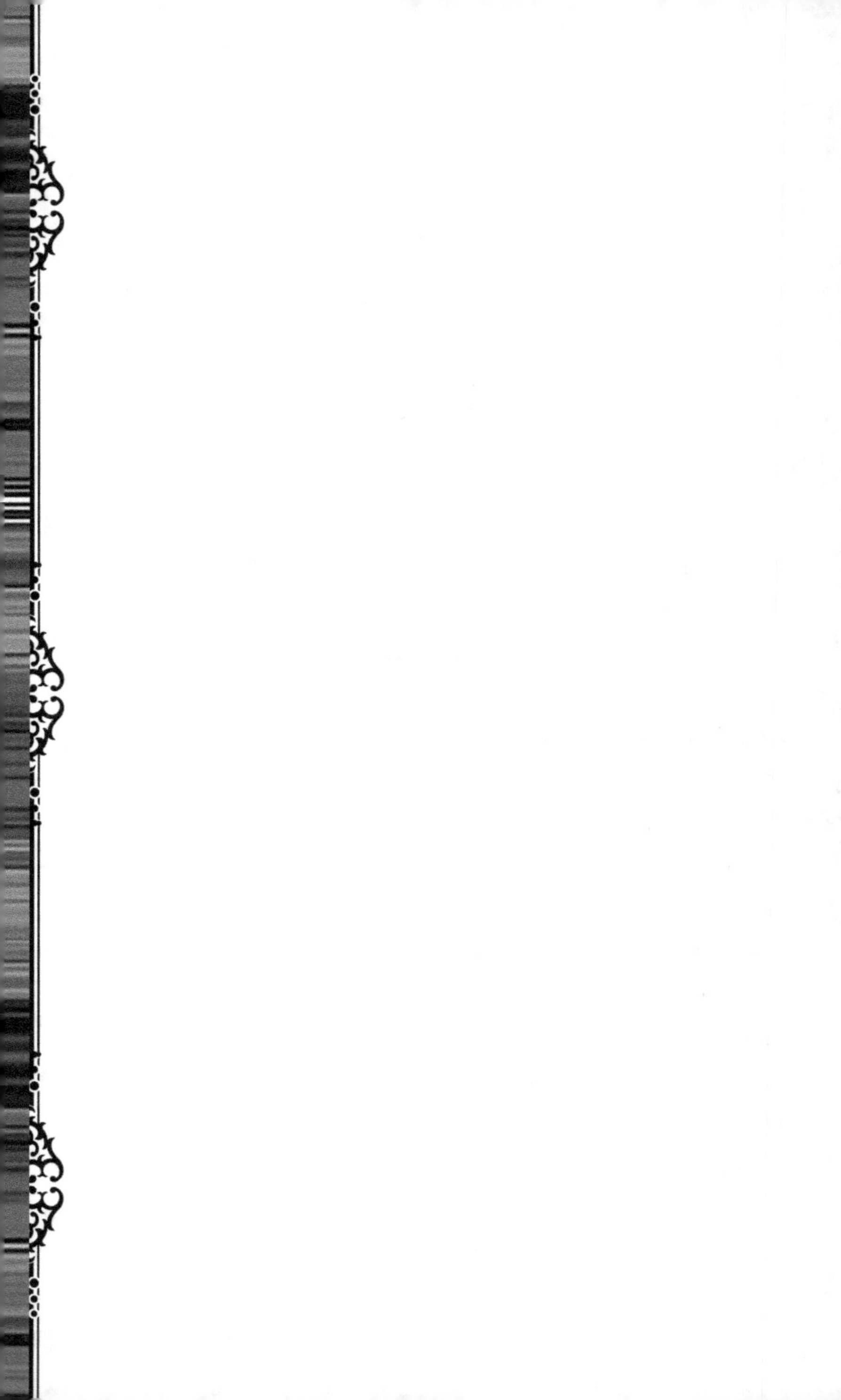

Acknowledgements

It's weird to think that with the release of Heaven Sent, I'm starting yet another series. I never in my wildest dreams thought I would write one book, let alone two in a single year. It's a been a wild ride of ups and downs writing this book, but at the end of the day, it's been worth it. I've met so many great people throughout the last year, I don't even know where to begin. Well, that's a lie. I should probably start with my husband.

Glen, you have stuck by me with this book. Writing took me away from our family time, and you dealt with that marvelously. I spent so many late nights writing, I barely came to bed half the time, but you never once complained. You knew I was doing something I was passionate about, and you stood by me until the bitter end. The night I typed the end, you pulled me against you, and I finally slept for the first time in over a month. Thank you for being the love of my life, and the most supportive man on the face of the earth.

The Betas (new and old) You lovely ladies have helped me tremendously with this book. Your helpful insight kept me on track and on task, when the story took a nose dive, or my late-night ramblings became apparent in my writing. You worked hard to help me get Heaven Sent on the market, and be the best book it could be. You are all gracious and supportive readers. I'd be nowhere without you.

Meet Avelyn

Avelyn Paige is a Wall Street Journal and USA TODAY bestselling author of romantic suspense and motorcycle club romance. She lives in a small town in Indiana with her husband and five fuzzy kids.

When she's not writing, Avelyn spends her days working as a cancer research scientist. Avelyn has been an avid reader her entire life, and it wasn't until losing her father in 2015 that she started turning all those ideas in her head into stories. She hasn't looked back since.

Join Avelyn's Reader Group: Avelyn's Angels

ALSO BY AVELYN PAIGE

The Heaven's Rejects MC Series

Heaven Sent

Angels and Ashes

Sins of the Father

Absolution

Lies and Illusions

The Black Hoods MC

Dark Protector

Dark Secret

Dark Guardian

Dark Desires

Dark Destiny

Dark Redemption

Dark Salvation

Dark Seduction

The Bastard Boilers MC

Property of Azrael